Silver's Threads
Book 3

Other Titles by Penny Reilly

Silver's Threads Series

Book 1, Spinning Colours Darkly
© 2012 First Edition
© 2013 Second Edition
© 2014 Third Edition

Book 2, Grey Weavings
© First Edition 2012
©Second Edition 2013
© 2014 Third Edition

Book 3, Warp and Weft
© First Edition 2012
©Second Edition 2013
© 2014 Third Edition

Book 4, Silken Web
© First Edition 2014
©Second Edition 2014

Reviews from Amazon.com

A wonderful book in a magical world…

November 6, 2012

By *Susan chambers*

This review is from *Silver's Threads, Book 1 Spinning Colours Darkly (Volume 1) (Paperback)*

This book is very, very special. The way it is written is amazing, it gets you in with the first page, it's a world I didn't want to leave when I reached the last page. I felt like I was knew the characters as dear friends, I could see the story in my mind's eye like a movie as I read. You won't be disappointed if you buy this book & you too will get enamoured of Sybil's world! I can't wait for book 2 to be available!

Woven beautifully, September 13, 2012

By *Marion*

Very easy enjoyable reading. If you enjoy books about the old ways, this is the old ways in modern times. Will pre-order book 2 as soon as it becomes available. Made extra special because I visit the real "Earthly Rites" which is as magical as this book. Thanks Penny for sharing.

Celestine Prophecy for Pagans! November 8, 2012

By *Niamh*

This review is from *Silver's Threads, Book 1 Spinning Colours Darkly (Volume 1) (Paperback)*

This book is more than just a story about women finding themselves and their purpose in life—though if it were just that, it would be enough. Penny has also incorporated a gentle education about the Old Ways, and the state of the earth as she is now, here and on other planes and is showing us ways that we can affect those around us and the planet in the way we were created to. If you let it, this book can change your life—yep, I said it!!

Her words are spun beautifully and create beautiful imagery and it is clear there is a plan coming together for those in the story. I can't wait for the next instalment!

The journey continues, February 7, 2013

By *Butterflygirl*

This review is from *Silver's Threads Book 2 Grey Weavings (Kindle Edition)*

Fly with the Ravens, travel the Skeins of Thyme, open your eyes and your mind to the 'unseen' as the search for Sybille continues and the crew at Covenstead delve deeper and deeper into the mystery of the 'between'. The second book in the Silver's Threads series is just as absorbing as the first, you will find yourself unable to put it down as you follow the paths of Sybille's' students and their friends as they continue to unravel the mystery of her disappearance and test their wits with the Dark Fae.

Love it! October 19, 2013

By *Valkyrie*

This review is from *Silver's Threads Book 2 Grey Weavings (Kindle Edition)*

So much information! Can't wait for the rest . . . this series is amazing, loved every page and can't wait to get my hands on book 3.

Another world, September 19, 2013

By *Kat*

This review is from *Silver's Threads Book 2 Grey Weavings (Kindle Edition)*

These stories by Penny Reilly take you to another existence and she makes it all seem so real and plausible. An enjoyable escape from our mundane existence.

Silver's Threads Book 2, June 23, 2013

By *Noelle*

This review is from *Silver's Threads Book 2 Grey Weavings (Kindle Edition)*

Again, I cannot thank Penny Reilly enough for your great work and having the list of characters grow according to the story line. I can't wait for the next book.

Silver's Threads, March 12, 2013

By *Patricia Hill—*

This review is from *Silver's Threads Book 2 Grey Weavings (Kindle Edition)*

*T*horoughly enjoyed books one and two—looking forward to book three—hope it is soon. The plot was easy to follow—would recommend it to like-minded people

Woven with wonder and joy, November 17, 2013

By Marion (Australia)

This review is from *Silver's Threads Book 3, Warp and Weft (Kindle Edition)*

I have been following this tale since book 1 captured my imagination. This is a well-written story that draws you into the world of the old ways through the lives of the

main characters. If you have ever had that moment of knowing something and yet not known why or how you know it . . . come explore with this story. Looking forward to book 4, which means I get to revisit the first three books as a lead in to the next part of the journey. Do we have a date for book 4 yet?
(Book 4, Silken Web was published 2014)

Silver's Threads

Book 3

Warp and Weft

Penny Reilly

ISBN 13: 978-0-9924759-4-9

Silver's Threads Book 3
Warp and Weft
© 2014 by Penny Reilly

Cover and interior design by Penny
Cover Art "Silken Spells" by Josephine Wall

Self-Published by Penny Reilly
Project & Series Editor Penny Reilly

Printed in Australia

First Published 2012
Revised 18/07 /2014

Dedication

I dedicate this book to all Indie writers worldwide,
struggling for recognition in their Craft
…let your creative spirits fly brothers and sisters.

Special Acknowledgement

The extraordinary artwork on the cover of this book, "Silken Spells", is by the very talented, Josephine Wall . . . her work has inspired me and thanks to this, I feel I could write a story for each of her paintings.
Please visit Josephine Wall on her Facebook page...
www.facebook.com/TheOfficialJosephineWall
Support the artist, visit her Gallery and buy her beautiful art at www.josephinewall.co.uk

Acknowledgements

My gratitude and my thanks go once again to my beloved husband David for his patience through the process of creating this book and in advance for those to come. He has seen me through the birthing of four books now!
To my amazing staff in our business, Jan and Leigh, who rally around to help me make more time for writing. Thank you Errol for your 'extra' encouragement. Many thanks go to the quiet and not so quiet followers of my Facebook and blog pages, especially Susan Chambers, Kat Lakie, Sonya Marshall and Noelle Hill. To the 'Reading, Writing Coven' who continually give support, encouragement and a few giggles on the way; you know who you are. Warmest thanks to my very special Grove members, Rhys, Jo, Richard, Louise and Susan for all the fun and inspiration, and to Rosalie Franklin and Donna Kelly for their professional encouragement.

Foreword by Penny Reilly

I am always surprised when I begin or continue a story, how the flow increases the more I apply myself. I did not imagine when I set out on this journey that it would be quite so extraordinary. Dreams have become vivid, and my peripheral vision flickers of the 'other realms', magnified.

Many friends and readers of my books have shared that they are experiencing strange and fascinating things, as the perceived veil between this world and other realms, thin to the point of almost non-existence.

Are these the changes we can expect; have the prophecies of the Mayan, the Navaho, the Celts, Nostradamus or Ramtha been, not about apocalyptic endings of the planetary systems but an increasing pressure on our senses, forcing us to wake up and realise, we are not alone? That we are not as important as we have perhaps led ourselves to believe; there again, if everything is now then everything is affected by us, what we think, say, feel and as a result, do.

My work is about that very thing, those experiences that so many have ignored, through embarrassment of what others may say, through fear that Magick is real, hidden away, waiting to be released from within each of us.

Why do we fear our own powers? When did we first think that they were something bad, to be buried like treasures horded for eons? When did we believe the tales of our 'fall from Grace?' When did the gentle teachings of so many evolved beings become twisted into a mockery of what they, in actuality, said? Why did the Wytch become the scapegoat for all the fear that humankind had of the women and men who knew the keys to healing, the plants to cure and the words to mend. What indeed, happened to the Cunningmen and the Druid healers of old, the Ovate, male and female alike, who were the teachers of their time in herbal lore and psychic phenomena, the walkers between the worlds?

When did we forget the Pantheons of Spirit who helped us to create ourselves, and forget we carry the same seed-spark that created them? Our only fall was into matter, "Mata," the Mother and it is in Her embrace we have always lived, together with the animator's flame of the wild forest, the Spirit of Place; indeed wasn't that our choice too?

If they exist then in truth we can awaken, we can remember all that we are, not in an egocentric or hierarchical manner, but in sheer awe and delight at our own magnificence as creatures born of darkness and light, matter, spirit, and of joy not fear.

Wake up humankin, wake up, celebrate the truth of yourselves; know that you have always been and will be loved, not in the human, confined, controlling understanding of love, but in the truly liberating kind unconditionally.

Blessings on your journey home …Penny

Contents

The search for Sybille has become more complex and intense. Morgan's sister Lily arrived unexpectedly from the UK, adding another twist in the relationship ties between the previously, close-knit group.

Max never truly recovered after the ending of his relationship with Lily and her reappearance in his life is forcing him to look at his motives, where magicks are concerned. Lily is a shapechanger, a singer like her brother and a skilled jeweller; she proposes to help the group in their task. Max's personal fear of magick, which he kept well hidden, is the decider. He finds he cannot cope with Samantha's constant companions; little leaf sprites that have taken a dislike to him, sensing he is not completely engaged with her. He is shocked into finding a different way to view magickal skills on his discovery that Lily is a changer.

Tara has taken Maeve to another thread in the tapestry after she came close to attacking Samantha, at the incitement of a curious creature, whose negative voice pushed her to the edge. She must relearn and remember her own skills from the Beyond. Her feelings for Morgan compromised too; when the little Merrow's irritating, haunting drove her to the brink of losing all self-control.

Flora and Cal, having sealed their relationship, are the most solid in the group in terms of clarity and personal control.

Bethan is becoming completely otherworldly after discovering her mother was also Fae, not human. Circaea, her grandmother, has given her an ancient instrument to learn, which enchants all who hear it with its sweet, haunting tones. Samantha is content to be with her wee folk and to spend some time in friendship with Morgan, an extraordinary singer and musician, the natural peace-maker of the group; a Ravenshaper, he works with Tara and her clan of changers.

Claire is rediscovering her mischievous side, and cannot help but tease her, soon to be ex-husband Harry, when he moves to Springsmeet to live with Annie. Flora would happily sack Annie from "Earthly Rites" if it were up to her, after the discovery of a younger sister Vanessa.

The Skeins of Tyme have not yet revealed where Sybille is but as the young men and women begin to travel the threads, back and forward through the warp and weft of the Wytchways, they are discovering new and amazing skills, strengths and weaknesses. All the knowledge they gain about their other aspects is overwhelming, yet they must stay focused on the task of finding Sybille and assist the Fae to stop the blight that will threaten all on the planet.

No mortal sees the hidden ways,
yet meddle they have since the dawn of days
and so they return once more, into life's fray
as each one from the Crooked Path will stray
Follow the road to the ends of Tyme
seeking the path that make sense of the rhyme
In dark and in light let your footsteps stray
let the Crooked Path lead you to the Goddess' Way
Follow the road into the Green
…look to the Lord and the Faefolk unseen
…to guide you home, never more to stray
…as the Crooked Path leads you to the Goddess' Way

…the journey continues…

Warp & Weft

Drifting through the warp and weft,
Fragile hands so pale and deft,
Weave the scrap of tapestry left
…upon the Skeins of Tyme

Flying spindle, curling thread,
Returning life the Earth to tread,
Once more Her Silver'n blood is shed
…upon the Skeins of Tyme

Forgotten life, forsaken light,
The silken threads, torn by blight,
Even the 'Onceborn' feel Her might
…within the Skeins of Tyme

Once Her threads so strong, were tight,
. . . Not to bind us but delight;
To stretch, to hold our Souls winged flight
…into the Skeins of Thyme

Arianwen Isil'Lindir & Aithlin Farandir
…from the Skeins of Tyme

Prologue

As the light softly fades, to draw in the dark
...on the Wolds silence falls, quiet now the lark
What waits in the glooming?
... as her scream rips the night
Eyes dimming, limp body falling,
...extinguished is her light

As the light faded from Rowan's bright blue raven eyes, her familiar spirit fought to release; the instinctual need to soar high, away from the deadly arrows she knew would follow, strong in her.

The shock of jarring dislocation when the arrow made impact into soft breast tissue and wing flesh, and the screaming agony that followed Rowan's fall, began to separate her disoriented familiar from her dying, fleshly body.

As the arrow pierced her to the bone, Rowan knew she needed to warn the one named Brandubh and keep him safe . . . he was crucial to the survival of many lives, including one day, her own.

She screamed at him to, 'Flee, FLEE!' and saw his horse take up the warning, bolting for home.
In her pain she changed, feeling the Wolf's Bane eating into her skin, pouring into her blood, taking hold of her senses, she flew through the veil, plummeting down to-

ward misty wet moorlands that seemed to be coming up to meet her at an alarming rate.

Rowan tried to bank but felt herself changing to human form again; too weak now to take control, her injured wing could not make the complete shift; instead, her human arm became a full size wing, the flight feathers remained imbedded to the bone. The Ashwood shaft broke off as she fell, pushing the arrow head deeper still into her flesh for the Bane to do it's task, seeping into her blood, freezing the nerve channels to her brain.

Dropping faster still, limbs flailing; her Raven-spirit tore free, alive but sorely damaged. In the final crashing dive, awareness fled. Rowan's blue gaze misted over, her sight gone. She tried to call her familiar back to her but 'Ruuuark...' was the last sound her Ravenkin heard as it echoed through the veil, vibrating the Skeins as she flew, 'Ruuuark,' she replied mournfully, 'Ruuuark...' hurtling blindly, into the 'Between'.

Chapter 1
Morgan Trethaway

Plummeting, falling, she broke through the veils
Light dying, senses failing, darkness prevails
All things must change when an immortal light fails
…as she plunges, silently screaming
…becoming human, becoming frail

'Ruuuark, Ruuuark,' the cry ripped through Morgan's silent contemplation in the forest. It echoed through the Aether in a chain reaction, re-echoing back and forth through the time-space continuum.

The Raven Ruark heard the call but could no longer remember where the distorted sounding of the name she bore, originated.

Tara heard, Lily heard, Claire heard as she sat in her Owl form in the tree above.

Morgan felt his aspect Bran reacting instinctively within him. Would he have been able to save her if he had returned? What could he have done if his horse hadn't bolted?

'Tara!' Morgan cried aloud. 'Where is the body of the Ravenchanger, Cal found on the Wolds?' There was no reply. Steadying his breath, Morgan relaxed back into his previous posture, calming his wildly racing thoughts.

This time, the cry had taken him by surprise, although he had heard the scream in his mind so often before.

Stilling his thoughts again, to consider the events of the past seven months; from the moment he had almost collapsed as an inexplicable grief hit him at Lammas, around the wheel through, Mabon, Samhain, Yule, and Imbolc and now almost Ostara, nearly, half a Wheel's spin to date, since he'd met the group of amazing people, his friends.

He remembered he'd been playing at a gig in the local pub and walked home in the rain afterwards. He'd known then that something had happened to his friend and mentor Sybille, who he'd known only from a distance when they'd met on the Aethers for his training. His connection with her had been so strong and then it had vanished, all but for an occasional tug on his mind. It was as if she leapt, stirring occasionally to mind-link with him but he could make no sense of it, when he focussed in, the fragile thread would instantaneously dissolve.

He'd known he needed to find her, when there was no reply from email or Skype. Morgan would sometimes see strange, otherworldly images of a tree so huge it defied description and of small lights; Makers, he'd later learned, flitted, tending to shapes he couldn't understand with the more logical part of his psyche.

These images became stronger if he didn't worry at them, for that only pushed them deeper into the mind recesses, designed to cope with the unknown. He wondered if he actually let it be, whether the answers would simply float to the surface. All knowledge was available, he just had to remember the 'how to' of it, wishing and not for the first time, there was a manual for the process.

Chuckling to himself at the thought, he stretched long limbs and stood; the Moon rose through the canopy of branches above. 'What the …!' he exclaimed aloud. 'The Moon shouldn't be there surely; it's too far round to the southeast. I'll have to check with Flora, she'll know.'

Pacing now in frustration, he thought of the last Sabbat, when he'd found himself in the Hearth of Scathach in his aspect Bran. He'd seen Maeve looking strong; restored to her former self. He recalled the experience when he'd first seen the Shapechanger Rowan as Bethan had described her and then, subsequently he'd scried, to see her struck down by an arrow from a Dark Fae's bow. She'd been lithe and slender, her hair wild elf-locks, cheekbones jutting under wide, tip tilted smoky blue eyes.

Morgan remembered the face of the Dark Fae female and always would; the hatred directed toward Rowan and he, a tangible force. How helpless he'd felt as his horse bolted, almost unseating him. Thing was, he felt he knew the face from somewhere, recently in fact.

With a deep sigh, Morgan relaxed back against a huge old forest giant, feeling himself slip into a calm, meditative state. His eyes glazed over, he felt glued to the ground, solid. He visualised small taproots sliding, probing down deep into the skin of the Mother.

Sybille, the very person he'd previously been thinking about, had taught him this method of grounding and so he relaxed deeper still, allowing the feeling of peace to wash over him. He became the tree, his skin the bark, his body the trunk, his arms and legs grew, dividing into multiple limbed branches, covered now in the last leaves of winter, too stubborn to fall. Small nubby buds were already thrusting towards the light of day, each one full of the promise of spring.

Just as Morgan felt he would lose himself entirely to the grip of nature; an owl's hunting scream tore through the stillness within him. He shook his head to bring himself back to physical awareness. Feeling light headed he tried cautiously, to stand, the better to sniff, to hear what travelled on the ethers on great heavy, wings and on the wind that had come up from the west. It appeared to be heading for Covenstead. He centred, steadying himself before sprinting off into the forest toward the farm, although it would have been quicker to borrow Max's car he thought as he ran. He didn't consider making the change amidst the canopy in the dense forest.

With the amount of physical, mental and psychic work the group were undertaking, he had become as solid as a rock, stamina had increased and he was feeling at his best.

As he ran, he could see the forest had begun its change to spring but sticky black webs festooned numerous branches, trap like, across the natural pathways made by wombats, wallaby, echidna and kangaroo.

We need to focus our attention on the healing side of things he thought; we've forgotten about the blight while we focussed on Sybille's rescue; perhaps she's just the catalyst to motivate us into action? Nature must have the answers; work in reverse as it were, before he pushed his way through the thicket of hawthorn and raced toward the farm.

Morgan screeched to a halt when he saw Claire locked in the arms of a large man, whose dark hair, streaked through with silver; he would recognise anywhere.

Chapter 2
Owl's Dream Too

Shifting, changing, morphing, rearranging,
…bones creaking, skin sliding,
…stretching …wings widening
…soaring, song outpouring, drifting, weight shifting,
…light gleaming, feathers streaming,
…eyes glistening, deepest listening
…body tightens; senses heighten,
…turns …spinning …dives winning,
…beak snatching, talons catching,
…load bearing, flesh tearing,
…hunger sated, warm, elated,
…strength fed …soon feathers shed,
…re shaping, almost breaking, freedom waning,
…shifting, changing …morphing, rearranging

Lady Moon hung suspended a fragile, transparent wraith, over the trees. Winters' grip encroached on the lives of all creatures, wrapping icy fingers around weak and strong alike. Yule had passed and the coldest weeks lay ahead, even after the release of Imbolc began to renew the life stirring in the freezing deep, underground.

Flora stood at the kitchen bench, hands blackened as she cracked open hard walnut shells to release the bittersweet flesh within. Sybille had taught her to roast the outer shell first to make the shelling process easier, the heat not affecting the treasure hid within or the second green skin that covered them. It was a messy job, the walnuts bled their oily residue; it took days to scrub it off her hands and out of the pores; it soaked like water, into a sponge.

She disliked using plastic gloves but sometimes wondered if she should. By the end of a batch, the oil turned yellow on her skin, particularly around the nail bed, making it look as if she were a smoker, not a good look for an herbalist.

It was late in the year for this chore, usually done in late autumn or early winter soon after the harvest, but the work of finding Sybille had been foremost in everyone's mind. The oil-soft nuts would be minced and added as a paste to cakes and pesto this year, being past their fresh best. Nothing need ever go to waste in the cycles of nature.

Flora watched the Moon rising over the trees; she felt queasy realising it was not quite where it should be in the sky for the time of year. How bizarre she thought to herself.

As she worked lost in her reverie, firm strong hands reached around her and a warm male body pushed up behind, embracing her in a huge bear hug. She relaxed back into him, Cal her lover, her friend; what a gift he was to her after her history with men.

'Can I pour you a glass of wine love?' he asked, 'I'm all done for the night I think. If I have to Google anything else, I'll go insane. They must have taken the word from 'google eyed" he quipped. 'How much more information is there to find for this exercise to be done?' he said in frustration, releasing Flora to run his hands roughly through his already tussled, brown hair.

'Well,' said Flora. 'Let's just sit and be for a while, will we? I can fix us a plate of fruit, cheese and biscuits. We can take a break from everything. Cal?' On hearing no reply, she turned; Cal was staring as if Moon-struck out the window.

Claire stood in the Moonlight looking skyward. A huge Owl flew, carefully avoiding the trees' bare limbs. Hooting softly, eyes fixed on Claire, he angled down to land on a low branch almost within touching distance. She remained, apparently unmoved, watching.

Flora, swivelled around rapidly to see what had captured Cal's attention, his mouth hung open in amazement. Only one expletive came to mind in the moment; they spoke in unison,

'SHIT!' Their first instinct was to run outside but a glance from Claire, sensing their angst, froze them to the spot.

Claire shimmered and changed into her Owl form Naboo, she lifted off the ground, talons raised in defence. In the same moment the other shifted, taking on human form as Claire hovered, before she too reverted.

'Pwyll?' she cried, loudly enough for Cal and Flora to hear. 'Pwyll is that you?' Claire launched herself at the tall dark man, at first with nails poised to strike, and then with the tears and kisses she rained on his face. 'Pwyll! Where the **fuck**, have you been all this time?'

'Ah, time,' he said, a grin changing his older version of Morgan's face to one unlined from the grief written there. 'I've not been too far away but, you know,' he hesitated, 'Harry?'

'Ever the gentleman,' she sobbed and laughed at the same time, none of which was audible to the waiting pair at the window.

Cal recovered first. 'Well I think they know each other.' He gestured to the pair locked in each other's arms faces alight with joy. Flora simply stood watching dumbfounded, her eyes smiling at her mother's obvious pleasure.

'It doesn't matter who he is, although I think that's clear from his face; just to see that look on her face after all this time is enough for me. I've never seen her change like that before though! Usually it's all bones and flying feathers.'

With that said, she grabbed Cal's hand and dragged him with strength born of happiness; outside to meet the man she felt she had always known would appear.

At that moment Morgan raced out of the forest at full tilt, screeching to a halt when he saw Claire locked in the embrace of a man as large as himself, his posture all too, familiar. At the unexpected interruption they broke apart, turning as one; the two men faced each other.

Morgan stared into the eyes of the man, alike to him as his own face in the mirror; except for the fact it was his future, more mature face, nonetheless striking for its maturity.

The tall stranger stepped forward and without hesitation pulled Morgan to him in an enthusiastic bear hug.

'Mor,' he said gruffly. 'It's been a long while since I saw you but I've been watching all these years.'

Morgan drew back abruptly, 'Dad?' He stuttered, unknowingly repeating Claire's words, clenching his jaw and his fists in an effort to control his emotions. 'Where the **fuck,** have you been all this time? We thought you were gone for good. Have you seen Lily, she's here too, and how do you know Claire?' Morgan broke off, gasping for breath after his dash through the forest.

Cal and Flora made their way outside just in time to hear what Morgan said, the similarity, startlingly obvious as the older man gave Claire a final hug and turned toward Morgan, hand outstretched in greeting. They saw him draw Morgan into a hug; a smile lit up his face, just as Morgan and Lily's did, his face the perfect prototype of their dark good looks.

'I'll explain all Mor,' he said. 'First I need to talk to Claire on an urgent matter.'

'What can be so urgent that you can't spare two minutes of your time to tell me, **where the hell you've been**,' bellowed Morgan, losing control; out of character for him.

From above, with a rushing of wings, Ruark crashed down to land on Morgan's shoulder.

'Ah, little sister.' said Pwyll. 'It's you I've come to speak to Claire about, and your sibling found on the Wolds in Yorkshire.' There was no reply as Ruark studied him unblinkingly. 'What's wrong with her said Pwyll?'

'She's just a raven I rescued Dad,' said Morgan. 'She's super smart but not a changer.'

'Nonsense,' scoffed Pwyll. 'Look at that silver streak on her wing; she's one of the Lady's' own, for sure.'

'I always thought the same Pwyll,' said Claire, 'but she's never spoken or made the change around us.'

'What's her name Morgan?' Pwyll asked.

'I call her Ruark, because that's the sound she was making when I,' …he trailed off, staring at Ruark as she moved down his arm a little, the better to stare back at him. He faltered as the world shifted a little beneath his feet; he heard a piercing scream he was sure everyone could hear …Ruuuark came the cry again and yet again, mournful and pain filled.

'Mor,' said Cal sharply, stepping forward to grasp Morgan's arm before he could topple over. 'What's wrong?'

He felt the world spin on its axis as Cal caught him, pulling him down to sit on the ground with his back against a tree. Ruark flew agitatedly between Cal and Morgan until Pwyll stepped forward to help. Morgan passed out.

He was gone, soaring through the 'Between', a large flock of his kin flying around him, and then he was shifting into his human form as the man named Brandubh, Cunningman; Druid Bard of the Isles. He knew again that many years had passed since the shapechanger Rowan had died for him, her body never found in any form. It was assumed she had been taken by the wolves or foxes, as was the Way of all Things, but he had been saddened and humbled by her sacrifice, which had enabled him the time to learn all that he had learned through concurrent lives. He was Morgan and Brandubh, 'Blackraaven' in one, sworn to The Morrigan as her Bard and Healer.

He would never forget the cry he'd heard as Rowan died; heard it echo again in his mind through the ages. He woke shivering; concerned faces looked down at him.

Pwyll reached out, placing his index and second finger on Morgan's brow just above and between his eyebrows. He muttered a few words, an incantation in the ancient tongue, circling his fingers three times on the spot.

'Seere a' lle, meiva a' lle, seere na' oira lle,'

Morgan's head cleared instantly; he grasped the proffered hand his father held out to help him rise. They exchanged a silent glance; on realising Ruark could be the lost Rowan's familiar spirit. Now was not the time, he couldn't get his own head around it; soon they agreed with a nod.

'What just happened,' asked Flora with concern? 'Are you okay Mor?'

'Yes,' replied Morgan groggily. 'Just a little light-headed. Thanks Flo.'

'So,' said the ever practical Cal. 'Who's going to do the introductions?'

'Sorry Cal,' grinned Claire. 'This is Pwyll a one-time friend and …erm …yes …erm friend,' she stuttered, trailing off somewhat sheepishly.

'Friend!' Pwyll roared, fit to burst with laughter but stopped himself from saying more. He saw Flora's quizzically raised eyebrow as she looked at Claire; he knew instinctively she was Claire's daughter, their similarity undeniable.

'Yes, friend,' affirmed Claire with a playful poke at Pwyll's ribs, 'and a long time ago,' she said, turning to her daughter with a smile. 'Long before Harry too,' she finished, stroking Flora's cheek fondly.

'This is my father,' said Morgan, speaking quietly to them. 'I haven't seen him since I was seventeen however, and I have no idea where he's been or who with,' he said somewhat bitterly. 'Where's mother?' he continued, looking his father in the eyes.

'Ah,' replied Pwyll. 'She's still around somewhere but you know her, ever restless.'

'Oh indeed I do,' sneered Morgan. 'Both Lily and I remember all too well the time we spent with each other, waiting for her to come home, for her to be a mother to us perhaps, you know **feed us** occasionally. It was always famine or feast, although there again, you're not to blame for her 'Fae-ness' either, I guess.'

Pwyll stepped forward; grasping his son by the shoulders, he looked deep into his eyes and said. 'I'm sorry son, I've always been trying to bring her back, always been looking for the moment when she would come home but it's never to be and for that I'm sorry. Searching for her took me away from you and Lily but at least I could be there in the earlier growing years of school for you, although I missed my little girl grow into a woman. How is she Mor? Is she as fine to look at as your mother?'

'Finer,' replied Morgan. 'She looks like me and like you, but in the most delightful feminine way of mother.'

'Then she will be a beauty for sure,' grinned Pwyll. 'You only have to look at us to see it.'

Morgan couldn't help but laugh at the dry wit of his father he'd missed so much over the last sixteen years, hugging him anew with a spurt of pleasure as the memories stirred. He'd never been able to stay mad at his Dad for long.

At that moment, Bethan and Max arrived. Pwyll glanced searchingly toward the direction from which they'd come, before turning to meet the others.

Introductions done, Flora invited everyone in for a drink and to share the platter she'd made before the unexpected arrival of Pwyll. She noticed that Pwyll grasped her mother's hand and they looked long at each other, joy evident on both their faces again. She smiled quietly to herself; catching Cal's eye, her smile broadened into her sunny, infectious grin. Cal winked at her knowingly, smiling back at her obvious pleasure.

Chapter 3
Maeve

Standing stones aged by the passing of Tyme
...call to the soul to remember their rhyme
...of the greening days when the world was new
...and the winds of song 'cross the planet blew

 Maeve woke to the sound of rain on the roof of the Hearth; droplets of water splashed off the leather of her jerkin and into her face as they leaked through the reed thatching. Icy cold, they were more than enough to bring her from the depths of sleep to wide awake in an instant.

She sat up, shaking the wet from her hair and clothing, wiping her face on her sleeve ...just another day in paradise she grinned to herself, thinking of her big warm bed in her room at 'earthly rites', but that story was fast fading ...she was still Maeve but which one ...was she truly an amalgam of both? She wondered long on what had sent her here; had she done something wrong; vaguely remembering the small being that had been haunting her, the constant gibes becoming like thorns under her skin. She was ashamed at how she'd behaved at the nasty urgings of the Water Merrow. Something else she was struggling to remember; the creatures' name had felt so familiar at the time.

She sighed and stretched, letting go her frustration yet again. Food was her priority right now she thought as the door flew open and the child Alma burst into the room excitedly.

'Come on lazy lugs,' she said, grinning from ear to ear. 'They're here, the Lady and the Bard for the Full Moon Rite. There'll be feasting tonight for sure!' Alma paused to tug at Maeve's sleeve instead. 'Come ON!' She said insistently.

'Alright, already,' laughed Maeve. 'I'm coming!'

They wandered out into the morning's wet, pulling up their hoods and huddling together for warmth, they headed to the Hearth for food and news of the night's events.

As they walked into the communal Hearth, the sound of fifty or more voices assaulted them, a wall of noise accompanied by the overwhelming smell of rich warm meats, fresh bread and the underlying, distinct odour of the wet hounds, milling around under the table and underfoot.

Maeve had overcome her predilection to non-animal foods rapidly, for otherwise she would indeed have starved. Wild bitter greens, roots, grains, meats and fish were the staple diet of the thread she now lived in and once again, she thought to herself, 'When in Rome.'

Alma and Maeve grabbed a trencher of bread filling it to overflowing with salty meats to share. Tearing off the ends and dunking them into the gravy. Maeve was sated first, she left Alma to finish while she went to rinse her hands and fetch water for the little girl, quenching her own thirst on the way.

The gossip of the day was all about the coming Full Moon rite. Maeve's first, after her final acceptance by into the clan; she was elated.

Life had become so simple for her that much of the time she was in the moment, becoming more spontaneous every day as she took on any chores given or training she received, with equal enthusiasm.

The little girl Alma, always seemed to be somewhere close by and every time she looked at the child she thought she should know her, have met her, but the answers wouldn't come. Alma brought out the child in her; she remembered her own playful side before the water Merrow had so disturbed her peace, causing the rift to occur between herself and Morgan. She taught the little girl to swim, talked to her of the changes soon to come in her growing, slender body. She had learned about the mosses used to stem menstrual flow and had shown Alma in turn, thus becoming big sister and mother to the strange, changeling-like child.

Maeve related to her differentness, her bitterness, which would come to the fore at the rare times she spoke about her village of birth and her parents.

Alma showed Maeve her skill with the Water Sprites but Maeve would at times discourage her, remembering the viciousness of the Merrow. Alma however would make it a fun thing but still the creatures never warmed to Maeve, remaining aloof and wary. If she strayed too close to the river, they would glare at her, baring their sharp teeth and warbling in their 'water rill' language.

Still, the days drifted by, hunting and fishing, foraging for roots, greens or mushrooms depending on the season and taking turns in watching over the livestock. She was even included in the search for the various healing plants, bark, moss and flower and time appeared to slow down as other chores learnt, were carried out; stretching and tanning hides for warmth and for leather strapping and her work as an artisan, making blades and such. One day flowed into another and for the first time in her 25 years, Maeve Hedinger was at peace.

From the moment, she had found herself pinned to the ground outside the Hearth at the feet of the Warrior-Lady Scathach; she had not really looked back. Her first thoughts of rebellion had vanished quickly when she saw the qualities and strengths of the others, born and raised to the lifestyle lived, albeit sometimes short and intense when called on to do battle, but never boring.

It wasn't that she didn't think of Beth, Flora, Sam and the others, especially Mor. There were the glimpses of Bran as he visited the clans and she knew that he was an aspect of the same, their faces identical only their colouring different, Bran's having the tendency towards reddish hair and pale, freckled skin to Mor's swarthy, darker looks. Indeed, she thought of her friends often, feeling frustrated that she couldn't tell them how sorry she was about her previous behaviour.

She often thought however, that as everything was occurring simultaneously she must have parents here somewhere or had she, literally, been thrown out of her own realm into this one? In addition there was, the child Alma, who had seemed to know her and even take to her from the onset, where did she fit in all this?

Everything flashed through her mind as she threaded her way through the mingling, animated folk, who were fast becoming her tribe, her clan, her Tuath.

On the peripheral of the seething group of, what he considered mindlessly, happy humans, Aerandir Sensarrius stood with the accustomed sneer on his saturnine face as he watched. Ah, so that's where the red raven went to, he thought as Maeve appeared. I'm sure mother will be pleased to know because where she is, so too will that annoying creature be.

Subjected to bitter embarrassment at the hands of his own people had not improved Aerandir's demeanour. Deep in the forest, several weeks ago in human reckoning and before Samhain, Fae elders had gathered to make Aerandir aware that his behaviour was unacceptable. He had crossed the line when he refused to give the first mutated Maker into Hercurin's keeping.

After the solitary confinement he had received as punishment for his insolence; he had taken to the forests of the world between worlds in isolation, although this time, of his own choosing.

He shifted restlessly, moving again through the trees and back to the realm where he had perpetrated the original mischief, looking for more, something new to stimulate him.

He had assumed the Elven folk had helped the little Dark Maker heal, by now. As he passed through the veil, he saw the creature hovering over a man sitting beneath a forest giant; one of the group of Bethan's followers, he recalled. Before the creature could engage with the oblivious man, the chilling scream of a hunting owl ripped through the peaceful forest.

Instantaneously the man leapt to his feet and ran in the direction from which the cry came; with a wicked grin, Aerandir was in pursuit in a second. 'At last,' he chuckled. 'Some entertainment perhaps but what is an owl making that noise for in daylight?'

The Dark Maker followed.

Chapter 4
Sybille's Book of Shadows

Full Moon Esbats

Feel Her light on your skin ...draw Her in, draw Her in
Breathe Her into your core ...deeper now than before
In your blood ...through your lungs Her Magicks' begun
.Through your breath ...to your Heart
Through your brain ...feel it start
Be aware in the now ...in Her Magickal light
Be still ...breathe Her in ...listen
...watch Her silver Orb glisten
She's still there on the 'dark of Moons' night...
While deep in the dreaming, the planet is waking
...oceans are rising the earth realm is quaking
...and yet through all of the doomsayer's fear
...we may feel fearful, tenderer, yet
...bathed in Her light ...we're STILL HERE!

The Moon in all Her phases has been a source of superstition, delight, awareness and even solace to folk of all countries and traditions worldwide.

It was the Moon, together with the menstrual cycles of women, which created the first Calendar of sorts. Life is cyclic, the regularity of the 29.5-day cycle of the Moon and women's menses was readily available to chart the patterns of

*nature and the associated elements, for celebration and hon-
ouring of the Lord and Lady, for once all fertile women
would bleed at the same time*

*Just as the Moon, viewed as having power over the
turning planets and cycles within nature, so too is she associated with having power over the forces of the inner tides of
humankind, the mind and the spirit conjoined. Therefore,
She can bestow the gifts of psychic visions and dreams but can
in turn, dispense insanity and delusion on people who exhibit
untoward, weak or egocentric behaviour.*

*In the Mystery teachings on the Crooked Path, dark
is the mother of the Moon and Her light. As the first power,
She is approached with both fear and reverence. The ancient
stories of Hecate, Aradia, Arianrhod and other Triformis
Goddesses, are associated with the power of darkness and the
Moon in the waxing, waning, new and dark cycles, by which
the eight Sabbats of the wheel came about.*

*In ancient times, the light of the Moon __was__ the pow-
er of the Moon, not merely symbolically but as the substance
of magick itself.*

*Of course, the solar Sabbats play their own role in
the literal sense of crop rotation and physical manifestation in
nature, but the Moon and Her mystery is the source of all
Magicks.*

*In the Esbat rites of the turning wheel, Dark of
Moon is associated with inner workings and for planning the
next phase. New Moon energy is for putting in place things
that are desired to manifest in the coming cycles as the Moon
'grows,' waxing to Full again, when the manifestation of last*

month's rites should complete. Onward again, as the Moon wanes, decreasing the energy needed for growth and manifestation in turn. From this, we can truly see where everything has a prescribed time to grow and to diminish. If the Moon controls the tides of this world and humans consist of 75% fluid, it would be foolish to think that, if the oceans and rivers are affected in their ebb and flow, we in turn would not be.

The ritual act of 'Drawing Down the Moon' is performed as a means to harness the energy and magickal power of the Moon at Her peak as she appears to shimmer between the edge of the world and then lifts, soars above, as our own planet spins within Her ebb and flow of tidal cycles.

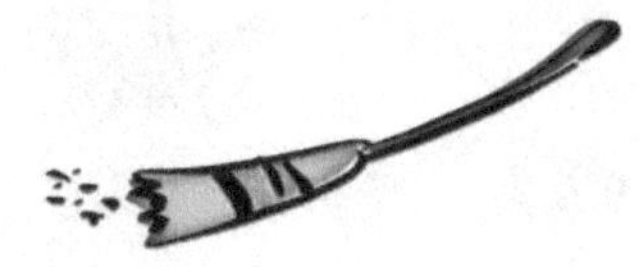

Chapter 5
Jay-Lily

The wytch wheel turns ever round
…winds blow strong over sacred ground.
Flow with the tides and love abounds
…fight and life's fire is no longer found

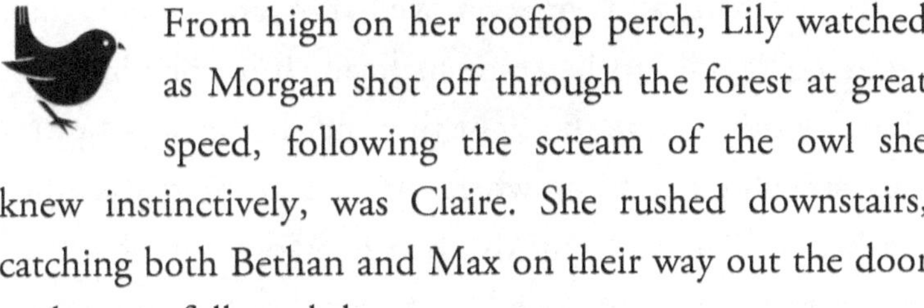

From high on her rooftop perch, Lily watched as Morgan shot off through the forest at great speed, following the scream of the owl she knew instinctively, was Claire. She rushed downstairs, catching both Bethan and Max on their way out the door as they too followed the cry.

They all ran, Bethan covering distance at such speed even Lily was panting to keep up. Max halted, bending over with his hands on his knees, gasping for air.

'Take your time.' Lily called over her shoulder with a grin, as she shifted to her Blue Jay form, faster than he'd ever witnessed before; it still freaked him out.

'Wait,' he yelled after her, but she was already winging her way after the rapidly retreating figure of Beth. 'How does she move that fast,' he queried aloud before following them as quickly as he was humanly able.

Bethan paused sniffing the air, her shape, fading in and out shimmered in the afternoon sunlight; she became almost translucent, glowing like a silver flame. Beth felt rather than saw the Dark Maker as it fled the forest, calling out in a harsh, haunting voice; she'd never heard it make more than a hiss. On the edge of her vision, she caught something else, a tall dark shape moved rapidly through the trees; she recognised Aerandir Sensarrius.

Lily and Beth broke cover together, Max not far behind, to see a stranger leaning over a seated and obviously distressed Morgan; reaching out he rubbed two fingers over Morgan's forehead.

Bethan and Max moved forward while Lily, changing rapidly to her human form, froze on the spot. She couldn't believe the sight that met her eyes as her father straightened from where he was leaning over her brother. Cal moved quickly to help Morgan to his feet; she heard Claire introduce him as Pwyll to the group who glanced toward where she was standing in the shadow of the trees; he knew she was there.

She watched as they filed inside as if it were the most normal thing in the world for him to be there. Morgan, sensing her there, paused a moment before calling out to her. 'Jay-Lily, come on. You can't hide out here forever.'

Lily didn't stir, simply stood with tears coursing down her cheeks. With a sad shrug and a shake of his head, Morgan followed the others inside.

Taking the time to control both her grief and her anger, Lily thought back over the years since their father had disappeared. Being a shaper, she had often picked him up on the Aether but never been able to pinpoint his exact position. Now he was here, just as she'd wanted night after night but had he left it too late she wondered, for her to forgive him for leaving them with a mother who didn't really know what it was to be one.

With a deep sigh, she wiped away her tears and straightened her back. There were a few things she needed to say to him and perhaps now weren't the time to confront him, not with the rest of the group there but 'hey' she thought, 'who cares.' Bracing herself much like a warrior would, she stepped out of the forest and walked towards the house. As she entered, she heard her father speaking of where he'd been and what he'd been doing.

'You should have seen it Mor.' He was saying waving his hands in the manner she so reluctantly, yet fondly remembered. 'It had a wing span this wide...' he tailed off as he saw Lily standing in the doorway and his face lit up, but before he could respond she was in his face...

'Oh yeah!' interjected Lily. 'Like that's an excuse for leaving us when we were only 12 and 17 apiece? Morgan practically raised me through all that time ...16 years Da,' she said, reverting to the colloquial, with a catch in her voice.

'Where the **fuck** were you?' she roared, unable to keep still any longer, she raised her fists to him wanting to hammer his broad chest but he grasped her wrists, holding her back gently until Flora put her arms around her and held her while she sobbed. It was not a sight often seen.

Well that's three times I've heard that yelled at me tonight, thought Pwyll; Cal, having the same thought, caught Pwyll's eye with a rueful smile.

Pwyll stood back waiting for his daughter to re-cover herself, he could see the tell-tale flush of anger, combined with embarrassment, that had always flushed colour into her cheeks, when she struggled to gain self-control. He knew well enough, even after all these years, to let her be.

When she recovered herself a little, Flora released her, handing her a handkerchief, she gave her shoulder a last stroke, in fondness. Lily sank into a chair. Words were not necessary as all could see the pain written across her face at Pwyll's sudden appearance after all the years. They were far from immune to each other's sensitivities.

Pwyll simply stood waiting for her to recover her composure before stepping forward to take the struggling Lily into his arms.

'I haven't been far away all this time Jay-Lily; I've been close in my Owl form, at times almost forgetting what it is to be human too. It's been necessary, as from the 'Between', I've been able to protect you better than I would've here. Your mother's a strange and cunning be-ing, with an agenda where cross-bloods are concerned. How we ever managed to conceive and birth the two of you is a constant source of wonder and the complexities of these altered bloodlines are at times, beyond me. As for explaining them …well,' he paused shrugging his shoulders as if throwing off a heavy mantle of pain and frustration. 'But this is all for another time. I want to celebrate with all of you my simply being able to be here, finally.'

He trailed off as he felt his daughter respond to his murmurings before breaking apart from him to blow her nose. He took the handkerchief from her and wiped her eyes as if she were still the little girl he remembered her being. It had indeed been a very long time; here she was a woman, and more beautiful than her mother ever had been.

As if a heavy blanket of sadness and stress lifted, they all began to talk at once, leaving Lily to recover.

Max watched, wanting to go to her but feeling at a loss. As he was looking longingly at Lily in walked, a giggling Tara and a grinning, yet he could tell somewhat distressed, Samantha.

Chapter 6
Sybille's Teachings: Spirit

Spirit sings within your frame
Water can put out the flame
Earth is solid, grounding, now
Air breaths the song all things allow

Spirit: the essence of all that is, our etheric bodies and all the layers of life in every all forms.

When we learn that all is made of this, we are well on the way to discover the truth of our being, for all is energy. Nothing exists without the embodiment of spirit in matter on our physical plane, for it is the animator.

Every breath we take, every thought, word and deed IS spirit as too everything is 'Spiritual' for if it were not it would mean, in effect it 'lacked spirit.'

Goddess, God, all directions, south, east, north, west, within, without, above, below.

Chapter 7
Maker's Dance

Makers dance to the tune of the All
…their rhythm accompanying the beat of your soul
…spiralling, circling listen to Her call
…an endless summoning 'twixt day and night
…tugging at you …pulling you home to the light
…dance to their rhythm, let your heart takes flight

The Dark Maker hid by day in a hollowed tree, she felt confused by the light, the pull in her core and frightened by the dark inner yearning the rhythm of night pressed on her.

She knew she'd not experienced darkness before it was a new concept entirely. She remembered that she'd come from a source of endless light and warmth but not how she came to be here, lost and confused; another new concept hurt her the most, loneliness.

She circled in the dusk at sunset before settling in a tree, close to the dwelling of the purest being she'd found to follow, in hope they might help her understand the loss she was feeling that often turned to anger and hatred, when exposed to the negativity of most humankin.

For a while, in that moment between light and dark, she would remember that primary source but then it would diminish as the grip of the night rhythms overcame her. An owl's cry, a mouse's squeal for a life, ended so abruptly or a rabbit caught, screaming with the piercing sound of a human child. All took their toll on her senses until they became a vile, sour mix and she no longer knew anything but a sense of outrage at the violence of such simple acts of innocent survival.

She remained stationary, almost reflective as she witnessed the passing of spirits between the realms of this thread and the otherworld. She could see in every direction threads of light and dark, twisting their way through the tapestry of the unknown. Some would light up for her, calling her to follow but somehow it was the darker strands that tugged at her most. Then a being would come, dark of hair and twisted of nature who would attempt to coerce her out of hiding; only the last remnant of her memories of light kept her hidden for now, but she was failing, her own light a dim shadow of itself.

Words would float to her on the Aether, from the dwelling she was drawn to watch and on the winds; words such as trust, love, home but then others would form on the sticky darker threads such as, fear, pain, revenge and death. She could still tell the difference, no matter how deeply she'd fallen into the humankin's threads but the return to her true self was becoming a distant dream.

She would watch the humankin come and go about their strange business, their faces sombre and pale or animated and excited by some small discovery. Occasionally, she'd hear the call of the tall Fae Aerandir who had saved her from the fire elementals; still she didn't feel right about his dark visage and his cloying perfume, which held the very stench of corruption she remembered, had caused her to fall.

Had he in fact summoned her, or was it his dark sister-mother; Aelish she was known by. Aithlin was the only other she trusted and the forest lord but if they caught her, would they destroy her or heal her pain …such confusion.

Flitting now in the darkening, she saw a man emerge from the dwelling; she could see by his energy that he was confused too. Could he help? He seemed to know of the dark and its call, pulled perhaps as she was by the effect of another's manipulations.

She flitted closer and he appeared not to sense her but then suddenly, turning toward her his eyes opened wide in surprise and yes, fear but too late, as she saw his mouth move and as if from far away the words, 'No, don't,' before she was caught in a fine web that pulled her into darkness again.

Mirdhaucha laughed aloud at the strange bug she'd caught in her net, wondered if M'lady would like it.

Chapter 8
Samantha

Gasping for air, Sam woke drenched in sweat and, to her immediate embarrassment and concern, her own urine. She hadn't wet the bed since childhood, when this dream had visited repeatedly. She recalled how often her parents chided her for the mess they considered she should have, 'grown out of.' As if she'd a choice in the matter, when ripped from the deepest sleep to find herself and her bed saturated.

In the nightmare, she was on a great pyre, alight, a living, screaming torch of pain. Then with the sounds of the crowd diminishing, she heard only the crackle and pop of her own flesh burning, the smell cloying like pork fat even over the stench of soot and smoke.

When the smoke parted like a veil for a brief moment, her last fleeting recall was of a pair of soft grey eyes looking at her, watching her burn with utter sorrow and horror, 'forgive me,' he mouthed to her before the smoke finally overcame her and she was floating free of a burned and blackening body.

She had never managed to fathom what this dream was about until now, when she thought about the concurrent lifetimes experienced, anything could happen. Would she have to relive this again physically she wondered if she were to merge with her other self. How in the world would she cope if that were so, could she go back, to warn Magdalena of this possible outcome?

She had really only wanted to take a nap in the afternoon quiet but fallen fast asleep. Rolling out of bed, still shaking from the raw agony of pain and fear experienced in the dream, she ripped the sheets from the bed, taking them with her to the shower to rinse both them and her.

Sam felt as if she were coming down with something, hot and cold at the same time and so decided she would head over to see Flora for a remedy to help her sleep and to release the fear from her body that would hold her back or make her sick.

Drying off and dressing hurriedly, she opened the windows to air the room; a swarm of bright leaf sprites descended on her, soothing her skin with soft little fingers even licking her hands, leaving a shiny trail of silvery-green sap, reminiscent of Aloe Vera. She calmed them in turn, and they caught her tears of relief as they rolled down her cheeks, so moved was she by their care.

Feeling much stronger, after a short while she slipped silently downstairs, out the door and to her car. More leaf sprites stirred in the trees as she passed and a single black feather drifted down to land on the bonnet of her car. Retrieving it and sticking it in her hair, she called out questioningly,

'Tara, is that you? I'm off to see Flora and Cal, do you want to come too?'

With a rustle of leaves and feathers, Tara dropped from the tree above. Her expression was serious as she landed close, looking deep in Sam's eyes; a frown creased her brow.

'Are you okay Sam? I heard you calling out in your sleep but your little sentinels,' she indicated the swarm of sprites, 'wouldn't let me listen in or even take a peek through the window at you. They had you barricaded in to all intent and purpose.'

'Yes, I'm okay thanks Tara,' replied Sam. 'It's just an awful old dream I used to have as a child of being burned alive, has resurfaced from Goddess knows where. Hold on a minute, what do you mean you heard me call out? I wasn't yelling that loudly, surely?'

'Hmm,' said Tara. 'Yeah I'll come with you but you realise I could teach you to change and you could fly with me.' She grinned.

'You're kidding Tara!' Sam exclaimed. 'Not everyone's a shifter surely?'

'Well Sam,' said Tara. 'In your case I'd be surprised if you weren't!' With that, she simply walked around the car, and got into the passenger seat, frustrating Sam with her all too familiar, obtuseness.

'You didn't answer my question Tara.' Sam said as they settled, fastening her seat belt.

'Well it's simple really Sam,' replied Tara. 'Every one of you, in fact everything known and unknown in the Universe has a vibration or energy, their own special note in the All. When it's disturbed by joy, a human note is enriched and, if another is involved, just for a moment it becomes a melody, but if it's in fear or pain, the note becomes discordant. When there's an argument, it's cacophonic. I guess it's a little like a mother recognising all the different ways her baby cries, one when it's hungry, another when it just wants a cuddle 'cos it's lonely. You should hear the sound of anger Sam, of war, pollution and greed; the sounds the little Maker heard that altered it so…' She trailed off.

'I remember the sound when we knew something had happened to Sybille, Tara. It was as if something beautiful had irretrievably ended. Nothing has ever really been the same again for me.'

There was nothing more Sam could say as they drove on in silence, other than to comment on the changing trees as they began to wear their new coats of greening buds and blossom. Ostara, Spring Equinox was almost upon them.

They arrived at Covenstead just in time to see Lily race out of the forest and into the house, slamming the door behind her in anger.

'Oh-oh,' said Tara, 'someone's in trouble! Let's go see,' she said, grinning wickedly at Samantha, who couldn't resist smiling at Tara's obvious delight at a possible human drama to investigate.

Linking arms, Tara led Sam to the house, peering cheekily in through the window, causing Sam to giggle outright at her wicked humour. Tara was always a breath of fresh air just when most needed and so with thoughts of her own nightmare fled, they entered through the kitchen door, where Flora stood, a sobbing Lily in her arms.

A large man stood with his back to them, watching. Mor, Beth, Claire, Cal and Max, silently looked on, the latter with unbridled longing in his eyes. Tension palpable, Tara took everyone by surprise, changing mid leap to half bird; half human she leapt onto the big man's back with a crow of delight.

'Pwyll, Pwyll!' She croaked in her husky voice. 'It's been forever!'

'Why as I live and breathe it's Tara.' Pwyll exclaimed with equal delight.

With a bellow of pleasure, Pwyll grabbed Tara and unceremoniously, waltzed her around the room. Tara broke away first, her grin slipping away, her face sobered, maturing the moment as she turned to Lily. Reaching out to touch her fondly between the eyes, she said 'Come on Lily, there's no time for personal grudges or bad blood between any of you. Your Dad may be guilty of not informing you where he had to go…'

She held up her hand as Lily tried to interject. 'NO, Lily he **had** to go! When the Lady calls you, there are no choices in the matter, not if you are totally dedicated to the Way that is. The trouble is there is a singular lack of dedication these days; only lip service given. This is a lesson in itself and much is learned from the sacrifices your father has given in the Lord and Lady's service. Sadly, it's a challenge for people not to be affected by others opinions of what one should or shouldn't believe or do. In this realm, other people's opinions seem to be more important than giving the self, permission to be who one is in truth.' She paused for breath, her face changing again, feathered, with piercing blue, raven eyes.

Lily stood her ground, but quieted with the strength yet compassion she saw there, sank slowly into a handy chair. Mor passed her a tissue and she mopped her face, giving him a watery, embarrassed grin.

In sympathy, the others left her for a while to her own thoughts. Tara reached out again to hug her before pulling a goofy face as The Morrigan left her and she reverted to her girlish self.

'I hate when that happens.' Tara said with a toothy grin.

Punching Tara on the arm good naturedly, Claire greeted Samantha with a smile and a hug, before introducing Sam to Pwyll, who gave her a deep penetrating look, a small frown of concentration appearing on his forehead; she had little time to wonder why.

Nobody questioned her reasons for turning up unannounced as they gathered around the table to bless the food and to hear the story of how Claire and Pwyll met, touching too on the approaching Ostara Rite of spring. Tara and Lily soon joined in, although the tension between Pwyll and Lily remained, it had lessoned to a degree of civility at least.

Flora, intuitive as always, shared a glance with Sam, a query in her eyes. Unwilling to share her dream with everyone straight away she mouthed, 'later' to Flora. Bethan, who reached out to give Sam's arm a rub in consolation, saw it clearly; Sam's dream hung like a shadow around her, a grey cloak of sorrow; the nature sprites were for once still, clinging to her in something akin to desperation.

Later that evening Flora and Bethan sat with Samantha to talk about her recurring dream. Flora had mixed a homeopathic remedy to help ease her stress, enabling more clarity in becoming the observer, rather than experiencing the horror, each time the dream manifested.

They had no idea why this dream should recur now and so couldn't really help Sam to understand it either. They could only offer their constant support and encouragement, while awaiting information that might be more concrete.

The next day being a workday, they said their goodnights, Sam staying for the night on the couch in Sybille's favourite room, where she found comfort in the familiar fragrance of incense that always lingered there.

Bethan, Morgan, Max and Lily wandered back through the forest by torch light. Having little to say, comfortable together in silence, they listened to the sounds of the night creatures stirring as the wheel turned toward Equinox again.

Drifting on the crisp breeze whispering through the forest, floated the sound of a flute and in harmony, a harp; Hercurin and Aithlin played an air in celebration of the coming spring. Frosty mists began to rise from the damp ground and pools of water crisped over with a thin layer of ice. Spring may be well on the way but, pre Ostara, there could be heavy frosts, even snow still to come.

Bethan and Morgan hummed quietly as they walked together. Other sounds intruded into Bethan's consciousness, whispering voices and guttural notes echoed through the forest but at first, only she could hear them. Slowly, they all became a little agitated, as the forest seemed to close in. Lily paused, changing into her Jay shape, better to see what transpired in the Aether, causing Max to start in surprise yet again, at the speed of her changing.

Morgan came to a standstill as he recalled his inner visions and the number of times, when he walked through the forests of the 'Between', the black lacework of blight beginning to cover the ground and climb the tree trunks. There were patches of forest that were so still, neither night-bird sounds nor the rustling of leaves, as creatures such as echidna wandered the pathways, were audible. Utter silence, even the sounds of Aithlin and Hercurin's shared music, faded from hearing.

They stood frozen as silence encompassed them. Drawing closer together for comfort, they watched in horror as the light frost that had been forming changed, from white to sticky black threads, and the pools of water to stagnant, stinking mire; the stench filled their nostrils with the scent of decay. Tiny creatures squirmed and wriggled in shallow pools, struggling for air, worms and beetles fought for life in the murk.

Bethan halted, shaking her hood back from her hair and pulling herself up to her full height, growing taller still as the antlers grew from her forehead in silver shafts.

Hercurin burst out of the thicket, running now on four cloven hooves for speed, as the Stag of his naming. He came to a halt before the frozen group, stepping between them in a defensive stance, changing to his huge human form, teeth bared and antlers rearing from his forehead, to match those of his Lady.

Aerandir stepped from the trees, greeting Hercurin and Bethan with a parody of a bow.

'Arwen, Heru,' Lady and Lord, he said. 'I have seen the small dark Maker recently Heru. I had assumed the Elders or you, would have healed her but she is unchanged. I saw her following the one here known as Morgan Trethaway earlier this day but more I cannot say about her present whereabouts, Heru?' He bowed again.

'Why do you care Elf?' Hercurin replied. 'Had you been a little more caring of the Maker previously she would indeed be well healed and returned to the Birthing Tree.'

Meanwhile Bethan watched, listening intently, her eyes not leaving Aerandir's face. She walked up to him as he made to step back into the cover of the trees.

'I know you,' she said quietly. 'How and where do I know you?'

'Look in the mirror Lady Arianwen and you will see me there. Somewhere in human 'time' we have obviously shared ancestry that is clear.' He grinned again, this time a little wistfully.

'Indeed that may be so,' said the now fully manifested Arianwen, 'but is there anything you know that may help both of us understand ourselves better, our differences too perhaps?'

'Alas Arwen,' Aerandir bowed formally to her without his usual irony. 'I am truly sorry that I have no idea of where we may share family ties.' The last words spat out as if they had a bad taste to them.

'Then shall we agree to find out for each other?' said Arianwen, compassion for his pain in her eyes and voice.

Aerandir flushed crimson under his pallor at her words and without a trace of his usual scornful attitude he bowed again, tears sparkled in his eyes. 'Yes, Arwen, I would be honoured to search with you for the hidden truths we both seek of our heritage.'

With that, he nodded to the group curtly, bowed with respect to Hercurin. 'Heru,' he muttered his natural aloof self again before he turned the forest swallowed him again. The forest came to life again and the blight withdrew. Hercurin knelt on the ground, tracing his hands over the still writhing worms and beetles until they were restored to new again.

'Mela en coiamin,' Hercurin said to Bethan. 'My love,' his smile, gentle. 'Spring is upon us; soon it will be our time.'

Turning to the group, he said. 'Mellon en amin, lemma vama eska.' 'My friends travel safely home. What you witnessed is a breakthrough indeed, for the young Elflord but be aware, his close proximity to the poor, sick Dark Maker has also affected his being. This blight appeared where he walked and so we must take him home to heal before it spreads further.' With that, he turned, changed again and sped away after the retreating Aerandir.

'Is there going to be an end to this soon?' moaned Max in distress. 'I'm beginning to forget what normal is!' He exclaimed.

Lily flew to sit on his shoulder and for once, he didn't flinch as she pecked his ear cheekily before slipping from his shoulder and changed to her human form again.

They walked on, arm in arm together, Morgan and Bethan walking behind as they head home to Wells.

Chapter 9
Sybille's Book of Shadows

Rite of Ostara

Heart of the wildlands ...spirit of old
...what do you teach us, so gentle yet bold
Whom do you call as this new spring breaks
...who will hear you ...who will awake?
Will we stay sleeping or will we wake up...
...to dance in your meadows ...to drink from your cup
Will we remember ...as time's speeding by
...remember the greening ...and fly

Eostre, Ostara, easter, oestrogen, egg ...the first fertility festival of the new year, stolen from the Pagans and taken as the death and rebirth time for the White God of the christian church to come.

It is a time of celebration for the rebirth of the young God as the sun/son returning and the Goddess as Maiden. Eggs feature as a symbol of the fertility of burgeoning life to come, just as rabbits, chicks and spring blossoms do.

Ostara is Spring Equinox, when cycles begin anew and the wheel turns once more to the power of rebirth and life over death. This is not a Great Sabbat but one of great joy, as the first rays of sunlight felt on the skin; send a promise of hope, for new life.

Our bodies crave green growing things after mostly, root vegetables and heavy meats, eaten through winter and of course the first wild dandelion and sorrel leaves are ready, there for the taking. These give our bodies the first 'green foods' of the year, rich in vitamin C and iron, if we eat in balance with what nature has to offer, rather than what the supermarkets provide, albeit out of season. When we eat foods out of season, they do not contain the nutritional benefits they would if harvested fresh at the particular time of year that is natural for their species.

This is a rite of pure celebration of new life, fresh air and returning light, the first bulbs break ground and the birds and beasts begin their own mating rites. The longest night and shortest day is done.

Gratitude is the key to this rite and a great time for the regeneration of things one wants to continue to grow within or without, in the garden of nature or in the garden of the soul; each bear equal weight in the death and rebirth of the human spirit and physical being.

It is the time for the seasonal planting of new ideas and the study of fresh spiritual ideals that, when begun at this time of year, should manifest by Autumn Equinox, Mabon.

Grow your gardens well …there's always an opportunist waiting in the wings!

Chapter 10
Arianwen

She walks with grace upon the earth
...with faery horns and wings
She listens to your every word ...listen as she sings
She sings to you of a planet green
...and food for all to share ...tread gently
...for she's watching, all who break the 'oath of care'

Bethan remembered being a silver pelted otter, swimming in a deep lake; it was spring fed and the undertow at its heart was strong. It would pull her toward an underground channel and up through the watery depths, to emerge at a rocky opening in the mount known as Chalice Hill, from where she could see the Tor and the tower, built after the White Christ had called his monks to these shores, with their temples of stone. Before that, the settlement on the Isle of Seers, visible occasionally across from the mount, nestled below hidden in the mist. Now, after building their chapel it was forever concealed, lest Her secrets be lost.

As her aspect Leah, she'd known the area intimately but there had been a part of her, long before she'd blended with any human aspects that had existed, deep in the heart of the dreaming, long before humans lived to control invented time.

In truth, she couldn't remember 'becoming' Leah, she only recalled standing on a jetty looking out over a vast lake between four hills, where a coracle waited and a silver otter swam. She remembered the different perspectives she could quite consciously achieve between human, standing on the jetty looking at the otter and then the reverse, the otter looking at the human; it was always with the same eyes, the same consciousness.

Then there had been the moment when a beautiful young woman had given birth to a child of the earth and the waters and one had come to kill them both. Aithlin had saved the child and given her to grow with strong humankin who still believed in the Mother's Magicks and in turn, this one had come to the jetty and repeated the whole cycle again.

She knew as Arianwen, there was a piece of the puzzle missing; there was another, who killed and would kill again for revenge. How had this creature become so dark, and when?

Now with the human aspects of Leah and Bethan merged together as one, Arianwen stepped from the rocky opening, water droplets raining from skin grown rosy with the cold, her silver hair turned a burnished red by the precious minerals in the pool.

Sitting by the spring was a small creature; she cradled a Maker in her arms as it passed from this thread to another and she wept little tears like pearls that shattered on the rocks.

'Twan't me wot urt er, Arw'n, t'was ...' she couldn't bring herself to say, fear making her little face appear old.

The Leah aspect remembered this one and wept with her; Bethan stirred and knew what she was. Arianwen held her, speaking softly to her grief.

'Magick feeds the land and land feeds our magicks,' she sang. 'Humankin have forgotten to believe and so our power diminishes, as too will the essence of the Mother. Soon they will wonder why their earth realm is suffering dire change and in turn so must they. Change or die; like us disappear into the threads beyond time. Those who appreciate their own powers of co-creation with the Mother, with us and who have the ability to project in all directions to restore the earth plane they believe is reality will only inhabit this realm. It is only one reality among many but which will they chose as their truth, one with anger, revenge, regret and deceit or a planet where the light and the Mother's Magicks return to empower the land again,' and the tears of the small creature dried and the Maker was gone.

She was otter, dragonfly, leaf sprite, bird; a tree, a breath of air; a droplet of water vapour, a tidal pool of emotion. She knew no differentiation between herself and all that is for she was, all that is.

Chapter 11
Alma

Watery depths of oceans and lake
...calling your innermost soul to awake
Float in Her darkness both salty and sweet
...ride on Her waves to the shores of deep sleep
Life is Her gift, through the blood in your veins
...the lymph that flows gently as it pools and drains
...through every cell and under your skin
...swim in Her depths, find your tail, grow a fin
...in Her cold, silent pools ...find your watery kin

After breaking her fast with Maeve, Alma wandered off by herself down to the edge of the fast flowing river. Maeve had training, even though the Hearth was holding a Full Moon Esbat that night, the next would be Harvest Moon as Mabon approached swiftly.

Alma was feeling a little out of sorts, wondering if she had eaten too much of the rich meats; she shivered as if with an ague.

Her belly ached and her back was sore. At nearly 12 summers, she was beginning to fill out a little, although the Cunningman, Bran had said she would always be a 'willow the wisp' of a thing, the first signs of burgeoning womanhood were apparent.

She had a secret hoped he would be wrong, that she might grow as tall and shapely as her friend Maeve. That she may be a warrior, a fighter but she knew in her heart that would be in her dreams.

She was training as a seer, even though her earlier time on the Isle of Myst had not been a successful attempt at seership, to say the least. After her parents had sold her into, what she considered slavery, she'd gone out of her way to be surly and uncooperative out of pure spite. She remembered the war she'd seen in her father's eyes as he'd fought for just a little decency versus his greed for the coppers, when he realised he'd sold his only daughter and why. Only when it was already too late had she realised that it was not the fault of The Cybil, Leah or even Brandubh, who'd shown her only kindness.

She'd gotten herself into so much trouble with The Cybil she recalled, even though she's tried so hard to be good. In the end, the Lady had lost patience with her inattentiveness and had sent her to Scathach's Hearth to learn with the Cunningman instead.

'When you can behave Alma,' The Cybil had said to her firmly, 'you may return to take up training with Leah.'

Alma had cried as Leah silently took her back across the lake to the shore where Brandubh stood wait-ing. She had felt the energy that moved between the Priestess and the Cunningman like a song of hope.

Leah had kissed the little girl of then 8 years fondly, stroking her cheek in farewell before Bran lifted her up gently to sit with him, high on his horse. Alma had felt an unfamiliar grief in the knowledge that she would not see Leah for a long time, in fact her gut told her …never.

Now, with her belly aching, she curled up against the trunk of an ancient willow that leant far out over the water's edge. She thought she felt a movement in its trunk but ignored it, thinking it a small creature stirring; she sought comfort in its deep root system, dry now and filled with dead leaves from autumn's shedding.

She dreamed again of the farm and village where she'd been born and raised to the age of almost 7 summers, before the Cunningman had taken her away to the Seer's Isle of Mysts.

She remembered how scared her parents had been when she'd raised the water sprites from their watery slumbers. Superstitions rife, the simple villagers acknowledged her as, 'touched', different. It had not made her popular and really as a wee girl, all she'd needed as any child did, was to be loved for simply who and what she was. Instead, she was lonely; her friends were the goats, chickens and any other wildling of this realm or other, it made no difference to her.

Water Sprites in particular had danced to her bidding and she'd never questioned it, thinking it perfectly normal to see the Mother's little Magicks. She'd often looked long at her reflection in the water puddles and wondered how she had come to be the child of two stocky, ruddy complexioned country people, blond haired and blue eyed to her red hair, bright aqua-green eyes and buttermilk skin.

She dozed a while, squirming in her slumber as the unaccustomed pain in her belly intensified; spreading deep, into her little womb and down the insides of her thighs.

A small scaly creature raised itself on slender arms out of the water to whisper to her but with a splash was gone again, it smelt the changing energy of her coming womanhood and the danger that surrounded the sleeping child; racing to find help.

Further, down the riverbank from where Alma slumbered, Maeve stretched her tired limbs. A small aqua-blue creature reared up out of the water to balance on its tail. The creature's face was a grimace of fear and agitation. After the experiences with the Mirdhaucha, Maeve, with an innate fear of anything that came from the water, yelled at the creature to go away. It dove below the surface, only to resurface a little distance away jabbering in a strange gurgling language, like running water over stones. Maeve picked up a rock, meaning to throw it at the Water Sprite, only to have her hand grabbed mid throw as the Cunningman Bran came out of nowhere from behind.

'What do you think you're doing Maeve?' He yelled in her ear, scaring the wits out of her. She struggled to free herself from his grasp but he merely twisted her wrist until she dropped the stone.

'I hadn't taken you for a cruel woman,' he said in his calm, clear voice. 'Can you not see that the creature was trying to tell you something?'

They both turned back to the river to see the Sprite disappear under the speeding current.

'They're shy creatures too, you'll not see them again, that's for sure and you need them to work with you for the cooling element at your forge too.' He almost threw her hand away as he let her go, stepping back in obvious disgust.

'I... but it's...' but he was already gone, striding away downstream, following the small sprite as it swam, trying to tune in to its frantic song of distress. More were showing themselves, racing with great speed on sensing the fear of their kin, through the watery channels and bubbles of the now fast-flowing river.

'What's going on?' Bran called to them, he saw the tidal river begin to flow harder and faster as if driven by an unseen hand.

'Of course, idiot,' he rebuked himself aloud. 'It's a King tide tonight and the Moon is already tugging hard on the inner tides of the Mother. What's spooked the Sprites though I wonder; the tide wouldn't faze them one bit.' He heard a weak scream and the sound of crashing timber, large debris and branches were already floating haphazardly on the speeding current.

Running round the bend in the river, he came to a halt when he saw an ancient, giant willow had fallen into the river. He could only assume the cries had come from the tree's Deva or the little leaf sprites, mourning the loss of their old home. Small Makers were gathering to help them reassemble into their Trueshape, their Tree Deva, giving them time to moan and cry at their loss.

Bran stood in silence as he farewelled the huge old being, lifting his cap and bowing his head. It still made no sense that the Water Sprites were behaving in such a manner, they were obviously in great distress over some-thing. Hundreds of them were lifting themselves out of the water, clinging to the floating debris, in particular to a large piece of the tree's root system, caught between the remains of part of the trunk and the middle of the river. All too soon, it would wash away downstream and rapidly out to sea, he thought.

As sad as this was, all things pass and reshape themselves, never dying merely changing form and so he couldn't see why the Sprites were so upset; the Tree Sprite too was refusing to go with the bright Makers, who in turn were becoming more agitated, concern ringing out clearly in their song.

He was searching within for an answer when Maeve came running toward him at full speed, waving and pointing in horror at something; what, he couldn't see from where he stood.

He climbed up the bank to get a better view of the water and saw a faint stream of red flowing out from the root bowl, spreading across the surface; from an Otter or some other water creature, he thought.

Maeve however, screaming now like a Banshee, headed directly into the strong current, swimming determinedly but with difficulty, the root bowl pulled out of her reach and away from whatever was causing her concern.

She grabbed hold of the remains of an overhanging branch, struggling to keep afloat, to reach the twisted root and the obvious blood that was streaming from below it. Somehow, she latched on, Water Sprites swimming around her, wary of her bared teeth and clawing hands as she fought to free the body of a small girl.

On seeing the limp body of the child, Bran sprang into action. Racing into the river, he swam strongly as he measured Maeve's rapidly fading strength. Between them, with the aid of the Sprites they managed to drag the roots in which Alma lay trapped, toward the shore.

King tide would have his prize no matter what, pulling the twisting root into an undertow and holding the still conscious woman-child under. They could see that, although her britches were a little bloodied she appeared otherwise unharmed. Gasping for air Alma broke surface, her eyes, boring into Maeve's, filling with horror. 'Help me,' she screamed. **'Maeve, help me, please!'**

Maeve and Bran struggled to pull her free but the root had twisted itself around her legs as if it had hung onto her as a means of halting its own demise. Water Sprites swam beneath Alma lifting her head above water and stroking her face, calling to her and to each other and then Maeve and Bran clearly heard…

'Let go, Alma …let go, come home to us now.' It was as if a light went on in Alma's face, she let go the struggle and let them pull her away with them, still entangled in the roots and debris of the dying willow.

Maeve screamed, fighting them off tooth and nail but they scratched and bit her fingers as she clung on to the floating wood, freeing the root bowl from the remains of the trunk. Suddenly, with a deafening roar the tree branch whipped back, flinging Maeve and Bran onto the shore, while the Sprites towed little Alma away, duck diving under the water they pulled her with them down into the watery depths of the river.

Sobbing uncontrollably Maeve tried to stand, to go back to the river, to find her little sisterkin and bring her home but Bran pulled her down again, trying to hold her; to quell her grief he said. 'You have to let her go Maeve. You saw her face; she made a conscious choice …now you must let her go.'

'Never!' she shrieked, beside herself with grief as a part of her died; her inner child died, weeping tears of blood; her innocence died, she changed bitter fury taking away the last remnant of sanity. Bran tried to hold her but she ran, back along the riverbank to the Hearth of Scathach, where she threw herself at the Lady's feet, begging her to put an end to her grief, to end her life.

Bran appeared, calling out for the healers as he ran to tell of the loss of Alma to the first Elder he reached, before collapsing into a trance where he would create the story of the child, write the tale of her life and sing the song of grief for Maeve. He would journey to the inner realms to find her missing child-self and help her heal …if she would let him that is …was his last conscious thought…

In the depths of his dreaming, words rose to the surface like ripples across a still pool. He heard laughter and crying and knew not if the sounds came from him, from Maeve, or from Alma but he saw the child sleeping in the depths of a watery grave, surrounded by Sprites.

They were shooing away an Otter, Oonagh, he heard her name called from afar by Leah. Oonagh was trying to wake the girl, tugging on her clothing to pull her back to the light of day. The Sprites had dragged her way down the river and out into the Lake of Mysts close to the Seer's Isle, where they had made a nest for her to sleep in. They were prodding the Otter with tiny spears made from the spines of some long dead creature; Oonagh was losing the battle.

Above her, she saw the outline of Leah; drawn back to the surface she refilled her lungs.

'What is it Oonagh?' Bran heard Leah call out.
She had not yet mastered the gift of the water creature's
language and so had no knowledge of what lay in the
depths of the lake below her.

Dragonflies gathered despite the cold water,
floating on the surface, their wings creating a
kaleidoscope of colour ...she heard sobbing
and the lapping of water against the coracle became a
song that the Bards would sing…

'Twisting willow limbs, pulled her in deep
…a woman-child sinks into the pools of dark sleep
Sprite's wailing songs that bubble and moan
…sing her now safely, to her watery home
Who's left to mourn her …who hears her song?
Is it a matter of right or of wrong?
Woman-child Alma just finding her way
…must now walk the shadows from night into day
The strength of her nature, the spirit of her will
…the legacy of seership, lost now, ever still
What will sustain her …where is her song heard?
…why, in ripples on water …in small cries of a bird

Chapter 12
Life Goes On

Moon dark draws near
...respect life without fear
Go deep inside to the shrine of your soul
...drink of Her cauldron; sip from Her bowl
Watch the wheel turn ...see the stars spin away
...as the wheel turns again ...it will bring a new day

After the excitement of the previous evening, life continued as per usual, each of them arriving at work as if nothing had happened. It was Friday and the weekend work began as shoppers browsed, and clients looking for guidance in a reading, flowed in and out.

Annie Savage, oblivious to anything but what she was herself experiencing, stood gazing into nowhere at the reception desk. She'd been having bad dreams that left her feeling off colour and had realised that, although Harry had moved in with her for the weekend, things were not as they had been between them. He was changed too by the experiences and memories that had begun to return to him about his wife Claire and he was suspicious of Annie, as if she were part of a greater plot. She had finally told him about Vanessa and his contempt had been clear, firstly, because she had kept it from him and secondly, he was unable to consider the thought that he had another daughter, his relationship with Flora being what it was. It was then Annie realised what an utterly selfish person Harry was…

'Too late!' she said aloud.

'What's too late Annie?' said Flora coming from the office behind the reception desk,

'Oh nothing Flora, just a late booking is all,' stammered Annie.

'That's odd, I didn't hear the phone.' Flora replied but on seeing the hostility return to Annie's face, she left well alone. 'I'm sure everything will be fine for the day,' she reassured Annie.

'Well of course,' snapped Annie, the accustomed haughtiness returning. 'I've been doing this job long enough I think.' With that, she stalked off to knock on one of the reading room doors, huffing. 'Tara always runs over time you know Flora. She must be told to keep track.'

'That's okay Annie, it's only when she knows that there's no one else following straight after. She likes to give the extra time to those who need it.'

'Well that's all well and good but it's not putting money in your coffers is it, giving all this free time!'

At that moment, Tara's door opened and a flushed but happy client came to the desk to pay for her session. Annie scowled, pointedly at Tara, glancing at the clock and sighing. Tara merely said. 'Morning Annie, nice day!' before walking toward the kitchen with a grin plastered on her face, giving her client a gentle stroke of encouragement on the way past.

'Erm, Tara suggested I might see Flora Jenkins for a tonic. Can I make an appointment please?'

Flora raised her eyebrow at Annie as if to say, see that's how the money flows; it's not always from the same source, before following Tara to the kitchen. She called back over her shoulder, 'Let me know when you need your tea break Annie and I'll relieve you at the desk!'

Annie muttered her thanks somewhat ungraciously and made the booking for the client for later that day with Flora, the happy client almost skipped out the door.

There came a loud rapping on the window in the office; Annie turned to see a small and unusual little bird and a large raven, sitting side by side in broad daylight. She could have sworn they winked at her. I'm hallucinating, she thought to herself, perhaps I should see Flora myself.

Moments later the front doors burst open and a grinning Lily and Morgan strolled in.

'Morning Annie,' they called out together. 'We'll be upstairs in Maeve's studio if you need us.'

'Speaking of Maeve,' said Annie, quickly recovering her composure, 'when's she coming home? There's customer orders' waiting for her.' Annie didn't miss the glance exchanged between Lily and Morgan.

'Ah,' said Morgan a little hesitantly.

'Not for a while yet,' finished Lily. 'You'll have to ask the customers if we can do anything for them instead, if it's an urgent order.'

'Where is she anyway?' said Annie.

'Away!' they replied in unison, making a detour to the kitchen, where laughter rang out, the familiar tones of Tara and Flora clearly heard.

'Well there's a woman been looking for her, tell her if you're speaking with her!' There was no reply.

Sam came in at that moment, 'I'll tell her when we speak next, thank you Annie,' as she too headed for the kitchen, the sounds of laughter drawing her in.

One by one, the group all wandered in to work; Cal using Maeve's room for study during the time Flora was at work. He liked to be close to her and their relationship was now on an established footing. His fear for them was that he would have to return to his position at the Uni in York but he was thinking of taking a sabbatical for study and was waiting for the paper work to arrive. He was considering Anthropology. What better mentors could he have than Claire and Alex, perhaps even Pwyll, he mused, with so much firsthand experience and Max to help with a thesis outline, or Sam perhaps.

Bethan had arrived early, settling herself at her loom for the first time in a while. Her work recently more focused on music but the search for Sybille was uppermost in her mind.

She was working on a bright emerald green wrap for a customer and as she wove, she remembered weaving a similar one for Maeve for her birthday.

Stopping the loom, she stood, stretched and walked upstairs, ignoring Annie as she passed through reception. She didn't feel like engaging with her today but knew; soon something must change, where the difficult woman was concerned. Sometimes a little knowledge was a dangerous thing and in this case very.

Continuing up the stairs, Bethan walked into Maeve's rooms; all was still and in the studio only a brief bubbling of water came from the cauldron.

Moving quietly round the room, trailing her fingers over Maeve's things, Bethan sensed her friend's energy was waning. Even in her studio where Lily had been working, her energy was diminishing rapidly; it was as if she was disappearing to this realm, this current life

'Where are you little sister?' Bethan sent out to the universe. 'Where are you?'

Beth felt restless and knew that all was not well in the life of Maeve wherever she was; a deep rumble and eerie laughter came from the cauldron, once more shooting up stagnant and stinking pondweed, bitter vetch that bubbled like acid on every surface it touched.

'Enough!' exclaimed Bethan sternly as all was silent again then, 'Please Lady we can't lose another kindred soul! Will you let her come home again?' …there was no answer just the sound of someone crying, deep, gut wrenching sobs. Bethan sent a small invocation out to the sorrowing one…

'On days that seem they are like no other; go deep within, reach out to the Mother.
She hears every word that your soul ever cries, whispering, 'Fear not, for you can truly fly'
Come with me; together we'll fly o'er the land, come with me, take full flight, don't be scared, take my hand.
You will see that life's more than just day-to-day plans as you soar on the wings of your soul.
Dear Lady let our friend be whole.' Bethan whispered, drawing a banishing pentagram over the door.

The whole building seemed to shudder as a flock of ravens landed on the roof above, nudging and pushing like children to see into the room through the skylight.

As Bethan looked up, a tall, raven-cloaked being, looked down on her as the raven flock morphed into one. She heard,

'Link with your aspect Leah and you will find your friend is not far away. She grieves a small child-friend and is close to losing her reason,' and the cry of a child echoed clearly through the room as the figure morphed back into a flock of raucous birds.

Chapter 13
Maeve

Through meddlesome ways so much is bound
...a young ones life is turned around
...and when the hunt rides out with the hounds
...once more the mists will this child surround
No mortals see the hidden ways
...yet meddle they have since the dawn of days
...each one from the Crooked Path will stray
...and so must return once more into the fray

Time past slowly as Maeve regained some semblance of rationale. She began to train with the tribe again but her training abruptly halted when Scathach saw that she was putting herself in danger willingly, wanting to fight with honed weapons rather than with the blunt staves they used in training. Therefore, given other tasks to do, her training as a warrior temporarily withdrawn, she was left alone to grieve and heal.

Maeve didn't think she would ever recover from the loss, taking it personally that she'd been unable to save Alma from the river; despite the fact, Bran reminded her often, that Alma had made a decision to go with her other folk. It was clear he said, that she'd been a changeling of some sort and that had been her challenge throughout her short life, not being accepted as 'normal' but also not knowing what 'normal' actually was.

She had never known any boundaries, the villagers being afraid of her and so even in her good humour; there had been an edge of something odd about the child. It took much for The Cybil to lose patience and Bran was the only other person Alma had known from her past.

Maeve would argue that she's never seen any of Alma's foibles as an issue; her mood swings from the height of frantic joy to the pit of brooding, dark despair, Bran's reply one day gave her pause for thought.

'That's because you were so alike Maeve. Have you not seen that and on occasion, the way she looked at you? I believe she really thought you were her sister-kin, lost who knows how or when and that one day you would take her away to find your parents and all would be well.

She didn't believe her parents were her real kin and I must say having met them, I agree with her. It may be time for you to find your way to the 'Seer's Isle' Maeve and to find the truth of your being. I will help you if I can but it must be both Scathach and The Cybil's' decision, for that to come about.'

After the candid talk with Bran, Maeve would walk to the river to seek solace and to see if she could see Alma from her new perspective. After all, the Water Sprites had loved Alma and had not meant her harm, whatever they were, Maeve was convinced of that fact, which meant that Alma was alive in some form or other and perhaps she would speak with her sometime.

She would often sit on the riverbank in the hollow left by the fallen willow and wait. She could hear the Sprites singing, see them playing in the fast flowing waters.

Alma had had a beautiful little voice, Bran said he would train when she had grown a little, her voice matured. On occasion Maeve swore she could hear Alma singing… a strange haunting song of loss and loneliness but she would put it down to her overworked imagination, until one day she heard…

Worlds within words …lives within lives
…fly swift as a bird …be a fish as it dives,
Smell the soil …burrow deep
…hear the earth …does She sleep?
Nestle in …worming down
…be the bug in the ground …be a cell in her skin
…go within …go within
…like the watery deep …all her dark secrets keep
Worlds change and decay
…fallen now …lost is the way
Soon all this world will watery be
…vanquished by tides …covered by sea
Then sinking down …deeper yet
…sleep forever …in a slow forget
Grow a tail … grow a fin
…go within …so deep within
Sleekly flow home …to your watery kin

The eerie song was disturbing but Maeve could not give it voice, cursing the fact that she had never been able to sing. Gazing into the river's depths, imagining she saw little Alma's face altered, changed, sharp teeth and tangled locks, small items snagged and woven into the red mane that now had taken on a bluish hue. There was no warmth in the eyes, no light remaining of the bright child Alma, who beckoned Maeve to come closer.

Then it hit her, Alma! '**Noooo**' …she screamed to the sky; the water, the earth and the fire within her core responded. '…It can't be true! Not Alma, she wasn't bad.'

Then she remembered the same cold eyes of the Mirdhaucha when they had looked into her soul, on another thread in the web of Ungwe, of life.

Here The Cybil found her, held her until she was dry of eye, and hollowed out, empty of anything; then she took Maeve home to the Seer's Isle that she might find peace for her soul.

Chapter 14
Sybille
...pre Lammas, eighteen months prior

Beyond the light of dreaming stars
...beyond the light of time
I reached within to find a space
...a place that's only mine
A place of light and healing sound
...darkness was its source
...and from the darkness light was born
...and matter its resource
From Dreaming ... by Sybille Madison

Dawn crept over the horizon and over the window ledge into Sybille's loft bedroom, the light gentling now as summer passed into autumn filtered through the giant elder tree that stood, boughs heavy with fruit, to shine dappled rays on her face.

She slumbered on, her dreams intensifying as the little Makers swarmed around her, forming and re-forming patterns in an energy maelstrom, swirling with colour and the essence of life itself. From far away she could hear voices calling to her.

'Wake up, wake up,' as she stirred in the dream, sensing she was not at home in her bed. She lay, held by delicate strands of thread, in a cocoon of it.

'Wake UP!' How often had she dreamed this through the years, a small part of her wondered but then startled she woke, dragged abruptly from the depths of sleep by the feeling of a heavy weight on her chest, Sybille knew it was morning. She felt the vibration of her cat Morgana's deep, rumbling purr and laughed despite the rude awakening.

Dawn had not yet broken but she was familiar with her cat's behaviour, when she called for food, *'**and now please, if you don't mind!**'* Sybille was aware there would be no peace if she didn't comply with her pushy cat's wishes.

Stretching out, she spilt a loudly protesting Morgana from her chest and sat up, better to view the weather through the window. She could see it was going to be a crisp, early autumn day. Mists were just clearing and a frosty smell lingered in the room, wafting in through the open window.

Just like any other day she could hear the sounds of life waking up, one by one. A distant Kookaburra, the wind in the Elder, chirping sparrows and the tap, tap of branches on the skylight above the bed. Branches, she thought looking up …no, birds the noisy local gang. Tara and her raucous clan were gathering, tapping and wiping sticky elderberry-incrusted beaks on the glass.

Tara morphed and changed, sliding down the glass in her human form, which always made Sybille hold her breath in alarm as she hurtled over the edge, only to change back into her bird form, crying raucously and flying back up again to land on delicate human feet, her cry changing to outrageous laughter.

Tara waved to Sybille. Morgana shot from under the bed, flying on velvet paws down the stairs and out through the cat-flap, leaving Sybille laughing aloud at the noise and boisterousness of her shapechanger friend and her raven mob.

Grabbing a robe, she padded bare foot downstairs, slipping into a pair of clogs she'd left at the door. Tara almost fell in as Sybille opened the door for her, eager to get inside, sniffing the air as she went. Despite Tara's usual good humour, there was a worried look in her eyes as she looked sharply around the hallway, pushing past and almost running into Sybille's study.

'Well good morning Tara,' laughed Sybille, following Tara into the study. 'What's bitten you this morning, lovely?' she questioned.

'Look out the window,' Tara gestured. 'Smell the air. There's the smell of foul Magicks abroad today but I can't tell where it's coming from,' she exclaimed with an agitation, unusual for her.

Sybille walked to the french windows, throwing them open to the frosty morning air; there was an acrid odour on the wind. 'It's probably something dead in the garden, by the smell of it,' she said. 'I'm surprised the foxes haven't been round with a rank smell like that out there.'

'It does smell of decay,' said Tara, 'but not of normal decomposing flesh. It's something else and I feel strangely agitated inside. Something's about to happen, Sybille and for once, I can't see what it can possibly be.'

'I've had strange dreams again, Tats,' said Sybille using her nickname for Tara, which came about through Tara's predilection for anything lacy to wear, no matter how tatty it may be.

'I've dreamed of renewal already and it's far too early for that surely? I've been dreaming of falling, and of travelling to an ancient land that feels and smells like Italy. I appear to be a mere girl, listening to the words of a wise young woman not that much older than myself in mortal years, perhaps 2-3 years or so. I can't seem to hear what she's saying but she becomes more agitated each time I have the dream. The older girl reminds me of someone but I can't grasp whom; in fact, I don't understand anything at all. I certainly don't have any recollection of this aspect as myself.'

'Hmm,' replied Tara. 'Something's definitely not right, but let's have some breakfast before we do anything else shall we?' Already she was off on a tangent and as usual, food was first on the agenda.

'Is that all you can think of?' grinned Sybille.

'Yep Billy,' replied Tara fondly, 'the best way I find to think, is with my mouth full.'

'Come on then, let's get some eggs and I'll cook you some french toast.'

In seconds Tara was changed, gone and back again; she carried several eggs carefully.

'I wonder sometimes you know Billy, if I should be eating eggs. It's probably a bit like eating my sisterkin's children somehow.'

'Oh okay then, just plain toast for you is it? Although you know I only eat unfertilised eggs,' she giggled as Tara's face fell.

'Well I did only say probably,' she smirked.

Over a shared breakfast, Sybille and Tara talked more about the coming Lammas and the fact that Samhain was over two months away. Neither of them could understand why Sybille was already feeling she was about to be whipped away at any time now, to renew. This time, however it was different in that she hadn't dreamed about her Trueshape Silver for ages, in fact she'd not put in an appearance recently, which was extremely unusual.

'I'll check this out Billy,' said Tara. 'I've heard some strange sounds echoing on the ethers but they make no sense; they're ancient and very disturbing. I think they may be one of my own sisterkin, lost to us millennia ago but why are we hearing it now? There's also the echo of a dying child's cry and strange stirrings with the tree and water folk too.'

'Perhaps I should call the Coven together for a working,' said Sybille with some concern. She too had sensed strange things, heard strange sounds on the night air and seen Fae folk moving through the forests between Covenstead and Wells more often than ever before.

'Is it time do you think Tara? Is Bethy about to wake up; I almost thought I heard the Heru's horn sounding early; not here in this realm but echoing through the 'Between'. I've never heard it before Samhain, even there.'

'Okay, get the gang together and let's call a meet as soon as possible. If you can get a full Coven all the better but at least those you know are strong enough to walk the 'Between'. Perhaps we should call on your students too, Sybille,' said Tara reverting to Sybille's whole name rather than the nickname she had for her. 'They're going to be very busy when you do renew anyway, as well you know; better to have them prepared don't you think?'

'Hmm,' replied Sybille, 'I'm not too sure Tats, Flora and Bethy perhaps and I'd love to think Samantha would buck up a bit but Maeve, she's the wild card!'

'Wild child you mean Billy, don't you? Even the Mother isn't sure of that one and the influences I feel have her entangled in something of which she has no conscious awareness. I just wish I knew what.' Tara scratched her head like the old black and white movie character Stan Hardy, causing Sybille to grin. Sobering, she said, 'Alright let's get the Coven together Tats. Will I text or ring them all or will you go, 'as the crow flies?' She was well aware of Tara's reaction to the crow allusion.

'Very clever Sybille,' she retorted. 'You know they say sarcasm is the lowest form of wit?'

'Oh,' grinned Sybille, 'and who might 'they' be.'

'Smarty pants,' hooted Tara, before disappearing in a flurry of feathers and lace. 'Out of here! I'll go see the first six on the list and you can ring the others. Let me know on the ethers if you need more people,' and she was gone.

A clatter of the cat flap announced Morgana's arrival for breakfast as with an audible 'harrumph,' she buried her face in her bowl.

'Morning blessings to you too,' chuckled Sybille, picking up the phone.

Chapter 15
Psychic Sigels

It cannot be felt except deep in your core
It cannot be seen but you know there is more
And when it is seen as, the first shoots break ground
...it happens in silence ...no noise, not a sound
What you have asked for will manifest the same
...if not simply wait ...whisper Her name
It will come, as it must
...in perfect love ...and perfect trust

Samantha sat as the desk in reception as the day-light faded. Annie had gone for the day and she wasn't due to meet with the others for another couple of hours.

Her rooms above 'earthly rites' were lonely after Maeve had been taken into the 'Between' the absence of the sounds that usually came from her studio as she creatively tapped metal into shape, was like a yawning hole in the night.

She often sat at the computer, late afternoon or early morning when things were quiet, to finish off the daily sales log, to work out tax or wages for the business. She had a good head for it, just as Sybille did and Flo had been relieved not to have to do it all herself. Running her herbal practice and her part of 'earthly rites', plus the farm was more than enough, she said. Business was booming and with the sale of her house, Sam had no financial worries, time to write and to enjoy the new freedom to work with the herbal grimoire and her little leafy friends.

Together, she and Flo had worked out the percentages for Maeve's sales and her profit share from the main business, putting it all in an account for when she returned, as they were sure she eventually would.

On top of all that, after the first year and a day was past, a substantial amount appeared in each of their accounts from Sybille's bank. They agreed to put it all into one account for Sybille when she came home although, when the automatic transfer occurred they began to realise it was pre-set by Sybille for when a certain amount of time had expired, and that meant Sybille was aware she would not be returning any time soon.

Her thoughts meandering where they might, Sam worked on as the daylight began to fade. Busy at her work, she didn't hear the front door open; it was more the quiet that brought her from her reverie. She felt it before seeing anything but it was akin to watching a movie with the sound turned down. She witnessed her Aunt and a host of others, some of whom Sam knew as Coven members, as they swept in through the door, shaking heavy droplets of water from their clothing and chattering animatedly; rubbing their hands together to warm them.

They moved on rapidly into the seminar room, she could hear their movements, muffled as if under water as they came and went fetching various items such as candles and incense. Sam could see Sybille's old carved chest and the beautiful Book of Shadows they had combed, both here and the farm, looking for. It had only ever been under the worst weather circumstances that the Coven had met at the shop for Sabbats and Esbats, so Sam could assume it was raining hard from their behaviour and by the simple fact of what she was witnessing. 'But it's not raining now,' she muttered to herself!

She sat quietly until the coming and going ceased and they closed the door, only ethereally however, as Sam could see the physical door was still ajar.

Slipping from her stool, she crept stealthily to the door and peered in. A very select group of only the most experienced Wytches, male and female alike stood solemnly in the centre of the circle; inscribed in the parquet flooring, usually kept covered by a large rug. Annie Savage was one of them and she wore a puzzled frown, clearly able to see Sam.

Sam knew immediately that this was no ordinary meet, no Sabbat or Esbat rite. Hearing soft footfall behind her she turned as Bethan and Flora came to find her. She gestured for them to be quiet and indicated to what she could see in the room. Flora gave her a puzzled shake of the head obviously unable to see what was happening; Bethan raised her hand to keep her quiet as she gazed into the room before stepping inside.

Sam wanted to grab her to drag her back as a strange feeling overcame her but too late, the entire group turned as Bethan walked in, two members parting the circle for her to enter. As if they had drawn back a curtain, Flora could see too; she watched silently with Sam.

Bethan, on reaching the circle's boundary, shimmered and changed becoming her Fae self as her antlers thrust from her forehead; she was once again standing in the forest grove of her dreams. She smiled at the group gently and walked toward Sybille; Silver stood behind her, whole, tangible real.

'There She is; She's come to us. Welcome Arwen, you honour us with your presence,' said Sybille and Silver in unison, the High Priest stood head covered by his hood. With a glance toward Sam and Flora, Silver made a gesture of warding and the physical door slammed in their faces; rattling and banging on it was to no avail.

'What the!' exclaimed Sam. 'Could you see what was happening in there Flo? That was Sybille and when Bethan walked in and they all turned, they welcomed her like an expected and long awaited guest.'

'Yes,' Flora replied, 'and was it really as if the room changed to a forest grove …in fact 'our grove' on the hill? That man was so familiar too …why that was Pwyll!'

'Well, more bizarre things to add to the collection then,' said Samantha. 'I hope Bethy knows what she's doing.'

Beth walked through the forest; there indeed was Sybille as she remembered her and the recently met Pwyll, Morgan and Lily's enigmatic father.

After welcoming Beth, Sybille drew her to the altar; the silence around them was absolute as if the other Coven members could not see their interaction.

'So Sybille, what do you have to say to me that I may remember what night this was and why you couldn't tell me about it before.'

'This is a meet I called just before I felt I was to renew,' Sybille replied, 'and it was important to link it in with the dream you told me you'd had so that I had a focus to draw you here. However if you are here and conscious this time of being who you truly are, then I am probably no longer of this world.

Do you know what has become of me? I had a vision time and time again about disappearing but I was unable to link it to my renewal with Silver and, speaking of which, where did she disappear to?' she said looking around keenly'

'I don't know exactly what's been going on Sybille,' said Bethan, 'or what really happened but I do know that you have somehow split yourself into several different realities simultaneously, yet not consciously. Then there's Annie Savage's strange behaviour but never mind that now...' she trailed off before continuing.

'I have strange dreams of you hiding yourself away but I'm not sure what part of you it is. Occasionally we see you floating around at home or at work like a wraith, especially around the chest where you used to keep your Book of Shadows. We knew that something drastic had happened or you would have simply gone on to the Summerlands and let us know later how you faired. I can only assume that it's your etheric double. Your physical body we know, Silver has safely hidden, where she won't tell us as if this was some ghastly game and your niece Sam, hadn't been beside herself with worry that your Littleshape has disappeared entirely. Without which, it must be hard for the Maker Souls to keep your body alive and breathing. I have no idea how that works Sybille, in all honesty.

We are doing all we can for you and we have a whole team together performing rites and scrying the Aether. There's Tara of course; Claire is changing again, Lily and Morgan are here. Cal Macintyre, I think you knew his father, a lovely man, who worked with Claire in the UK, came back to help. He found a raven shaper's body from centuries ago, obviously murdered while caught in the change and so was unable to renew.

Susan and Alex come and go; they've moved to Springsmeet and of course Sam and Flora. Everyone is doing their upmost to help.'

'You said where I used to keep my Book of Shadows. What did you mean by that?' said Sybille with the first signs of agitation.

'It's gone Sybille, replaced with a blank one.'

'So how are you all coping without it,' she queried, 'and what about Annie Savage Bethy, or should I say Arwen,' Sybille amended with great respect. 'Why she was just here, we called her to this meet!' She paused looking round, thinking intently before she said, 'Maeve, you haven't mentioned Maeve, is she okay? How is my wild girl?'

'Well we suspect Annie of taking the Book of Shadows in fact but we're managing without it and she's been behaving very strangely. There's a lot of jealousy and anger projected toward all of us from her; she seems agitated about something all the time. She got herself into a lot of trouble with the Fae, we witnessed her rite at Mabon and it was almost taken over by the essence of a couple of very dark Fae.'

Beth took a shuddering breath before continuing. 'As for Maeve, Tara's taken her to another thread in the 'Between', Sybille. A rather unpleasant little entity was goading her and Maeve almost attacked Sam as a result. She stirred the pot between Sam and Max too.

Tara wouldn't let her stay to interfere, when we have enough to do looking for you and working out what this whole ordeal is about for each of us in the first place.'

'Oh Goddess, this is terrible, what could have happened?'

'A Maker fell, Sybille. That much we do know and the result of that's a blight affecting the ethers, which will eventually affect us here; we've already seen it and smelt it in the forests.'

'How can that be Bethy? What could've caused it?'

'I can't answer that but I know that its fall is part of why you have not been able to return. We're working hard and we have many helping. Don't worry Sybille; we'll keep working to bring you home.'

'The most important thing is to save the Maker, Arwen, imperative that you do,' Sybille said in great agitation.

Beth reached out to touch her in reassurance but the vision dispersed and she was back in the seminar room; the door opened by itself, returning everything to how it had originally been. Sam and Flora rushed toward her as she returned to her human vibration.

Immediately she told them of the events as they walked to the Harvest to meet with the others for dinner. They all felt strangely calm as if this was more the norm than not, which in fact it was fast becoming.

'What's your role in all of this Pwyll? You were there as Sybille's High Priest, so there's more to your being here than you've told us.' Pwyll remained impassive as he heard Beth speak in his mind. He looked at her briefly but made no reply.

'I can command you know, as Arianwen I can order you to speak.' Sparks flew from her hair making Lily jump, but she said nothing, sensing the silent interchange between Beth and her father.

'But you won't,' the reply came in Beth's head. 'It's not how you are Arwen, you know of free will all too well.'

Chapter 16
New Threads in the Weave

In the world that we know it, what is time?
How does it flow; is there reason or rhyme,
Is it random or fated?
Affected by love or by hatred
In the world as we know it, what is time?

'When you think about it,' said Morgan, reaching across to grab a bread roll from the basket in the centre. 'It's actually quite a breakthrough to think that Sybille herself was aware enough to lay little 'time-line' scenarios. Trouble is we don't know how random they might become with our conditioning about time. For all we know there may have been others that we've missed, simply because we didn't have any idea of the concept.'

'Yeah,' said Max, through a mouthful of bread. 'We've always thought about time-space as future and past, rather than zigzags through the continuum. I mean, it makes sense but our brain still works on the linear idea, so we lose a lot in the translation.'

'There has to be a way we can tap into some of these, what can we call them, 'transmissions' perhaps?' chimed in Lily. 'There's probably some sort of fragment or energy remnant left that we could chase? What do you think Beth?'

'That's a thought Lily but the question as always, would be how I guess,' replied Bethan. 'Although I do know her song-line, I'd recognise it anywhere and as Arianwen, I can travel just about anywhere to follow a trail as long as I start at the jetty by the lake, which is apparently where so much began. My challenge is to remember as Arianwen, not as Leah or Beth,' she grinned bemusedly. 'Boy that sounds complicated!'

Cal spoke up, 'Well I read somewhere that every magickal or psychic event leaves an impression in the ethers. Perhaps a little bit like a traumatic event or a happy one come to that. Therefore it's more a matter of finding out exactly what Sybille's 'imprint signature' would be.' His words made Tara and Pwyll sit up straight, exchanging meaningful glances.

'Very clever,' Tara grinned at Cal, pinching an olive from his plate, '…and, we can probably work that out by looking at the one you just experienced Sam,' finished Pwyll for her.

'But that would mean we would have to make it happen again, wouldn't it?' queried Sam. 'How would we do that …erm, gauge the time it happened?'

'That wouldn't work,' said Pwyll. 'There's no way that an event can be harnessed by the time-space continuum to the same moment …hmm, let's say daily or weekly, even annually.'

'So, how then?' said Sam, thinking that her dream could also have an imprint she might be able to follow but didn't say it aloud, storing the thought for later.

'Let's go back and see what we can find,' said Tara. 'It's only been a couple of hours, so with any luck we may still pick up a trace of the event but first, have you finished with that Sam,' indicating Sam's half-eaten meal.

'Yes, of course here you are, where do you put it all Tara?' answered Sam, a little distractedly.

'I can't stand waste,' she said. 'That's my excuse and I'm sticking with it.' She smiled cheekily, as they rolled their eyes at her familiar words.

'Okay then,' said Claire. 'I'll go get the bill, shall I?' They each put their money on the table; collecting it together, she headed to the desk to pay.

'Come on,' said Lily. 'Let's go take a look; although I'm not sure what we can do, it's worth a try to get everything moving ahead.'

'What's the rush Jay-Lily?' Tara piped in. 'You got somewhere better to go?'

'Well not necessarily better but I came to help and yet I still have to get back to the shop or I'll lose the deal if I'm not careful.'

'We can help from here,' said Sam. 'Perhaps we could develop a sister company between the two?'

'That's food for thought,' she replied, Flora and Bethan nodded enthusiastically in agreement, Max looked somewhat dejected. Morgan didn't miss this however.

'Have you thought of coming back to the UK for research Max?' he said, making a huge effort not to smirk. A punch in the arm was the reply from Max, with a sheepish grin at Lily.

Sam stood to follow Claire to the desk. Lily said. 'You guys might want to be just a little more sensitive perhaps?'

'She's fine now,' said Max losing his grin. 'We've talked it through.' He rose abruptly and strode to the door, holding it open for Flora and Bethan who gave her brother's arm a quick squeeze in passing and a gentle smile.

Taking their time in the cool early spring evening, they walked and chatted quietly amongst themselves.

'It really is all okay you know Max?' whispered Sam as she passed him.

'Thanks Sam, I'm such a fool,' he replied wistfully.

Chapter 17
A Dark Weaving

Weft and warp ... warp and weft
... only the shadows of truth are left
Deep in the flow of nature's weave
... find the thread made to deceive

Entering 'earthly rites' through the courtyard at the back, they shed coats and scarves, donned against the cool night air. Walking through to the front desk, they stood where Sam had sat as she relayed to them what she had witnessed as the vision unfolded.

'It was like watching a movie, but now I come to think of it everything was quite translucent; not slow but somehow floaty. It's hard to describe when I think about it now.'

'That's alright Sam, we saw some of it. Beth saw more obviously but then the veil was very firmly brought down the moment she entered the circle,' she trailed of thoughtfully. 'Now I come to think of it Bethy, how did you manage to just walk in like that? Sybille was a stickler for protection in every way?'

Pwyll and Tara chuckled.

'Beth's not really human Flora', said Tara, 'and although your circles are strongly built to protect you, they don't keep anything out that really wants to enter;

just nothing can perform negative stuff, is all. It's kinda the law.

It's a bit like some hackers on the internet; they don't necessarily mean harm, they just want to see what can be breached, how deep they can invade your space. It's just a game to them really, pure mischief. The threshold wards at your front and back doors are more protection, as we have to wait for an invitation, whereas circles always have an etheric corridor running between the boundaries and the Watchers.

It only takes a strong connection with the elemental spirits and anything is breachable but as I said, they can't work the negative in a mutually exclusive sacred space. Everything is energy, vibration, so safety is dependent on the individual's belief in their own ability to be safe.'

'Hah, remember how upset Maeve was after the Fae just strode into the circle to collect Bethy at Samhain?' said Max

'Exactly!' said Flora, 'and I'm a bit freaked out too by thoughts of what may be wandering through the circles we always thought were so safe!'

'Anyway,' said Tara, 'we can debate this another time. We have work to do here,' she said, whilst gazing at the door to the seminar room and the surrounding area.

'What can you see Tara?' asked Morgan, 'It still looks sort of misty around the door frame, or is it my imagination?'

'I can see it too Morgan,' said Sam, it's not very strong but it's still there.'

'I can see something but there appears to be another energy superimposed on it; its darker, somewhat tainted, like the little dark Makers' in fact,' said Beth moving forward to run her hands tentatively over the area, without actually coming in contact with the door.

'You're right Bethy,' said Tara coming up behind her. 'It would appear we have someone or something tailing our every move.' She turned to look at each of them carefully.

'Well Maeve's gone; the Mirdhaucha hasn't shown herself again...'

'She's still hanging around Maeve's studio Tara,' interjected Lily. 'I often hear her laughter but it sounds almost happy, playful at the moment; the sounds come from the water tank.'

'Ah, I wish you'd said something before, Jay-Lily,' said Tara sternly. 'Every piece of information we can put together is vital ...each new strand in the tapestry becomes a thread in the warp and weft somewhere else. We'll deal with that issue later.'

'Sorry!' said Lily seriously.

'Alright then, let's stay focused here,' said Pwyll.

'I've an idea,' said Flora suddenly as she dashed away up the stairs toward her rooms. 'Come on Sam I need your help here.' Sam followed, shrugging her shoulders at the others as she left. She caught up with Flora at the door of her apothecary. Moving fast, Flora said to Sam. 'Quickly, can you grab a smudge bowl, lighter and an owl feather smudging fan please?'

'Sure, but what's the go? Why do you need me Flo?'

'You've been working with Airmhid's satchel of herbs, what would you suggest for a blend that may 're-veal' things; light it up so it's visible, so to speak?'

'Ah I'm with you. Yes, let's see. I wish I had the Grimoire here but it's back at Covenstead.' At that there came a swish of wings and a tearing sound as the Aethers parted and Claire tumbled into the room from out of nowhere in her Owl form.

'You'll need this,' she said dropping the bag on the table in front of them.

'Oh wow Mum, thanks, you're brilliant …but how did you …no never mind,' giggled Flora, Sam joining in.

'Now,' said Sam. 'This would come under seeing, seeking, questing so if we were doing a full working it would be in the West quadrant. I'd use a scrying bowl of silver and a silver candle.

We really need a waning Moon but at present, it's waxing toward Ostara of course. You're right on target with the Owl feathers Flo, but I don't have to tell you that.' She grinned at Flora who stood open-mouthed star-ing at Sam as if she were crazy. 'What's wrong?' asked Samantha, 'are you okay?'

'Yeah, fine,' said a stunned Flora. 'When did you learn all this though?'

'Ah, it's a long story but it comes in the dreams when I sit speaking with Nina, in my Magdalena aspect …anyway, moving on. We could use some of the big guns but in an enclosed space they could be too toxic.'

'…such as…?' queried Flora.

'Well, monkshood, poppy even belladonna are plants for seeing, mistletoe just makes me gag so I was thinking more like, eyebright with sage to strengthen the sight and good old mugwort or black sage, as people are calling it now …that's a tried and true for psychic dreams and vision quests. I guess this rather falls into that category.

We could all participate, if we don't make too overwhelming a brew,' …she trailed off again. 'Sorry, I'm running off at the mouth here and we don't have the time to do a full working.'

'We don't really need to,' said Tara, wandering in casually, the circle was cast in the room and the potency of that is obviously what caused the imprint to linger, along with some help from Sybille of course.' She grinned at them. 'Now, we know where the Moon is and although it's waxing right now toward Ostara, as you said Sam, it's better than the dark or new phase and you can still bring candle, scrying bowl, blessed water, smudge bowl and the herbs. You may want to add some silver birch, bark and leaves too,' she finished a little breathlessly.

'Well that seems to cover all bases then,' said Claire. 'Come on let's get the things together, now where will I find an Owl's wings,' she grinned, changing one arm to a wing and back rapidly. '…Oh silly me, there it is,' and she and Tara went off into fits of giggles together. Flora and Sam could only shake their heads and follow, once they'd assembled all they needed.

'I'll have what they're on,' said Sam poker faced, making Flora giggle again. Tara's piercing blue gaze fixed on them and they could see The Morrigan lurked not far behind her faint smile.

They assembled hurriedly in the fading light, an eerie silence falling amongst them as Sam and Flora filled the scrying bowl with blessed water, eyebright drops and silver birch leaves, adding white sage to strengthen the potency. They lit a smudge bowl of silver birch bark, mugwort and more sage. Lighting the candle so that it reflected in the water, they then wafted the now gently smoking herbs over the bowl with the Owl smudging fan.

At first, they thought nothing would happen but slowly as they squinted through the smoke, an outline appeared as if etched into the woodwork of the door itself. A Sigel, Sybille's double S-shaped seal appeared, but on its side like an infinity symbol ∞, over-layed with something …it looked like a reversed A, ∀ and there was something else, a symbol of sorts but it was small, making it too hard to see for its intricacy.

'Well,' exploded Pwyll. 'We certainly have been busy here. That looks like Sybille's Sigel but it doesn't look quite right, as if she's actually trying to tell us something by not getting it right …and the A could be Aerandir or Ailish or even Aithlin for all we know of their signatures…' he trailed off scrubbing at his face with both hands in frustration.

'I think I recognise that symbol Da,' said Lily. 'I've seen it recently.'

Bethan stepped forward for a closer look and remembering something shapechanged rapidly, bringing out every detail she could remember of her merged aspect Leah, wearing the midnight blue priestess robe; searching through the folds and pockets of the cloth she appeared to be looking for something specific.

Frustrated she changed again, 'Hmm,' she said, 'Leah must not have been carrying it with her when we merged but there was a stone that the Otter, Oonagh gave her, I have to find it, it had this symbol carved into it I'm certain. I took it for a nut or a bud.'

'Ostara will soon be here and we'll be more than half way around the wheel again,' said Claire. 'There must be away we can look for it, if I can find the fold in the warp and weft I should be able to bring it back.'

'No,' said Bethan. 'I think this is something I can do. It shouldn't be too hard to go to the point where Oonagh gave it to me as Leah. I'll go tonight when we've finished here. Will you sit with me Tara?'

'Of course, Arwen,' said Tara respectfully. 'I think we can go now. Where do you want to be while you travel?'

'Here in the Seminar room. I think would be the best way to link the threads. Can we pull back that carpet so I'm working in the same space Sybille did when she left the imprint. Somehow, they link up.'

'Okay folks, in that case we will need to cast a circle first and then you can all wait elsewhere while I help Bethan on the journeywork.'

'Let them stay if they will,' said Bethan, 'this is not just for me and the more energy lent to the process the easier it will be.'

Morgan immediately stepped forward, 'I'll cast for you Bethy, if you don't mind male energy in it,' he said with a smile.

Beth laughed aloud, 'As if, Mor!' she exclaimed, as he lightened her mood.

Using the same incense blend for revealing secrets, Morgan cast the circle, simply and securely for Beth to travel. He cast alone and everyone watching was awestruck by his working and the power of his presence.

Lily stood by and smiled proudly, 'Wow,' she said, 'I haven't seen him that potent before,' as she glanced over at Sam watching from the doorway, she was smiling gently to herself and there was a look in her eyes never seen before, even when the spark was there between her and Max.

Claire and Tara caught Lily's eye and they smiled at her knowingly. Could it be, they all thought, could it be? Max saw it too but was more relieved at being off the hook, out of the situation they'd found themselves in so suddenly. Ah chemistry, they all thought.

'Pity Morgan's oblivious,' whispered Claire to Tara who let out a hoarse chuckle, breaking the moment; Morgan almost dropped his Athame at the sound.

'Ha ya think,' she chuckled, quickly covering her mouth with her hand; off they went, both giggling like children again.

As Morgan walked to the centre of the circle for the final cast, chanting, the energy crackled with static.
'I cast thee oh circle that thou be the boundary between the realms of man and the realms of the mighty one; a guard and protection which will preserve and contain the energies we do raise within thee, wherefore do I bless and consecrate thee.'

He executed a perfectly balanced last turn, ending up directly opposite the Altar. His azure-blue energy still spinning from his Athame, he consciously quieted his breathe. Bowing to the four quadrants he walked to the Altar to collect the blessed water and then to the northeast to open a doorway for Tara and Bethan. Drawing a doorway in the ethers with his Athame, he took first Bethan's hand, pulling her gently through, splashing her with the blessed water and kissing her on the lips, then Tara.

He closed the doorway, warding it with his own Sigel and Tara with hers. Bethan walked to the four quadrants to salute and call on them for aid, Morgan drew her to the cushions before the Altar, where she sank down into a perfect lotus position.

He completed a circuit of the circle before settling on the floor with Tara, behind Bethan, stilling his own mind to lend her energy for the journey.

It was as if she'd grabbed him by the hand as they spun off together, out of the realms of earth and through the Skeins of Tyme before plummeting down into the waiting aspects of Leah and Bran, just as they were, in another thread of the warp and weft.

Somewhat stunned, they could only look at each other before Bethan walked off; heading toward the lake and the little coracle she knew would be there. Bran looked hard and long; it was Leah and yet it was not. He could smell the magick on her, he could mind sense his other self, closer to her than he had ever been.

She smiled quizzically at him as she turned, knowing he would remember when he returned to the everyday, but for now his consciousness had focus more specifically as Bran, rather than Morgan; one day they too would merge aspects to become one. Bethan didn't think it would be long in coming either, she could see his energy field quivering as he fought for concentration between the two aspects. It was like watching a hologram, warping in and out of sync.

A part of him knew he needed to stay close to the priestess who had collected little Alma that day at the edge of the lake and yet he was torn, something felt wrong. Leah sensed it too and faltered before turning away, walking to the coracle purposefully, she unhooked the rope from the post at the jetty. She had hoped that Oonagh would appear straight away but that was not the case, the lake was quiet and yet not peaceful, a drift of smoke swept across the water; not a ripple stirred below. This smoke did not carry the familiar apple wood aroma but rather something sour and unpleasant.

Struck again by the eerie silence, she pushed off from the shore. Strange shapes floated on the mirror still water but she couldn't see what they were in the approaching dusk of an autumn day.

No lamp hung in the prow of the coracle as would usually be, which concerned her more. Where were the birds, fish, and otter, the water sprites that would carry her across? Nothing stirred except the smoke, turning red through the haze as the sun sank lower.

Realising she'd been standing like a statue for several minutes; she threw her hood over her hair and pushed off from the jetty, moving painfully slowly toward the lake's centre. She slowed to a halt, balancing herself in the coracle carefully before raising her arms in the age-old way,

'*Part the mists of Tyme;*' she lifted her hands palm upwards. '*Let fall the woods of nine;*' reaching into the pouch she pulled out a small pinch of woodsy fragrant ash, letting it fall over the water. *'Together air and water blessed,'* she dipped her hands in the lake, kissing the water droplets on her fingers, she blew them away; *'dispels the veil into the West,'* with a banishing pentacle to the mists. *'To hear the sacred chime,'* and a bell sounded from afar. *'Mother, may you guide this seeker home,'* she sang…

…the veil parted but she could see nothing through the reddish smoke that began to swirl around her as a wind came out of nowhere.

A strangled cry came from her as she saw the tall figure, long red hair snarled and tangled, standing on the jetty ahead. Blood covered her hands and clothing and her eyes were that of a lunatic. Another appeared from behind her, dishevelled and obviously grieving yet sanity remained. Beth waved to her frantically but there was no response. Nearing the jetty, she could see flames lit up the ancient settlement of the Seers, the source of the smoke she realised. Objects, at first of unknown or unidentifiable origin, floated in the waters that lapped the shoreline like a dirty tidemark. With growing horror Beth saw there were bodies amongst the detritus, raven, sparrow, owl and her beloved otters; she realised they were wrapped tightly with the blighted, sticky black threads, covering everything.

She screamed aloud in pain and outrage. 'Who did this, what did this? Who dared to violate the sanctuary of the Mother?' She fell to her knees, sobbing; the force of her grief propelling her and Morgan back to their waiting bodies. Beth, white faced and shaking, looked at Tara as if she had lost the power of speech.

Tara and Morgan reached forward as one before she could try to stand.

'It wasn't real Bethy,' said Morgan. 'I was there too; I was Bran. Someone is trying to distract us. Everything was fine at Scathach's Hearth, except they are all very sad for Alma and for Maeve who is grieving the drowned child Alma. The Cybil is sending someone to fetch her and she will be going to the Isle of Seers soon, to heal her grief. I remember clearly, seeing through Bran's eyes, I was just as helpless to save her as Maeve was; the child gave up the fight and went willingly with the Water Sprites. Someone has been there before us Bethy. This isn't real. It can't be real!'

'It's okay Morgan, my senses tell me you're right but the aspect of Leah is strong when I journey there. Yet, she would know if this is something that could happen depending on what we achieve in fixing what needs fixing. I think this may well be an outcome if we can't.'

So saying she stood unaided, shaking off the sticky residue of her experience. She said simply, 'Poor little girl, how she reflects Maeve's wounded inner child …hmm I wonder,' she trailed off thoughtfully, exchanging looks with Tara, who gave her a slight nod in understanding.

'I didn't see what you saw Bethy,' said Morgan, 'I was still on the mainland but I heard you scream and smelt the smoke. I could see through Bran's eyes and almost through yours but the one thing I do know is this hasn't happened…'

'…Yet,' finished Bethan for him. 'Still, there's one thing positive that came from it all at least; mission accomplished,' she said a little bitterly, putting her hand in the pocket of the floaty dresses she had taken to wearing. 'Leah was carrying this,' she held out her hand on which sat a perfect jet black, river washed stone, like a cabochon; etched in its smooth surface in fine filigree silver was a quite legible, symbol…

'Why it's larger and clearer than I remember! I wonder if this is the same stone?' she mused.

Tara and Pwyll stepped forward almost simultaneously, 'I think it's enough for tonight, Bethy, don't you?' said Tara.

'Yes indeed,' said Pwyll. 'You must be exhausted Arwen Arianwen,' using her formal title before whispering quietly to her. 'Keep it well hidden and guarded please Bethy, it is a sacred stone of blessings that is not for all to handle or even see.' From his pocket, he produced a small, midnight blue velvet pouch with a silver cord. Holding it out for her to drop the stone into then, tying it tightly, he placed it around her neck, bowing to her formally. They all knew not to question when one of the birdkin stepped forward and spoke in such a formal manner.

Wearily closing the circle down, putting the tools safely away in a locked chest, they went to the kitchen where Flora had brewed some 'journey tea' to help them ground themselves back into the physical realm. They spoke little, giving Bethan and Morgan the chance to debrief what they'd experienced and, when Flora was satisfied there were no ill effects, Morgan, Lily, Bethan and Max bundled into one car to go home to Wells.

'It's not good to be alone here Sam,' said Cal. 'We …erm …that is Flora has room. I hope I'm not speaking out of turn Flo.'

'No love,' she replied, her dimples flashing. **We**,' she emphasised, 'have the space.' Turning to Pwyll and her mother, she said. 'Are you guys coming back to Covenstead to roost tonight?'

'Ha, ha, very funny,' laughed Claire, and yes we are. We can all fit into one car.'

'I'll drive,' said Pwyll. 'Come on let's go home.'

Claire smiled, despite the tension of the evening's events as if it were the most natural thing. 'Yes, home,' she said, 'I'm hungry again.'

Cal laughed outright. 'Now I know where your incredible appetite comes from at times, Flo!'

Chapter 18
Spinning Tales

The next day being Saturday, the busiest day of their week, Sam was again at the front desk, early. Claire had loaned her, her car; Sam's left at the centre the night before, saying she would 'fly in' with Pwyll in the morning, which had been cause for raucous hoots and catcalls from Cal and Flora.

Sam wanted to take a good look at what was going on behind the desk for the weekend. Annie was still behaving very strangely secretive and they agreed one of the Ravenkin should follow her unobtrusively; they needed no new surprises.

One thing was certain, Harry had moved in with her. They were not sure what hold she had over him; of course, she was an attractive woman but he was dead set against anything magickal. It was a miracle he'd ever become involved with her at all.

'Perhaps it's 'glamour',' Tara had said, one eyebrow raised, when Sam had approached her on the subject. Claire and Flora refused to talk of him at all, not through any rancour but simply because they were just not interested any more.

'Too much water under the bridge,' Flora had said when Sam had quizzed her and so, done with was the topic of Harry, finally.

Max stayed at Wells to research and write. He had been reading Sybille's teaching notes with great interest; it gave him more insight into the nature of the woman all is friends and family adored. Despite the fact he had attended rites with his parents since childhood and his leanings were most definitely Pagan yet, unable to understand completely what he believed, he remained sceptical.

Lily, Bethan and Morgan had driven in early together to practise for a special event planned, a book launch for the following Wednesday, which would be Ostara eve.

Before Sybille had disappeared, she had finished a book ready for publication. Sam had edited, revised and created an unusual illustration for the jacket and the week before, a hefty box of books with her stunning cover artwork had arrived.

They had been aware it might create an assortment of problems with Sybille nowhere in sight to sign copies but they thought it might draw some of the less friendly members of the local Wytch set out of their proverbial, broom closets. They would need to know soon whom they could truly trust, should they need a larger circle when they finally attempted calling Sybille home.

Strangely enough, it was often the most reclusive that were trustworthy, the other 'fresh out the closet candy-floss Wytches', were usually the most trouble. Sybille had referred to them as dangerous; a little knowledge badly applied, only caused trouble.

Morgan, Lily, Bethan and Tara formed an interesting, eclectic, musical group and with the addition of Sam on flute, they were creating an amazing sound together; their band 'Unearthly Tones', was becoming popular in the town of Springsmeet. Now, instead of Morgan finding his gigs externally, he could work from the centre teaching and playing, when they had exhibitions, book launches or other functions for local talent in the arts and science.

They gathered in the studio, Bethan had made her own to demonstrate her spinning and weaving, giving classes in both. It was a lovely sunny room with french doors opening out into the courtyard. It was too early to open them in case they disturbed the neighbours but they could at least, start to map out the parts they were all to play or sing.

Tuning their instruments to vibrate in harmony, Morgan struck a note, Bethan following on the Uilleann pipes; she was just beginning to master their sound.

'Let's try the ones we're sure of first to introduce the pipes too and then we can try something new, yes?' said Morgan. 'All right then …erm Lily do you remember the piece I wrote, Enchantment?'

'Yes I think so,' said Lily, and she trilled the first verse…

'Water drips from ancient trees, silent the birds, still the bees. Rivulets of water, currents run deep, soon to wake earth from Her long winters sleep.

Gone longest night and the shortest of days, there's cold still to come but spring's on the way.

Not yet visible, not yet seen but below the cold ground the trees thoughts are of green.

Slowly, roots stirring, She stretches to wake, drinking in water, new buds to make.

Ice and snow form but in darkness below, new life awakens in beauty and flow.'

'That's the one,' he grinned at her. 'Okay then let's try it. Are you confident with the lap pipe and vocals together, Bethy?'

'Sure, let's just go for it shall we?' They lost themselves to their music, until the sounds of the shop stirring and voices of customers could be heard.

With everything else that was happening in their lives, work was almost their source of relaxation as the shop hummed with life, people came and went, most feeling better just for having wandered through the various rooms filled with beautiful things, from the practical to the exotic.

The small room, set aside as a magickal apothecary was filled with draws and draws of herb and resin complex' and simplex' that fragranced the rooms with their earthy and floral scents.

Customers could mix their own blends or ask for assistance to create something unique for their magickal workings. Simple white sage smudge bundles were stored in pots, handmade incense cones and sticks were stacked in piles of same fragrance. Giant cinnamon sticks, soused in oil of roses and whole, slender, vanilla bean pods, filled the air with spice.

Flora, focussing more on the medicinal side of herbals, was pleased to see how Samantha had taken to the task of serving clients in this area, like a duck to water. Rich essential oils added by pipette, a drop at a time, blended carefully, so that customers could find something that resonated absolutely, to their vibration. It was as if she were remembering ancient teachings, she could not recall from where or when, although her dreams of studying with a teacher in her aspect of Magdalena, were returning strongly now. She knew however that she must collate all her understanding of that thread, to better blend with her current consciousness. She wanted to learn from the experiences of Magdalena, so that Magdalena could learn from her in turn.

'Nothing happens in isolation,' she muttered aloud to herself as she dusted and checked draws for contents.

Flora had created a wonderful space for herself and for her clients. She loved the one on one, sessions that dealt with an individual's issues, be they mental, physical or emotional; she encouraged people to see themselves as one whole, living organism rather than parts. Every action, thought and deed has an outcome; the law of cause and effect, will not be denied. Teaching people to be self-responsible was not an easy task but Flora's gentle way, made it possible for people to resonate with her and in time, truly embrace their own self, fully.

Lily's work was growing in style and grace; her work was finer, more delicate than Maeve's robust pieces but both Morgan and Cal were interested in helping with items such as wands and even Athame. Morgan was remembering how much he had known of the art of smithing fine blades and what he had in fact learned from Maeve, in his aspect of Bran. As much as he had attempted to help her bring out her psychic nature so too, had she shown him practical magicks for working with metals and now he was replacing her in much of her work. It made him sad to think of her away from her life and friends.

Max the research buff, together with Alex his father, were finding out more about the twists and turns of the Celtic history and the mythology of their time.

Overall, their workdays were smooth and easy, other than the constant reminder for Claire, of Annie and Harry. She knew that soon it would have to be nutted out between them all and Vanessa considered part of the family, being Flora's sibling.

Claire was racking her brains for a way to help the young woman, who was living in a poky flat in the city with some of her friends from Uni.

Annie had never mentioned Vanessa being Harry's child, but Claire and Flora could see potentially the same things happening to Vanessa as it had with Flora's relationship with Harry.

Susan had also found her niche and was working hard with her painting, recalling the way she used to create doorways into the 'Beyond.'.

Chapter 19
Sybille's Teachings: Magicks

Magick is real, powerful, strong
When abused or misused you will feel when it's wrong
Like a fire in your gut, your Magick will burn
…the pain of wrong doing your Magicks will spurn

When I teach you about magick, I try to instil an awareness of what it is, to truly experience life in the moment. Most Wytches have an innate love of all things natural but if they are not really present and aware in the moment, then much is missing.

When you sit in nature, do you completely drink it in with all the senses or just one or two? Can you say you breathe the leaves, not only their odour but also their very essence?

Do you realise that just as you shed hair and skin flakes, droplets of moisture; as you speak or sneeze, laugh or sing, so too do the trees and every other creature that inhabits your world. Spiders and tiny microscopic mites are teeming everywhere, never more than an arm's reach away, leaving little particles of themselves behind as they move.

A tree sheds its leaves, bark pieces and dust thereof, twigs, branch and seedpods; droplets of water and sap from *their woody skin all fall, just as those particles of you fly off into the air. As you breathe in, so do you breathe their essence and particles; in turn they inhale yours. How can we then ever say, even on this basic physical level that we are separate, that we have no knowledge of one another ...the trick is to remember how it is to be a tree, a bug, a bird ...in fact all things, for part of you already is and has memory of it; its own Sigel. ...blessings ...Sybille*

Chapter 20
Hidden Truths

Eight the trees of Wytchways known
...and in between the five are sown
Five the Sabbats round the wheel
...five the elements that harm or heal.
Spirit the fifth that binds the five
...as the Wytchwheel spins all human lives

Cal worked in the wilder part of the gardens at Covenstead, always left for the nature spirits to play. Planting a traditional Grove of thirteen trees, he was enjoying the feeling of the sun on his back, working up a sweat as he dug. He was used to colder climbs but was relieved to have spring in sight at last.

He was different he realised to the others, with no obvious magickal skills and yet his vision at Yule had been potent, he felt he'd a new role to play. In finding the body of the Ravenkin on the Wolds, he'd wondered why it had been him and not one of the magickal kin themselves,

'Because you are solid and strong, my friend,' came the reply as if from nowhere and yet everywhere...

Cal paused, wiping his face on his sleeve and looking round for the source of the voice; its owner stepped from behind a large tree.

'…and because you are trustworthy, think before you share information as to its value or if it will harm or heal the cause set before you.'

'Lord Hercurin,' Cal bowed a little stiffly to the large, handsome Forest-lord who stood before him smiling.

'It is due to this, I would share some things with you that are not to be shared until it becomes obvious as a clue. Will you trust me Callum McIntyre?'

'Without question,' replied Cal. 'You are the God I dreamed of as a child, although I had no true Pagan upbringing and it's you who brought me to the path of archaeology and now anthropology. I have always known that nature held all the answers.'

'Then I would ask you to sit with me a moment and I will show you a vision that will not be shared. I ask you say nothing of what you see, but I need to know that it is stored in a human vessel that one day will make a difference to the outcome desired by all, namely the return of Sybille Madison.'

'How could I refuse?' Cal replied; as the Green-lord looked deep into his eyes, he thought he would drown in their benevolence.

Hercurin invited him to sit, his back against a tree, offering him a few drops from a small bottle he carried in a pouch. It tasted like amber nectar and Cal felt himself lift gently out of his body; no fear no dizziness, only a lightness of being and a sense of joy.

Suddenly, he was gliding over treetops above snow-covered hills at sunset; below he could just make out two shadowy shapes moving through snow. Ravens were flying, screaming in their usual raucous way and he recognised amongst them several of the raven-shapers; he was sure Tara was one of them.

He watched as they climbed a trail higher into the hills, through rugged terrain and as the smaller of the two shapes appeared to falter. His vision became telescopic; he saw the larger figure reach out as if in encouragement. As his vision panned in, he could make out a very tall male with burnished hair much like his own and who was of a similar size. He reached out to help the other, a small dark haired young woman, as she stumbled and fell. He shimmered and changed into a large fox form, shaping the girl, as she lay unconscious, into a young fox the easier for her to manage the harsh cold. He revived her and they continued into the hills to a small stone cottage.

Cal thought he recognised the countryside, Scotland, Ireland, Wales he pondered. He would know if he found it, he thought as he drew his vision back further away from the foxes, padding on through the worsening conditions.

He could see a wide strip of water and wild moors, and drew a picture in his mind so that he could look at a map when he returned to the everyday. He realised that his gift was distance scrying and his memory, always sharp, would always allow him to find a place again if he had a few landmarks to go by. He felt elated at the thought, he had a working tool by which to help the group, before he found himself back in his body, feeling a little drunk on the energy of the potion the Greenlord gave him, with a smile and a pat on his back.

When he came to the sun was going down, a grove of thirteen trees grew in a perfect circle and his tools were clean, leaning against the trunk of the tree from which Hercurin had emerged. Cal smiled to himself in quiet joy and went to find Flora to show her the Grove. Every tree was budding, some such as hawthorn, black-thorn; rowan and elder were in flower. He knew he wouldn't take the credit; it wasn't in his nature to lie and the Greenman smiled at the man's honesty.

Chapter 21
Alma

Alma felt herself pulled, tugged on, in her drowsy state, where she lay curled in the cavern of a great and ancient willow. At first, she thought it was Maeve, her big strong sisterkin but then she realised that she was looking up through a coloured spectrum that sparkled and sang to her of peace and playful companionship; no more chores to do, no expectations on her behaviour and civility; a song of Alma, finding Alma.

She tried to sit up, but found her legs and arms entangled in the root system and she could see the ancient willow's trunk, as it lay at right angles to the riverbank. That's not right, she thought to herself as she felt the tree split wide open and the root bowl swung out into the river's flooding tide.

She tried to scream, water filled her mouth and nose but then something was holding her face out of the water. Water sprites were calmly holding her yet tugging her along, towing the root bowl that trapped her.

Even with her ears underwater, she could hear her one true friend Maeve, screaming to Brandubh the Cunningman to help her but he was too far away to know what was happening.

Alma felt peaceful until Maeve and Bran emerged from under the root bowl trying to save her, trying to untangle her arms and legs. It was then the water sprites went crazy, biting and scratching at Maeve's hands as she tried to pull her free.

Suddenly Alma was fighting too, at the fear in Maeve's face she panicked, feeling the sprites pulling even more strongly, on her senses as much as her physical, weakening little body.

She screamed aloud as her head went under again; she breathed and gulped the cold muddied water. Maeve, pulled away by the currents was crying out in frustration but something in Alma knew it was useless, the sprites were too strong and too many.

Alma gave a last scream, gasping for air her head broke surface, her eyes filled with horror bored into Maeve's, 'Help me,' she screamed. 'Maeve, **help me please!'**

With a roar the ancient tree split in two; Maeve and Bran catapulted back onto the riverbank. Alma heard the songs of the sprites as they called to her, beckoning to her to let go, to come with them, to come home; she simply let go the struggle of her young human life.

Centuries passed in human reckoning and Alma changed as the spirit of the waters infused her, their emotions infected her, until she altered. Gone the human child she thought she had been until finally, gone too were the memories of being, even partially, human.

She began to find her way further and further from her watery nest with the sprites. Eastward, flowing northward, into the largest valley of the Great Wold and on, into underground streams and rills, breaking ground with the Gypsey Race as it rose to the surface, who knew why, from its source at Wharram-le-Street, through the northern Yorkshire Wolds and out to the sea at Bridlington. It would often appear when least expected, with no reason known to the watching humans, while she drifted invisibly by with the currents; played with the seals and sea otters, caught fish as she remembered she did once somewhere, with someone. Mirdhaucha would find her way, until she found a special place that called her to stay a while longer.

Throughout the centuries, she would be banished and bound by Wytches and Cunningmen, hounded from every settlement's well, when they thought in her fierceness she meant them harm or that she would poison there water supply. By then, she was composed more of water than anything else; she questioned why they thought so badly of her and why she would consider poisoning, the very element that sustained her.

One day Alma woke to find herself in a soft bed, in a strange space. Briefly, she was an ordinary little girl but when she felt the fear in the child's heart, she withdrew in anger to a space of vengeful thoughts and feelings of helplessness and despair. She would hear a woman screaming at the little girl, hiding away in a cupboard or under a bed, for fear of the large, smelly men who would try to entice her out with sweets, for who knew what purpose.

It was a different space from where she had first known her power over the water folk. The people of the tribes who didn't understand her, had constantly confronted her, so different was she to her so-called parents. Her own kin had sold her to the Seer's Isle Priestess, The Cybil. From there, when her behaviour became unacceptable, sent to Scathach's Hearth to find and hone other skills than her true one of seership and to tame her wildness. Once there, she'd met someone, a young woman whose name she could no longer recall.

Every now and then as she changed and grew in spite and anger, for what she had long forgotten, she would find herself in a great cauldron of water in a strange place that looked like an alchemist's cave. A large oven, benches with strange tools and contraptions, coils of fine metal wire, nuggets of precious metals but worse than that, there was a strange hum in the air, constantly buzzing in the background. It was as if a nest of bees had taken up their home in her ears, an irritating current of sound, making her shake her head anxiously; the sound made her angry.

She would watch from where she perched on the top of the large water cauldron, a tall redheaded woman, who seemed strangely familiar. The woman, Maeve she heard her called, would work, sweating and swearing rudely when things went wrong; it would make her giggle. Still there was something about her strength and feistiness that called to Mirdhaucha the Water Merrow, once known as Alma.

She began to show glimpses of herself and to cause the great water cauldron to bubble and splash, until one day; seeing Maeve with a man named Morgan a shaper, she became agitated and angry. Who was that man, she knew his essence, and the woman; who was she to her.

It came to her in a surge of longing, followed by anger, at the memory of the day she had drowned to humankin and became a Water Merrow. She forgot she had made the conscious choice, seeing these two people to blame for her loss and so she sent a geyser of stinking, acid, pond water over the woman, burning her hands and chest with its lime content. Jealousy raged, as she watched the tenderness of the man toward the woman; this just wasn't right, he wasn't the one. She didn't know what that meant; just that he wasn't the one. Mirdhaucha vowed she would drive a wedge through their friendship, sneak and poke at the others in the group, who together were looking for a lost friend.

She spread dissention and anger amongst them, tricking them into believing their relationships were in jeopardy, until one day she managed to cause such friction between Maeve, the man named Morgan and the woman Samantha that the great Raven bird clan had arrived and whisked Maeve away. Chuckling with glee Mirdhaucha had followed, only to find her worst nightmare repeating itself, she again forgot all else to become the child Alma once more.

An endless pattern through the threads of Tyme, until one or the other of them would understand they were in fact one. The Water Sprites watched and waited and a Sylph, Minhiriath, known once as Sarah to her human friends, watched from her other form and hoped that the small Merrow would wake up and remember the truth of her being.

Chapter 22
Sybille's Teachings: Water

Earth you are, compassion grown
Fire and water becoming know
Air will sing, when fire alights
…and water washes all things bright

Water: our emotional self, all we feel and sense intuitively and physically, all the fluids of our physical body, and the fluid tides of our environment; classified as a feminine element.

The Moon governs everything that is fluid on our planet, including our own inner tides that pull us directionally, in accordance with the way we react or respond, to our environment.

We are 75% liquid and so it's easy to see why we can be such emotional creatures, especially the feminine aspects.

When we can learn to flow with the tides of life, including the tides of the planetary and seasonal phases, our life becomes easier, we stop trying to 'push the river' or paddle upstream against the natural currents.

Undines, nymphs, sprites, autumn, west

Chapter 23
Maeve

Fire is harsh and anger sings
...don't go too close you'll burn your wings
Earth yourself go deep within
...let water again become your kin
Let air breath you, let laughter ring

On the shores of the Seer's Isle Maeve wandered, gathering small stones to throw in the water, skipping them like the live things they were across the surface.

Peace eluded her, sleep had flown away to hide in a dark corner of her psyche; she would never be herself again, but there again who was that self anyway? Surely not this burned out shell, with reddened eyes and hollowed cheeks that she caught glimpses of in the glass clear water.

The Cybil had given her much to think about in the short time she had spent here in reminiscence, retreating from the world of humankin.

Often the Water Sprites would gather, Sylphs of Air and woody-fragranced Earth children, caught on occasion in peripheral vision. Sometimes a Salamander would spit fire at her as she attempted woefully, to light the forge again. A boiling hot or icy cold splash from a bucket of water would show her that she was too much out of favour with both these elementals, to ply her art.

She didn't know how to cope with the last thing that defined her, denied her. Art was her life, her wands, Athame and sacred jewellery, the alchemy of changing metal to a molten mass and into a shape of mutual choosing. Perhaps after all that had been the problem, she hadn't listened to the essence of the material's spirit more than a few times in her endeavours. She realised, with shame at her own arrogance, when she remembered the beautiful crystal shard that had a will of its own.

Therefore, the days passed, her tears cleansed her, forging her anew through her own pain. The Cybil gave her parchment and writing sticks of charcoal for her to try writing down her thoughts, sketching pictures of things she would perhaps, one day bring to life through her art after she'd healed; the latter she couldn't imagine or how it would feel to be whole again.

She missed her Hearth sisters and her friends from another thread, although they were fading into the Mysts of Tyme. On occasion, a raven would visit, crying Ruark to her, muttering sounds she thought could be words and another would come, bringing a completely raucous gang with her to tease and bring a smile to her face; it never quite reached her eyes.

One of the beings, the noisiest of them all, would come close to her peering deep into her soul, whispering to her that her name was Tara. She challenged Maeve to

wake up now and remember the journey she had under-
taken was by choice. At any time, the being told her, she
might have made a different choice on any matter that
had presented itself to her, as a lesson to learn and grow
from.

Maeve would laugh bitterly and say. 'Yeah as if I'd
choose for Alma to die!'

'No indeed,' the being said, 'but Alma did and
that was her choice to make. You are arrogant to think
you know better than the one choosing,' before flying
away in disgust, calling out. 'Have you not learned anything Maeve? Have you forgotten all that your teacher
Sybille taught you and right here, right now, the princi-
ples The Cybil can show you? Have you forgotten your
friends so quickly?'

Then suddenly one day, the being morphed
changing, in a flurry of black feathers and layered lacy
cloth into a small, exquisite woman with piercing blue
eyes. It was as if the veil parted and Maeve could see the
faces of her friends, overshadowed by those aspects she
recognised here in this thread and others she didn't.

There was Bethan, the beautiful priestess Leah,
Morgan the ever-watchful Cunningman, Brandubh. Flora
the little, elder herb woman and Samantha looked out the
eyes of a young, dark haired scribe who looked like a
shapechanger; Cal was there, a solemn faced boy who collected firewood for the Hearth and Claire in her Owl
form, who often sat on The Cybil's shoulder. Faces they

may not even know they bore, depending on the importance of the connections they held in the search for Sybille.

'Ah Sybille,' she sobbed and the raven woman returned to stroke her gently between her eyes and hold her in a musk-scented embrace. 'Hello Tara,' smiled Maeve through the last of her tears. 'Enough now,' she said, 'enough. I want to go home.'

'Soon,' replied her friend, 'soon. There are one or two things still left for you to do here. From now on, don't shut Bran out, he cares for your wellbeing and will be able to send messages to the others from here to the thread where they are. I think you are ready to return to Scathach's Hearth though.'

Maeve gave in gracefully and for the first time in months, smiled a weak smile as Tara handed her a scrap of paper before disappearing again through the veil, the words written in Sybille's hand were for her alone…

Fire is harsh and anger sings, don't go too close you'll burn your wings. Earth yourself go deep within, let water again become your kin …let air breathe you, let laughter ring…

…and she remembered the day they'd all begun to think about the little notes left for them by Sybille; how disappointed she'd been that the riddle of her disappearance wasn't going to be an easy thing to resolve. She'd been selfishly aware of her irritation toward Sam in particular, and at the others seeming acceptance of the whole situation without question, such was their loyalty.

All of them had proven their worth without agenda, even Sam, so hurt by Max hadn't complained once, she'd not shown a scrap of real compassion for her; driven by the Merrow's barbs of dissension and then, Tara had whisked her away. She now of course realised why that had been necessary, she could have hurt Sam severely in her uncontrolled anger.

She unfolded the note and re-read the five simple lines. 'Hmm, let's see,' she said aloud to the elementals, flocking to her side at the scent of Sybille's song.

'Fire is harsh and anger sings…'

…her anger at her mother, her child-self and her earlier circumstances, hadn't tempered her and so she went too close to the flame of the past and did 'burn her wings'; then to be taken to Scathach for 'tempering' as a battle maiden.

'So much for that lesson,' she scoffed at herself, as she read the clear instruction…

'…don't go too close you'll burn your wings.

…Earth yourself go deep within…'

…she interpreted this as finding her centre as a warrior maiden, grounding herself in the moment; and I'm still a virgin she thought ruefully, instead of earthing my fiery qualities and tempering them in the water of emotion. Does water not hone and temper metal, after all?

On reading the last lines, her tears welling again, she read aloud…

'…let water again become your kin.'

Alma, her little friend, whose magickal abilities to call up the sprites had been phenomenal and yet Maeve had been afraid of them. 'So what was I remembering?' she said to herself. 'Who is Alma to me?' She read the final line…

'Let Air breath you, let laughter ring.'

This one really puzzled her until she put it into context with Alma's playful nature and her own fear of the unknown Merrow. She realised they were one and the same being, altered somehow through the changes wrought by the sprites but there was still something she was missing.

'Ahhrrrrrr,' she screamed in frustration, screwing up the paper and stuffing it in a fold of her robe unceremoniously, the thought so close she could almost smell the answer before it dissipated on the wind.

The Cybil and Tara stood watching her from a distance, the sound Tara made, echoed Maeve's own frustrated cry. 'She's so close!' she exclaimed. 'When she grasps her intellectual and spiritual gifts as real, she'll truly breathe again, laugh at her own stupidity and the fact that she takes herself and everything else so seriously.'

The Cybil sighed sadly, as the memory of another thread in the warp and weft, rose to the surface. Sybille, her perceived future self, would know what to do to help break down Maeve's fears, her terror being that what she thought about herself might be true. She wondered if she could find a way to speak with Sybille in the thread, prior to her disappearance.

Chapter 24
Mirdhaucha

Tyme is an illusion all threads are one
…in the tapestry of life, unravelled, undone
Finding the Way through the channels of light
…reweaving the threads to heal them of blight

Mirdhaucha swam through the waterways in the 'Between'. She could hear a sweet sound far away vibrating the Skeins of Tyme; it called to her, hauntingly melodious, the pipe perhaps that the one known as Bethan, Arwen Arianwen played?

Ah, that one was a danger to her mistress she thought. She knew she mustn't approach her directly, biding her time while her mistress worked her dark magicks; they scared her.

Often, she felt the pulls and tugs on her senses from other threads that she knew were entangled, due to her fall from her original path. She shrugged the thoughts off, the sound continued to call to her, humming softly; she could smell fresh water. Not an instrument then, she thought!

Following the scent, she pushed her way through a small opening in the veil, to find herself in a darkened room where an old woman sat, her head buried in her arms on the table. A beautiful bowl, shimmering with crystalline spirits sat in front of her; the scent of sweet water emanating.

She approached carefully, her diminutive height barely reached the table, so she stretched up to take a closer look for the cause of the sound that sung to her being.

Eyes wide in awe, she saw the bowl held moving things, shadows and light; it sang their song quietly. As she reached out, up on her tiptoes, there came a loud retort as the crystal cracked, crazing over with fine web-like lines before exploding with a roar, which to the Merrow sounded like anger.

She covered her head, ducking under the table, barely avoiding the legs of the sleeping woman. Splinters of flying glass flew through the room in every direction; a large shard fell close to the frightened creature. With hardly a pause, Mirdhaucha snatched up the piece and fled back through the gateway in the veil, gleefully clutching the shard to her. Finding it sharp and cumbersome for her small hands, she broke it in two the sound of it snapping echoed through the Skeins of Tyme, to shake the cocoon where Sybille lay. The Merrow paused a moment, fear taking hold, before she wrapped the shards within the folds of her cloak. Fae and Greenlord alike paused to listen, pain on their faces as they covered their ears; human-kin stirred in their sleep or paused in their day, to sense the changes approaching, unnamed.

Swimming the channels of underground streams, she immerged again in the lands of the Fae. She was always careful not to show herself to the silver haired Fae, seeking only the dark ones who followed a different path, much of it hidden even from their own kind.

She found her Lady, the dark Fae Aelish, seated on the bank of the river with her son Aerandir. He always scared the Merrow with his frightening glares of anger and contempt but the Lady would soothe her with a touch and a sharp retort to Aerandir to, 'let her be.' Under the auspices of Aelish, she would smirk at him, spit at or nip him when she could sneak closer. Today she didn't even glance at him, so excited was she to present her Lady with the crystal shard treasures she'd found.

Bowing and nodding to Aelish, she placed the shards at her feet without a word, not daring to look in her eyes.

'What have you there, Merrow?' Aelish said to the small childlike creature. 'Is it a gift for me?' she almost smiled.

'Yer, M'lady …s'alls fer yer,' trilled the Merrow happily in her watery voice.

'Well they look interesting,' Aerandir quipped. 'What's so special about pieces of glass?'

'Ah not glass,' said Aelish looking closely at the shining pieces. 'It's volcanic obsidian crystal, from the core of this planet. If you listen carefully, you can still here the echoes of its song,' Aelish almost crooned.

'S'rite M'lady, t'was t'song wot led Mirdhaucha t'it,' chirped the Merrow happily.

'You did well little one,' Aelish replied, patting the child like Merrow on her head almost fondly, 'but scurry along now. I need to take a closer look at this treasure.'

Without a thought, the Merrow dipped a bow to Aelish and leaped happily into the river, dousing Aerandir before swimming away through the watery channels of the 'Between' to her nest beyond time, in the lake of the Seer's Isle.

'How do you stand that creature?' Aerandir sneered, shaking water from his hair. 'She smells of pond-weed and worse.'

'She's a useful little ally, always poking around in other people's things and on occasion has brought me a trinket or two that were dropped in the rivers. This one is particularly special and I know exactly who to pass it on to.' She smiled secretively to herself.

Later that day, on the thread before Tara had whisked Maeve away to a different realm, prior even to Sybille's disappearance, a woman visited Maeve in her studio. She brought her two magnificent shards of Lemurian Crystal to make into a wand, the other for a strange gift she suggested she make for her friend Bethan's forthcoming birthday.

Maeve had been stunned at the ridiculously low price the woman had asked and had a moment of doubt that the pieces were perhaps, stolen. Shrugging off her suspicions, she bought them and the woman, never seen again, forgotten.

Chapter 25
La Stregga

Dreams are like gold when answers they give
…what will you ask for the life that you live?
When dreams are disturbing listen, you must
…or the gold of your dreaming will fall into dust

Annie Savage struggled to the surface as if coming up through gelatinous, thickened water. She knew the dream was real but her psyche screamed no, it just couldn't be; she could never have been such a bad person.

Her guilt at the thought, brought her wide-awake, only to see a shadowy figure in the corner of the room, 'Lady?' she queried. 'Is that you?' There was no reply; the figure seemed only slightly built but stockier than her benefactor.

She sat bolt upright, as the figure moved toward her and she saw clearly an aged woman with an olive skinned face, her eyes were wet with tears. She was wringing her hands in obvious distress and Annie could see her lips moving but couldn't make out what the woman was saying to her.

Then it was as if someone had pulled a plug from her ears and a stream of beautiful Italian washed over her. It was a language that Annie had always loved, part of her ancestry in fact. When her parents had gone back to Italy a few years ago, to nurse her ageing grandmother and never returned, she started going regularly to a conversation class in Melbourne. Her other relatives gave her a wide birth due to her prickly nature and her inability to understand the relationship a true Italian family had.

She understood, 'We are one you and I. I have been so wrong and know I must make recompense to the young Magdalena but I do not know where she is now. I cannot find her in the Aether and my Lady Aradia has deserted me, I fear. I am lost. My bowl was shattered and pieces disappeared mysteriously. I died alone and lonely and am fearful for my Littleshape.'

'So Aradia is her name then, I did wonder but what is a Littleshape and are you a ghost then? What sort of bowl did you break, and why is it so important? Slow down you are not being clear.'

'I am sorry I cannot find the words to describe what has happened and what I did to cause it. I am a treacherous person and I sense you have been too but perhaps together we can make amends to those who have been so hurt by our actions.'

'I don't know what you mean,' said Annie returning to her usual haughty demeanour as soon as she felt threatened. 'Who are you and why do you think we know each other at all?'

'I am La Stregga an aspect of you as you are of me; we are one in the Trueshape and if you help me I will show you the way of the Stregga.'

'I am already a Wytch,' said Annie, 'what can you teach me?'

'Well,' replied La Stregga, 'I can perhaps at least teach you to be honest with yourself, for that has been what I have learned!' and with this she simply vanished.

'Well!' snorted Annie, 'what on earth was that about?'

She fell back on her pillows again, convinced she must have been dreaming but sleep would not find her again that night, she kept hearing the sound of glass shattering and felt a wave of energy wash over her that resembled all her fears manifested. For the first time she realised she really needed someone to talk this through with but there was no one, Harry the last to understand. She sent out a silent plea to the universe and to her one time friend… 'Sybille,' the cry echoed through the Aether and Sybille stirred in her multiple aspects throughout the Skeins.

Chapter 26
Vanessa & Annie Savage

Fragile wings drooping she sits to muse
…what humans are doing …the resources they use
There's a limit to what sustains us
…and what equals abuse …so beware
…even Fae folk can have a short fuse!

Annie had not been sleeping well for some months now the strange dreams interfered with the depth of rest, the result was she felt she was losing the plot. Her temper frayed and her tolerance, both at work and home, was zero. She had pushed the encounter with the strange Italian Wytch conveniently, to the back of her mind.

She'd only recently, had a confrontation with her daughter Vanessa who, on meeting Harry by chance on a surprise visit, had been shocked to look into a face so similar to her own, in masculine form. Both she and Harry had turned to look at Annie in horror as they saw the obvious written all over her face. There was no gainsaying the fact that she had hidden this from them and denied them both knowledge they had right of.

'You lied to me,' screamed Vanessa at her mother. 'You said you had no idea who my father was and I thought you had been a promiscuous slut but in fact it's actually worse because you knew and you lied to me. By the look on his face,' she indicated with her head toward a stunned looking Harry, 'you didn't even tell him he was a father!'

'Yes she did,' said Harry coldly, 'but only recently. It's a shock to see you in the flesh,' he trailed off weakly.

'Well, if it's a shock for you when you already knew, how do you think it is for me?' said Vanessa equally coldly before she turned, saying over her shoulder, 'I'm done here,' as she stalked out the door proudly.

Vanessa heard her mother call after her but she simply kept on walking. Spring sunshine had turned to sleet, so pulling the hood of her coat over her head she began the short walk down into town, heading for 'earthly rites' and hopefully to find Tara.

A sudden realisation hit her, just as she was pushing open the door.

'**Shit**,' she swore aloud, 'that means Flora is my half-sister!' but instead of the anger she expected to feel, she felt a sense of warmth at the thought. She remembered Flora offering the food for Lottie's little gathering and the genuine feeling of caring that had exuded from her and from the other young woman, Samantha too.

Had they known something she pondered? 'Oh yeah, great!' …she swore again. 'Claire must have known that day too.'

She paused at the door, not wishing another confrontation that day. Too late, Samantha was opening it for her, having witnessed her hesitation; she gently drew Vanessa into the warm shop.

Vanessa turned away from her avoiding her penetrating gaze, her anger changed to tears of hurt and as she turned, she walked straight into the arms of the sister she hadn't known she had, until now.

Flora led the now sobbing girl upstairs to her room. Saying nothing, she poured Vanessa a glass of water, adding a few drops of 'recue remedy' to ease the pain and shock written clearly on her face. Pulling her to a couch, Flora sat with her, wordlessly emitting compassion and caring toward her little sister. She smiled ruefully at the thought.

'What's so funny?' said Vanessa, seeing Flora's smile. 'I personally find it hard to see the funny side of any of this,' sounding more like her mother in that moment.

'Oh I'm not laughing at you Nessa,' slipping naturally into the nickname she'd heard Tara use; 'I'm smiling at the thought that I have a little sister, is all. It isn't an unpleasant prospect! I was wondering why you're here today in such a state. You've been to see your mother I presume?'

'You mean you knew,' said Vanessa pulling back to look in Flora's face, 'you could have told me!'

'No Nessa, I believe our shared parent and your mum should take full responsibility for their actions, personally. No one told me either but it wasn't hard to see

Harry's resemblance when I met you and remember, you're actually not the only one who was in the dark about this; my mum Claire was for years after all. It means when I was just over four years old her husband was having an affair.'

'Yes, I'm sorry Flora, I'm just in shock, can't think straight. I know I can be difficult at times but I'm not unfeeling. It must be a dreadful thing for both you and your mum. I for one can't, and I'm sorry if this seems rude, understand what my mum would see in your dad,' she gave Flora a watery grin.

'Yeah I know, go figure,' and, 'eeuw,' they said simultaneously.

There came a knock at the door and they broke off their laughter almost guiltily at the ease they were handling a tough situation.

'Yes?' Flora called.

'It's me Flo,' Claire said, 'can I come in or do you need more time.

Flora raised an eyebrow at Vanessa questioningly before calling out, 'No come in,' at Vanessa's shrug of agreement.

Vanessa stood up as Claire walked in hesitatingly she walked towards her. 'I'm so sorry Mrs Jenkins,' she said quietly.

Claire looked at her for a moment, gauging the girls' unexpected response. 'Well,' exclaimed Claire. 'You're nothing like either of your parents are you?'

Vanessa could only smile. 'No, thank the Goddess, I'm not Mrs Jenkins.'

'Claire,' said Claire. 'Please call me Claire, Nessa.' With surprising ease, the three women sat to get to know one another.

Vanessa told them about her mother's inability to communicate with her and so she'd opted to go to a college that had shared accommodation close by.

She worked in a supermarket at weekends and some evenings to pay her way; her mother didn't have a lot to give her and hadn't complained when she'd moved out of home.

'So, what are your plans now Nessa?' asked Flora. 'Will you keep doing what you're doing?'

'I'd actually called in to tell my mum that I wanted to leave college; I've just turned 19. I want to find a way to learn photography, perhaps an online course, a cheap rental and a job to pay my way. I want to get out of the city and thought mum might let me stay with her until I found somewhere affordable of my own.

I'll get good references from the supermarket, I never missed a day; I couldn't afford to anyway, so I could apply here in Springsmeet for a position,' she finished with a sigh, before continuing.

'That's all changed; he's living with her now,' she said, her emphasis on **he's,** clear in meaning, contempt oozed from every fibre of her being.

'I couldn't possibly share space under those conditions even if mum agreed so…' she trailed off, tears welling.

'Well,' said Flora, 'I can certainly understand that and I had a pretty normal time growing up; that is until I disagreed on a career course; sorry mum,' she directed at Claire.

'Oh no apologies necessary, as you well know Flo,' laughed Claire. 'I don't know what I was thinking staying around so long, hoping he'd actually see someone else's side to an argument and then there's his disbelief in my magicks…' this time Claire hesitated, glancing at Vanessa.

'Magicks?' she queried. 'I don't understand.'

'Sorry Nessa, it's probably too soon to talk about it with you but I will I promise, very soon.'

Recovering herself before Vanessa could reply Claire continued. 'I'm sure we can work something out to help, can't we Flo?'

'Well yes,' there's room at the farm…'

'…or perhaps with Susan and Alex,' interjected Claire.

'Oh I wouldn't want to impose on anyone, particularly people I don't know at all,' Vanessa said in obvious discomfort. 'Even you two don't really know me!'

'We simply know you're blood,' said Flora gently, causing another round of tears from Vanessa.

'It's true love,' said Claire. 'You're the innocent party in all this and you're my own girl's sister, so no matter the circumstances you're family now and this is how we,' she indicated to Flora, 'look after our own.'

'I don't know what to say,' said Vanessa. 'You're both so kind.'

'Then let's sort what needs to be sorted as soon as possible,' said Flora. 'Do you need a hand moving stuff from town?'

'I don't have a lot and the girls I share with already have someone to move into my space,' replied Vanessa. 'Clothes, my camera and a few bits and pieces I love, so I'll have to find some furniture locally.'

'Oh, we have plenty of pieces between us all,' laughed Claire. 'The boys have collected a few items they don't use anymore and Alex and Susan brought far too much with them for a small house.'

'Who are the boys, Alex and Susan?' asked Vanessa. 'There seems to be a whole group of you who know each other so well, I'd hate to intrude.'

'We're a pretty diverse bunch of Wytches,' laughed Flora, 'but we work together here and we're...'

'...working on a project about magick,' finished Claire rapidly, glancing at Flora with an almost imperceptible nod of negation. Flora heard clearly in her head. 'We can't risk trusting her completely yet Flo, she is her mother's daughter and we don't know what her abilities are where the Way is concerned.'

'…we're forming a music group too,' finished Flora with hardly a pause, the interchange not missed by Vanessa.

'If you chose to move in with Cal and me,' continued Flora, 'you could earn your keep until you find a job, helping with the chores at the farm or even here at the shop, although I'd have to run that past the team for confirmation.'

'I can read the Tarot,' said Vanessa after a pause. 'Tara taught me and she said I'm good at it; clairsentient,' she said. 'Oh and I can sing and play the harp a little and can certainly help with graphics for your web site.'

'Well we always need good readers,' said Flora. 'It would mean you reading for someone so that we can assess your style and ability, where to fit you in the team and it would mean you would occasionally be working with your mum when she's on the front desk. I'm sure we can work around that.

As for the voice, you'd have to speak with Morgan and Bethy about that and whether you'd fit, but I can't imagine why not; our dad's got a pretty good voice when he loosens up enough to sing.'

'Oh wow, this is all happening so fast; you don't waste time when you make a decision do you Flora?' said Vanessa with a grin. 'Don't you have to speak with your, er partner?' she finished.

'Well no not really. I will as a courtesy of course but the decision is mine to make. Sybille has left the farm to me. I mean in my hands,' she covered rapidly for her slip.

Vanessa was somewhat confused, 'Where is Sybille then?' she asked in apparent innocence.

Again, Claire and Flora exchanged glances before Claire said. 'It's a long story Vanessa and we have to bring the group together to introduce you and to tell you about what's been happening here. Yeah, it's a complex story and…'

'…well time is something I have now Claire and I sense there's a mystery here. I did when I brought my friends down and realised that mum had lied to me about her owning the shop and being the 'High Priestess', to use her terminology, of Sybille's grove. I mean, why she would fabricate something like that to impress her own daughter is beyond me and I haven't had a chance to ask her,' she paused, thoughtfully.

'I met Sybille a few times and that just didn't seem to fit with what I can remember of one feisty and sure of herself, woman,' she trailed off at the look of surprise on the two women's faces.

'I remember you Nessa,' said Flora. 'You came to a few Sabbats when you were just a wee girl. You showed incredible aptitude for sensing people's emotions even then. You're an empath aren't you?'

'Yes, I used to come to the lesser rites, solstice' and equinox'. I loved the energy and watching the grove work their magick in circle casting for the seasonal changes. Tara said I was a natural. It's one of the things that the girls I was sharing with got spooked about, my ability to sniff out a furphy, but that didn't apparently work when it came to my own parent.' Vanessa finished, in obvious frustration.

'Well,' said Claire, 'with all the skills we have between us, it's always those closest to us that we seem not to 'get'. I think we must have a personal buffer built in that allows them to get away with all sorts of things.'

'Anyway, let's go talk to the others who are in today and we can get some things sorted. That is, if you'll let us?' asked Flora.

'Oh yes of course,' replied Vanessa. 'You guys are the greatest, thank you so much. I didn't dream today would turn out like this when I plucked up the courage to talk to mum.' Her words trailed off as her thoughts slipped back to the man who was her biological father. That's all he is to me, she thought sadly.

Sensing her mood swing Flora gave her arm a friendly rub. 'Come on Nessa-sis,' she said playfully, 'let's go meet the tribe.'

There was a raucous sound of ravens and a great flapping of wings as Tara manifested in front of them, hooting with laughter. Vanessa paled and simply slipped onto the couch, mouth slack, her eyes vacant.

'Oops,' giggled Tara, 'I should have knocked on the roof ya think?' before cracking up with laughter, she flopped down on the couch next to Vanessa, reaching out to rub her between the eyes with her long slender finger. Claire was smothering her giggles behind what now appeared to be a few feathers.

'You two!' said Flora in frustration. 'Hasn't she had enough of a shock for today?'

'Well I just thought I'd lighten the mood,' grinned Tara, reaching out again to stroke Vanessa's forehead.

She came to, a puzzled look on her face. 'Er, what just happened?' Vanessa stuttered. 'Did I really see what I thought I saw?'

'Yes!' Tara laughed. 'Sorry but we have to bring you rapidly up to scratch with what's been happening; I thought that might wake you up a bit.'

'I'm having trouble remembering but I'm sure I saw you do that when I was a kid. Mum wouldn't believe me, told me not to tell fibs and I never mentioned it again. I used to try to be a fox but it never worked, except a couple of times in dreams and…' she trailed off as Tara and Claire exchanged a wordless glance.

'…and?' questioned Claire. 'What were you about to say Nessa?'

'Oh, well once I found short red hairs in the bed and there was a smell of earth. It reminded me of my puppy when I was a kid and the smell of her paws when she'd dug in the dirt.'

'Well this is a wonderful surprise,' said Tara. 'We'll talk more about it tonight, when you meet the gang.'

Vanessa smiled a sweet smile and said. 'I can't wait! It's all too exciting for words.'

'Alright then,' said Flora. 'Let's round up the gang and introduce you properly.'

Chapter 27
Sybille's Teachings: Trueshapers

Beyond the light of dreaming stars
...beyond the light of time
...I reached within to find a space
...a place that's only mine
A place of light and healing sounds
...the darkness was its source
...for from that darkness light was born
...and matter its resource

A Trueshaper is the greater aspect (over-soul) of all the combined aspects of an individual, (new agers call it soul-self) and they in turn are an aspect of the highest ideals; Goddess or God-self if you will as of course, even Deity is one in Primordial Source.

Each of the aspects of a concurrent life, (as you know everything is now), are known as Littleshapes, sparks of life-essence that fly between lives, animating the physical body and creating the lessons and experiences of the individual's journey.

At present in this realm, the journeying is unconscious for most and most believe, if they believe at all, that time is linear and that they must die first before they can have an understanding of other lives, other aspects of self, known as sleepers, innocents or Onceborn.

Our job when we awaken is to protect them, for they are not bad, even when their fearful behaviour causes them to do dreadful, destructive things to themselves and each other. They are innocent to the extent of their true selves and therefore need to awaken, each in their own time and yet, every so often we reach, what may be described as a critical mass in our planetary evolution, which pushes us inwardly toward change; these are the moments of opportunity for spiritual growth that can awaken a sleeper. We are at such a moment now in our history.

We understand our challenges better when we know these things for even the White Christ of the Christian peoples said, 'They know not what they do.'

Eastern philosophies speak of Karma and this of course is a version of what I have outlined but still perceives time to be a linear process from past to present and on into an unknown, 'fated' future.

This is a fabricated concept, for life and the universe do not understand the meaning of the invention of the clock and man has looked to understand time, by attempting to harness it, which in turn limits understanding of alternative concepts.

Of course, we see the sunrise and set, the length of day and night, a lunar or solar cycle etcetera yet, under the laws of the universe, this is but an illusion. We would probably go insane if we were to attempt to grasp the entirety of the known and unknown worlds all happening at the same time and ourselves as vast, eternal beings; miniscule parts, cells of ourselves, flitting and animating our aspects in continuum.

If we can see it rather, more as a tapestry of threads, each thread a separate life, and yet one thread in the tapestry links each life, one to the other, not just our own journey but everyone's journey; through this our understanding of same is broadened, becoming less insular. We can then 'jiggle' one of those threads from our current life perspective, drawing to us the knowledge our other aspects have collected to assemble a body of knowledge that may become 'whole' to itself. Is this how a new philosophy is born, perhaps?

If we have a particular skill, we are successful at but have no formal or even fleeting training in during this consciousness, chances are we have brought this quality with us or are remembering that we have achieved this in another aspect of ourselves. In turn, we can glean information from these other aspects of self as we link with them in consciousness. In reverse, when we feel confronted by characteristics, we just cannot own as our own; those that are negative, spontaneous outbursts of violent behaviour, for instance. This may well be where ancestral memory strands may overlap; we may not use this as an excuse to make our behaviour okay, however. I have seen many who would blame their 'other lives' as an excuse for their bad behaviour, using them as a crutch, instead of something to work through or integrate within, much as people with addictive traits must do. They know it is a part of them to monitor, until the origin is found.

It is also advisable to realise that the goal is not perfection in the individual aspect per se but rather in the True-shape acquiring knowledge, through all the countless possibil-

ities, within multiple and concurrent lives; and this is the desired outcome to all our meanderings. We may liken this to something that is rare on this planet, other than in sport and in some rare families or tribes, namely 'teamwork'.

There are theories today that promise separation from ancestral and cellular memory in this life and that would be valid, if we were to see beings who were in fact the equivalent of the White Christ, The Magdalena, Brighid, Buddha, Mohammed, Cerridwen, Hecate and other such worthy beings who have walked this realm but what happened to them? In other words we have to actually know, (or at least have some idea), **where we are going** *when we speak of 'ascension' (although this speaks of a hierarchy) to other planes or we may indeed become lost in the 'Between'. Therefore, we may consider finding/creating, a place that becomes so real to us on the inner; we then manifest it as the place that becomes* **where we will go** *, (rather than where a hierarchy tells us we will go, scaring us with fear or wooing us with pleasure).*

Is this another aspect or a final coming together of all aspects; that is of course up to you to decide!

When we understand this, all egocentric agendas fall away; we know we do not die but merely change form, our essence remaining the same yet growing, as we gather all the aspects of self into one being, united in consciousness and without fear, for fear is egocentric and is the controller. Fear is the self that believes having things and accumulating assets will make the ego-self happy and keep them safe.

Fear has created hierarchical orders including wealthy and poor, weak and strong, religious right and wrong in a judgemental manner.

Sadly, the wealth associated with the accumulation of things cannot sustain or indeed be eaten, when one is starving.

Chapter 28
Maeve & 'The Cybil'

On days that seem they are like no other
...go deep within ...reach out to the Mother
She hears every word that your soul ever cries
...she whispers, 'fear not, for you can truly fly'
...come with me; together we'll fly o'er the land
...come with me, take full flight
...don't be scared ...take my hand
You'll see that life's more than just day-to-day plans
...as you soar on the wings of your soul'

Maeve felt as if she'd been asleep for a very long time, a sleep of nightmares and pain. Pain for her little friend Alma and fear, when she'd discovered the truth of what Alma had become; Mirdhaucha, the Merrow who had haunted her at home in Springsmeet.

The wheel turned again and it was a strange feeling, not knowing what time of year it was or where her friends were. She could only reason that if it was Beltane here then it may be Samhain there but how many turns had there been. Life on the Seer's Isle had no sense of time passing, no one really seemed to age or ail; those who did were, like herself, not from this thread on the Skeins.

The Cybil was teaching her to find peace within, no matter what else happened to or around her; techniques to understand the opportunities presented were to learn the truth of herself. Her relationship with her mother on the thread where she'd been born as Maeve, who Alma truly was, all became clear as she followed the evident trail, with the blessing of hindsight. She realised she couldn't help Alma become the child again if she didn't heal the child within herself, healing her adult self in the process.

Standing on the lake's edge, she'd scry in the little pools the waters left behind in the tidal ebb and flow of the Brue River. She would see her friends going about their daily business, seeking for Sybille and planning the next stage of their personal journeys into the 'Between'. She'd seen a design for a knife, an Athame she realised and was suddenly excited at the thought of working again. There was a working forge here on the isle too she thought, perhaps they would let her use it.

There again, perhaps Tara would let her stay with her friends although; they were her friends here now too and at the Hearth. Rhiannon, Brighid, Iwerydd, her female warrior friends and of course, there was Bran who she recognised clearly, as Morgan. Then there were two other young men she'd come to know as strong warriors and friends, Fionn and his older brother Jamie who looked so much like her, he could be her twin brother. Their relationship was one of teasing just as siblings would do; the blade she realised was for him and she would present it as a naming day gift, if she could complete the work in time.

Excited now, sensing the sprites gathering, she hurried to the forge and was happy to work for the smith in turn for creating her own piece.

It wasn't an easy start to her return journey, water and fire sprites made it hard for her, burning her with their sparks or droplets of boiling water as she dipped the blade again and again after beating it to shape, making her work to reclaim their trust and for her to lose her fear.

Day by day, she increased her physical strength as the work progressed; an Athame was born, one as never before. Rich, dark woods made the hilt smooth after rubbing with precious oils until burnished. It was strong, longer than a normal hand span; Jamie was a large man. Just before his naming day, it disappeared and she feared the Mirdhaucha was up to her old tricks; she failed to see the fox that carried it away through the veil.

On the day, Tara surprised her; taking her to visit her friends at the Journeyman, she was ready. She forgot about the mysterious disappearance of her prize piece, after all The Cybil had taught her well about the acquisition and ownership of things that were simply that, 'things'. She'd proven to herself that she could overcome her fear of the water and fire sprites and once more reclaim her gifts; after all, she could always make another blade.

She couldn't believe her joy when Tara arrived; she was ready to return to Scathach's Hearth and had no idea where they were going only assuming it was there. She giggled and shrieked with glee as Tara took her at full speed through the veil; she could have sworn she felt feathers or perhaps fur against her skin as they flew and the smell of Tara's musk filled her senses, along with something else unidentifiable.

Chapter 29
The Day before Ostara

If you could live inside a book
…the one you read in a quiet nook
…where would it take you, how would it look?
Would it be sumptuous …a travelling feast?
Would it have dragons and other such beasts?
Would it be sad or a place of content,
…would it be in a castle or in a red tent?
Who would you be in the pages you read?
…a saint or an angel a vampire that feeds.
What would you look like …would you be fair?
…would you have ringlets …long tresses of hair?
Would you have friends or be on your own,
…would you be happy or constantly moan?
Who would you be in the pages within?
'Relax, enjoy the journey,' she said with a grin.

Wednesday arrived and the shop was a flurry of activity, Sybille's books displayed throughout. Samantha was aware that there would be many questions as to Sybille's whereabouts and they'd put together a solid story of her being away on a writer's retreat, working on the next volumes of her books and no, she did not want visitors or emails at this stage.

It was getting harder to explain her long absence; Sam felt dreadful every time she explained this to people; she hoped only that they could bring her home soon.

Now as the excitement of her first book launch kicked in, Sam felt alive and happy the terrible dreams that plagued her, dissolved in the spirit of achievement. Along with that came the first feelings of spring fever as if the sap rising in the trees was welling up inside her too. Her little leaf sprite's colours changed to those of fresh budding leaves and pale apple blossoms. Birds began to nest in the eves, the air filled with fragrances as magnolia and fruit trees blossomed, crocus, hyacinth, daffodil, bluebells and snowdrops broke ground throughout the landscape.

They closed shop early to set up the refreshments, keeping an eye out for the reporter who was coming to interview Sam about her aunt and who would then write a review for the book which, in turn gave credence to the shop. Sam was also aware she would need to be careful when she spoke of her aunt, not give anything away.

Invitations sent weeks ago had sparked an over-whelming response; Sybille's reputation as speaker and author, always well met. Now, as editor, publisher and artist, Sam could with confidence, put her name to the book, Earth Rites, the Way of all Magicks proudly, in honour of the aunt she loved and missed.

She could hear music wafting from Bethan's stu-dio, low voices from the reading rooms where Tara and other readers were busy with clients and the sound of laughter drifted from the kitchen, where Flo and Cal were cooking up a storm of, 'finger-food' delights.

Max, who having set himself up as the official food taster after missing lunch, lounged comfortably against the kitchen bench while the others worked and chatted. He and Sam had found their way to a mutually satisfactory friendship, unspoiled by their brief interlude of intimacy; they were both unembarrassed by it and were instead, best friends.

Max, slowly gaining confidence, was overcoming his fear of shapechangers and manifest, magicks. He worked happily and tirelessly on both research and the renewal of his relationship with Lily; she was reticent. To be hurt again as she had been by Max was not on the cards she said.

All in all the days moved on smoothly, tomorrow was Ostara, a rite of renewal and spring equinox, a rite of balance; the timing for the book launch was perfect under these auspices.

Putting the last of the work sheets and other paraphernalia away, Sam was free to wander the shop, taking in the scents of fragrant candles and incense; she gave a silver chalice inscribed with the symbol of the Goddess Triformis, a quick polish with her sleeve, where a clear fingerprint marred the shiny surface. She worked quietly as she saw others that were smudged and dirty inside and vowed to face Annie the following day, about the necessary cleanliness such a shop needed. Dirt equalled dirty energy and repelled sales. Who would buy a dirty chalice as their sacred tool, she mused.

Sam worked quietly, moving through the various rooms, straightening an object here, putting a book back on a shelf there. Engrossed in her tasks, she realised that the comforting background noises from both kitchen and studio had diminished. She felt a surge of energy and sounds, muted further, were akin to being underwater; she shook her head in an attempt to clear her ears.

Lights flickered and dimmed; once again, the eerie feeling of someone or something watching, overcame her. The leaf sprites, unusually quiet that day came to her in a sudden rush of melodic song, surrounding her with their protective and united force, little thorn swords raised in defence.

A misty figure walked the passage between the bookshelves, appearing to be searching the titles in agitation, ghostly fingers unable to make physical contact with the books making their frustration palpable. They paused at the table where Sam had made a display of Sybille's earlier published books, bright cover art dulled by the dim light. The figure seemed to be that of a young woman no more than 18 or so, pale under her olive skin tone and frail, weighing no more than a child does. Long dark hair, unkempt and tangled, fell around her shoulders and down her back. She appeared to be weeping as she searched but again the sounds muted, as if from far away.

Sam stood still, watching the sad figure compassionately as it came directly toward her. Sudden recognition came. It was Nina, she realised the girl she tended in her Magdalena aspect. Nina looked up from her search and froze as she saw Sam,

'Magdalena!' she cried. 'Is that really you?' She advanced towards Sam, joy replaced grief in an instant.

'It's true then, we don't die!' she exclaimed. 'Where are you and what happened to your book, I can't find it anywhere?' Again, distractedly she moved on, searching the shelves.

Sam had no chance of reply or to find out more as the door to Beth's studio burst open and the group tumbled out, instruments in hand, on their way to set up for the evening. They all came to a halt as they saw Sam standing, apparently gazing into nowhere.

Morgan passed his lute to Lily as he stepped forward in concern, 'Sam,' he quizzed, then louder. '**Sam, are you okay?**'

With the light and sound returning to normal, Sam almost shook herself, attempting to centre into the moment.

'I'm okay,' she managed, blinking rapidly to clear her sight. 'I just saw an apparition. It was Nina, the girl from my Italian, Magdalena aspect. She was distressed, looking for a book she'd lost, Magdalena's …my book? She looked sick and sad but she recognised me as Magdalena and was happy to know that death was not real, so I assume I must have died and ...oh of course, the dreams, Bethy?'

Beth took her hands and reassured her, 'If Magdalena died in that aspect she is still here in you Sam. Knowing this might in fact make it easier for you to merge with her aspect and to find the connection between Nina, Magdalena and Sybille, just as Morgan is linking with Bran and I merged with Leah. As hard as this is, it's a breakthrough, the more we connect with our aspects the more knowledge we gain to find her. We might then find out more about the book and Airmhid's herb lore.'

'Strange she should also have lost a book, don't you think,' said Lily, sharp as always for detail.

Sam gave her a watery smile. 'Yes of course, it's just she looked so sad and tired; not ill though for a change but whose aspect is Nina? She seems to connect with Flo but she's sure it's not her aspect. The link appears to be through Airmhid's bag of herbs and the little spirit Nangini. Do you remember me telling you about Magdalena's fear of her and that Nangini would visit Nina instead, making her the intermediary?'

'Sure,' said Beth, 'but Flo has followed the journey to being an herbalist and Airmhid gave her the bag of herbs; why not you I wonder, although you're working with them now more than Flo!'

'Whoa,' cut in Lily. 'Aren't we making this more complicated than it need be? The most important thing is that Sam is working with the magickal side of the herb lore and Flo with the medicinal and in that they're doing what Nangini wanted but through two people rather than one. If Nina isn't Flo's aspect, what we really need to do is find out who is, in the here and now. Who can help us with that, is more the question.'

'Your brilliant,' said Sam to Lily, 'genius in fact but who can help? Who would know?' She paused looking from one to the other of her friends.

'Tara,' said Lily, Beth and Mor in one breath.

'Of course, Tara,' said Sam, 'but she's not always easy to get straight answers from, is she?'

'What about Da then, Mor?' said Lily.

'We can try.' he replied. 'Let's do it later after the launch, he's coming with Claire shortly, he's singing a couple of pieces with us.'

'Is there no end to your family's talent?' said Sam. 'Alright let's finish setting up and then we can enjoy the night. I don't want anything spoiling it and then we can get down to some serious business, I'm over being the guinea pig in this, I need answers,' finished Sam with conviction.

'Yes, I'm with you,' laughed Morgan, taking her arm and leading her toward the kitchen. 'Come on, I think we all deserve a small drink for Dutch courage and to celebrate Sam's literary achievement too.'

Putting aside the challenges presented for a couple of hours, they threw themselves into the evening, setting up, cleansing the shop with sacred herbs and blessed waters before finally, greeting guests as they arrived. Susan and Alex were there early to help serve food and drinks.

Guests, dressed in bright coloured clothes echoing Sybille's own style and black clothed, more corporate individuals rubbed shoulders, stretching their necks and pointing at beautiful pieces of art and Sybille's latest book with equal enthusiasm. Sam was caught up in the whirlwind of their excitement, signing books as if it were the most normal thing in the world to be doing.

'Unearthly Sounds,' played and sang to the room, greeted with spontaneous cheers and applause that quietened as Bethan began to sing…

'Dark colours spin a muted blight, each note a chorus of the night; spinning fast the dying light, upon the Skeins of Tyme.

We did not fall descent was slow, on gossamer wings in ebb and flow, we came, a planet's seeds to sow …upon the Skeins of Tyme.

Then in sleep, we tumbled 'til, the darkness every thread did fill. Humanity birthed, forsook Her will …upon the Skeins of Tyme.

Webs are woven by intent, spiraling out the weave is bent. Earthly tides are almost spent …upon the Skeins of Tyme.

Grey the threads once coloured weave as all souls this realm must leave; that man himself could so deceive …the failing Skeins of Tyme.

Each mortal a thread that woven must, in perfect love and perfect trust; to rise above the cut and thrust …that snaps the Skeins of Tyme.

Where to mend and where to sew, loose threads fly no

colours glow as all beyond this realm must go …into the Skeins of Tyme.

Through the gateway once, star bright, its edge now tainted by the blight, into shadow's darkest night …beyond the Skeins of Tyme.

Drifting through the warp and weft, fragile hands so pale and deft, weave the scrap of tapestry left …upon the Skeins of Tyme.

Flying spindle, curling thread, returning life the Earth to tread, once more Her Silver'n blood is shed …upon the Skeins of Tyme.

Forgotten life, forsaken light, the silken threads are torn by blight, even the 'Onceborn' feel Her might …within the Skeins of Tyme.

Once Her threads so strong were tight, not to bind but to delight; to stretch, to hold our Souls winged flight …into the Skeins of Thyme'

…there was a moment of utter silence then bedlam broke lose, haunting notes from Bethan's lap pipes lingering on as they took their bows.

Cash flowed, for books and beautiful pieces by Lily, Tara and Beth's; a large Athame found its home with a tall auburn haired stranger dressed in black, his smile, belying his somewhat sober gothic apparel, lit his saturnine features with warmth.

'James?' queried Beth as they exchanged the sacred tool for money. Smiling, he stepped forward to hug her. 'I haven't seen you since Uni; what have you been doing with yourself?'

'Well I'm here to buy this delightful piece and would love to meet its maker,' he said looking round with interest, expectantly.

'Oh, that's one of Maeve's pieces but she's not here at the moment.'

'Well that's a pity and that makes two people I'd wanted to meet, absent this evening,'

'You came to see Sybille?' queried Beth.

'Yes but in her absence it's Samantha, Sybille's niece I'm to interview.'

'So you made it then James? You always said you wanted to be a journalist. Congratulations,' Beth smiled at her old friend from student days.

'What's going on' Bethy,' said James, reverting to the familiar. 'I can smell magick and it's the strongest around you and around the very girl I'm to interview? What's going on?' He repeated a little more forcefully.

'Why I'm really not sure what I can tell you James but it's lovely to see you anyway. Perhaps we can catch up sometime for a drink?' With that, she gently pushed past him to serve another customer who was waving for her attention, leaving James standing.

'Can I help you at all?' asked Cal, who had witnessed the interchange between them, speculatively and recalled seeing him in the vision, Hercurin had shown him weeks before. Now I understand he thought to himself, this man is a potent force and apparently, a force for good.

Snapping back to the moment James muttered, 'No thanks,' before walking determinedly after Bethan. Mor caught Cal's eye from across the room and moved in silently to intercept James.

'Hi,' he said, thrusting out his hand to James. 'I couldn't help noticing you bought that stunning Athame. You beat me to it. It's strange though, I cleaned all the Athame only this morning and I don't remember seeing it until tonight,' he said questioningly. 'I'm sure I would have remembered it if it'd been there then.'

'Ah, really,' said James, trying to see past Mor's large frame. Morgan simply moved to one side, further blocking his vision, giving Beth time to disappear from sight.

'Yes it is isn't it; a stunning piece that is. I couldn't resist it.'

James realised what was happening but it only made his journalistic self, more determined to find out the truth of what he sensed. Magick was part of his very nature and his skill was literally that he could 'smell' it but he was also concerned that the woman, who had written many amazing works, should not put in an appearance for her most recent publication, Earth Rites.

In truth, he smelt a rat. Where was she, he mused? There had been a few rumours circulating, implying that she had mysteriously disappeared. It was well known, she had the ability to become invisible when she retreated to write but the whole building reeked of fresh, untainted magick.

Turning to the large, dark-haired man, taller even than his own six feet, blocking his movement, he smiled. They each knew what the other was up to and a silent challenge passed between them before with a grin, Mor stepped aside to let James pass.

'I'll go do that interview with Ms Madison's niece then,' said James.

'Yeah,' Mor said. 'I'll see you again I'm sure.'

'Oh you can be **sure** of it,' replied James, not returning Morgan's smile and ignoring his outstretched hand this time.

Morgan watched him walk toward Sam; he knew that James could one day be an ally or an enemy.

Evening drifted into night and into success, wine flowed, mouth-watering odours filled the room as savoury pastries, spiced nuts, and citrus-scented olives passed around, for hungry guests to enjoy.

Their plans to speak to Tara later were however thwarted, when Tara didn't appear; Pwyll, reluctant to comment, merely said, 'These events have been to make everyone think outside the square in order to find Sybille, heal Silver, stop the blight and whatever's causing it. It's all up to you. Tara and I are but mediators, we can't do more than we're doing to help.'

'Well thanks then Da,' said Lily scornfully. 'Why is it no one from the otherworld can fix this and why do they think we can? It's like a grail quest out of a novel!'

'I can't answer that Jay-Lily,' said Pwyll. 'The Lady alone knows the answer and you need to remember that you are more than a little, 'otherworldly', as you call it.'

After finishing the clean up, Flora stretched and yawned. 'Come on folks, let's go home. We have an early start tomorrow and Vanessa will be arriving at the farm soon. I'd like you all to meet her, and we can continue this conversation then.'

'There's a lot we have to explain to Nessa too,' said Claire.

'Has she decided where she wants to live, Claire? We do have room if she needs some time to think and we'd be happy to help out,' asked Susan.

'She's coming out to the farm to live,' Claire replied...'

'...and Sam's coming home to live too,' said Flora with a grin.

'Who's going to be living here then?' said Lily.

'No one,' said Sam. 'It's too lonely and sad here without Maeve. We still have to come in to work in our studios, but it's nice to go home at night to the farm. It's easier getting together there or at Beth's, than us all meeting here in the evenings. It's not so far for everyone to travel, other than Alex and Susan of course, but they said they're happy to.'

With that they closed the shop, piling into the cars; Vanessa was waiting at the door with the cats and Honey, who'd found her way over through the forest from Beth's, as had become her habit of late. She seemed to know when Morgan wouldn't be coming straight home to the cottage.

Chatting and laughing the group made themselves at home and Vanessa, introduced to everyone. She was nervous but the friendly banter soon put her at her ease, she joined in animatedly and happily accepted the invitation to the Ostara Rite in the morning.

'Don't you think the whole thing will freak Vanessa out?' said Max to Sam, quietly. 'What if the Fae turn up or Silver, trailing blight behind her.'

'Vanessa is Flora's sister Max. Although they're not full blood siblings, there is enough of Flora in Vanessa and of her mum Annie come to that, for her to be able to handle the Rite. She's been exposed to Magick all her life and is a competent reader, empath, seer and one would imagine, Wytch!'

'I still think it's dropping her in the deep end a bit though,' replied Max.

'None of us were prepared for what happened to Sybille, especially me come to think of it. We need all the help, psychic gifts and magickal talents we can get to help find my aunt, and anyway Max, Claire and Pwyll are going to talk to her tonight about what's been happening. She'll either be able to help or will be scared witless but any Wytch worth her mettle will come to the party,' Sam finished.

'Wow,' said Flora overhearing their exchange. 'Go Sam! I wouldn't have imagined this conversation only months ago.'

'Well we've all grown a lot since then and this isn't the place for the fainthearted,' she said with a glance at Max, causing him to colour up as Sam moved away to help Vanessa who was brewing a pot of the sleep tea Flora kept on the shelf; her sprites, stirring and rustling as she walked away.

Cal had taken Vanessa's things to what was now her room in the attic, while Sam had shifted hers into the room her aunt had loved the most, her study, which was a beautiful space. With the couch replaced by her bed the room was cosy and yet spacious, the bonus being Sybille's energy and her vast library of books, all around her.

After a brief discussion on the Rite of Ostara, they decided to prepare the things needed for their ritual early the next day, placing them on trays to carry to the Grove first thing.

Soon done, they sat around the huge old table to say a blessing and to welcome Vanessa formally into the group.

They chatted as they dipped or painted colourful eggs with natural dyes for the following day's celebration, for breakfast and for hanging in a tree in the Grove.

Sam sat quietly, mixing the incense they'd chosen to use for the Rite; the fragrance filled the room as they chatted.

'Can you teach me about the herbs, Samantha?' asked Vanessa. 'I have a strange leaning towards them and yet I have no idea why.'

'You'd be better asking Flo,' replied Sam. 'She's an herbalist. I'm a novice in comparison.'

'It's not so much the medicinal aspects for healing, although that's fascinating too, it's more the magickal aspects, also the darker plants that can be used as 'heal or kill'. I know that sounds odd but the homeopathic qualities are amazing. To think a plant that is poisonous, used in miniscule doses can actually protect a person from poisoning by the same plant. You know, like the roman emperors took a little of the local snake venoms in small doses every day to protect them from snakebites that the assassins used to kill them.'

'Wow, you seem to know bit a bit about the dark arts of those times!' exclaimed Flora, joining in eagerly.

'It's an interest I've had,' continued Vanessa. 'Especially roman times, the Borgia family, the decadence of the roman Caesars and Emperors, the growth of amazing medicines that were a result of that whole period. We may see them as debauched but there were some amazing

minds of that time that resulted in our medicines of today, particularly homeopathy.'

'Have you ever considered studying it formally?
We seem to have a lot in common, so it must be in our
blood. Even though dad's convinced modern medicine is
the bees knees, he at least admits that it came about
through the original study of plants that were then syn-
thesised.'

'No not really, it's just an unknown urge and I really want to study photography, but wouldn't you say Flo,
that today's science is what magick was to earlier civilisa-
tions?'

'Undoubtedly, Nessa and I've had that very same
discussion with our father too,' she laughed ironically.
'He won't be pleased with me encouraging you either.'

'Well to be honest I really couldn't care much
what he thinks about me. I know he had no idea I even
existed and I don't know how my mum could've covered
it up, if they were still seeing each other either, but his
whole attitude to my existence has been nothing short of
cold and impersonal and more about his own feelings,
than anyone else's.'

'Sounds as if you've got him pegged, Nessa-sis,'
said Flora; they exchanged grins knowingly.

'So,' said Nessa. 'What's in the blend for tomorrow Sam? It smell's quite floral.'

'Absolutely, when you think of what spring means
with the bursting buds at the moment, even though it's

still cold there's no doubting its arrival by the scents; this is what I'm trying to capture. I also have this amazing old Grimoire of Sybille's to work with and the blends are particularly subtle. So this one is a combination of what is most evident in the landscape right now, borage, known as 'bee balm', clover for its sweet honey fragrance and cherry blossom. I found some broom and wattle flowers that had just popped, they're yellow for spring and the element of air that spring represents. Then there's a little dragon's blood oil to invoke the returning light and oakmoss, for the return of the Oak King's power.'

'Wow, that's incredible, I bet it will smell heavenly too' Nessa said, 'and I'd love to see that book.' Sam promised she'd show her the next day.

At that moment, Pwyll and Tara approached Vanessa, asking her to come with them to Claire's, wanting to fill her in about what had been happening and what her role may be in the coming days. She was keen to know what was going on and left, smiling over her shoulder at Flora and Sam excitedly.

Flora yawned and said she needed to head for bed; Susan and Alex said goodnight, while Beth, Morgan, Max and Lily gathered their things for the short drive home, squeezing Honey into the back was the hardest thing and they said their goodnights amidst gales of laughter from the back seat as Honey sprawled across Mor and Lily's laps.

Cal stood for a moment breathing in the scents and listening to the night sounds, full of the calls of owls; small bats flew, hunting the early emergence of gnats and moths, before moving inside and to bed.

As Beth drove away, Morgan noticed a large fox sitting watching the farm from under one of the old birch trees. He appeared to be listening intently, full focus on the old dairy that Claire had made home as a silvery, wraith-like shape, floated across the ground towards it. He could see she was small and slender, fitting the description of the apparition Sam had said she'd seen at the shop but he couldn't make out her features as she drifted silently by, accompanied by a smaller fox; a vixen.

The spirit paused momentarily, as if listening to something before turning in his direction; he heard clearly. 'Help me. I have to find it. I have to help her but I'm so weak now but if I don't Magdalena will suffer unbearably.'

He relayed his thoughts to her as they drove on. 'Tell me how I can help and I will do everything possible.' Too late, they were too far away for him to hear her reply.

Lily touched his arm. 'Are you okay Mor?' she queried.

'Yeah I'm okay Lily but I just saw, what I'm pretty sure is the same spirit Sam did earlier today. It seems she's only manifested since Vanessa's been around so perhaps we need to look for links there?'

'Things are certainly hotting up,' said Lily in reply. 'It's hard to tell what'll happen next. Kinda exciting and daunting too. I feel as if things are starting to come to a head but I'm not sure how or why I feel it.'

'Yeah I know,' said Morgan, Da and Tara both know more than they're letting on too.'

Lily laughed aloud, 'Oh you can be sure of that Mor!' she exclaimed.

Her laugh startled Bethan from her own reverie; she'd seen the spirit, knowing instinctively it would be a major key as things unfolded.

Chapter 30
Ostara Morning

Water drips from ancient trees
...silent the birds...still the bees
Rivulets of water...currents run deep
...soon to wake earth from Her long winters sleep
Gone longest night and the shortest day
...there is cold still to come but spring's on Her way
Not yet visible, not yet seen but below the cold ground
...the trees thoughts are of green
Slowly, roots stirring ...She stretches to wake
...drinking in water, Her new buds to make
Ice and snow form but in darkness below
...new life awakens ...in beauty and flow.

Ostara; dawn approached on silent icy feet, frost covered the ground and only the hardiest blossoms and bulbs survived its death grip. Instead of the usual banter as they gathered again in the Grove to cast a circle of flowers, the group were quietly, introspective.

Vanessa swept away the autumn leaves that lay like a carpet on the ground, renewing the grasses pushing through, which had kept the delicate shoots warm under their covering. She had not needed asking, taking on the role of the new member as maiden in place of Maeve, as if she had always been there.

They all realised just how clever and intuitive she was, her original somewhat prickly veneer, had been just that, this too being so much a part of Maeve's personality. Nessa's long wild hair was black as jet, rather than red but of the same curling texture, which reminded them of Maeve, giving them pause for thought where she might be and what she was doing; they knew from Morgan it would be Mabon where she was.

Vanessa chanted as she swept, feeling lighter and happier than she had in ages as she felt the surge of spring energy flowing up her legs through the soles of her feet, traversing her spine, leaving a warm tingle where it travelled, which settled in her womb, a small flame in a cauldron. She sang of renewal of new beginnings, new projects in fact, a new life…

'*Three times the circle round …thrice to bless this sacred ground. As the flowers bloom and small birds sing …to welcome in the spring,*' she crooned uninhibitedly; they all paused to listen to her enchantingly rich, contralto. Morgan and Bethan joined in. Tara arrived with her usual unruly mob, to lend their own vocal magick in husky tones, to the choir…

'*The Lord and Lady return to play …young and vigorous, greeting the day. New life awakens; they dance the circle round …to welcome a new season …breathing life to the ground.*

Where 'er she treads sweet flowers bloom …soon she'll prepare for her Greenman groom. As they grow in strength, love grows anew …and when hawthorn, flowers white …you'll feel the sap rise in you too.

Therefore, we sweep as we dance …to bless this sacred ground. On this day, all things renew, we dance the circle round …we thank our Lord and Lady for all the gifts of spring …as the flowers bloom fragrant and the small birds sing.'

Then, instead of the cold and gloomy start to their rite, suddenly the sun burst through the clouds and the frost began to melt. Water ran in small rills that sped down the hill and dripped off rooftops into water tanks. Laughter rang out as they joined in song before falling silent, raising their arms to greet the sun as it rose above the treetops.

They hung their eggs on the bare branches of an ancient elder, tying notes in yellow ribbon to hang alongside, each one a plea for help in their task to find Sybille. Each lay a flower offering on the Altar with the pledge to renew their personal courage or skills for the journey yet to come.

As if rehearsed, they fell silent again, meditating on the egg's shape, so representative of the feminine principle; the edges of their sight blurred, the tree appeared to grow in size; swelling to become a giant so vast, they couldn't see the top of the canopy or its outer most branches. Egg shapes softened, the ribbons became festoons of silken drape; what appeared to be a host of cocoon-like butterfly pupae, hung from the tree, small lights flickered as they flew from cocoon to cocoon.

Only for the briefest moment, they saw the tree was weeping blood-like sap and one of the cocoons, blackened, hung from one delicate thread that the light beings were fighting to secure. Just as suddenly, they were blinking at each other wordlessly. They'd all witnessed the same thing but no one understood what it meant.

As one, they turned to Pwyll and Tara but Tara was gone and Pwyll was in the midst of his change, flying as a huge Owl, despite the daylight. They glimpsed his face focused and stern as he disappeared through the veil, Claire not far behind.

Beth changed instantly, her antlers rising from her brow faster than they'd ever seen before, then she was off through the forest her shape flickering in and out between fleet silver-white deer and her Fae form, soon joined by the familiar shape of Hercurin.

Vanessa broke the stunned silence with a sudden outlet of breath, bringing them all back to the moment in a rush. They looked at each other, searching for answers,

'I've seen that tree in dreams,' said Sam.

'Yes me too,' said Susan. 'It's one of my recent paintings in fact I….' she trailed off, as there came a rustling like dried leaves.

The small entity Nangini appeared evidently distracted. As Sam's leaf sprites rose from her robe in an agitated cloud, she realised they were green leaf and blossom now, yet Nangini was still dressed in autumn russets and brown. She appeared to be fading in and out, her tiny fingers like dead twigs; her face more wizened that before. They barely heard what she directed to Flora, so faltering was her energy.

'*Remember the bag of herbs. Remember. They hold the secrets to all. Remember Lady Airmhid. I told Nina to tell you Flora, you know of the birthing.*'

She crumpled, becoming nothing more than a pile of dead leaves, blowing over the ground to come to rest at Sam's feet.

'Ah no,' she cried, 'that's too cruel,' but her sprites formed and reformed shapes and patterns on Nangini's scattered remains until she became a green version of herself.

Nangini smiled at them through eyes that sparkled again briefly, the floral gown she wore flowered with apple blossom, 'everything changes,' they heard as she lifted and flew on the breeze.

Exchanging glances Sam and Flora gathered what they could of the leaves that had clothed her before placing them in a basket to see what species they were and to work out what she'd meant by her brief exchange with them. Sprites came from all directions, carrying to them every remnant of leaf and twig before settling in a cloud around Sam again.

'There's that reference to Nina and Flora again,' said Lily, somewhere in there is perhaps the answer we've been looking for.'

'Something's not right,' murmured Vanessa. 'Sam can you show me the Grimoire you told me about?'

'Sure Nessa but what's that got to do with this?' asked Sam.

'I have no idea but something just triggered inside me. Perhaps it's nothing but…'

'…no buts,' said Flora. 'Everything is important, even when we think it may be irrelevant we have to check it out. My instincts tell me you may have a big role to play Nessa-sis, so when we can let's take a look together at the Grimoire and see if it triggers anything with you.' Sensing a great change about to occur, they smiled at each other, their excitement hard to contain despite what they'd witnessed.

Taking time to recover they sat, slowly feeling the life returning to the land and into their bodies as they sat to eat a simple libation of almond cakes and apple juice before packing up their tools to prepare themselves for the coming day; life and their work continued. Today Vanessa would give Sam a reading as a trial run.

Again, a large fox sat to watch the gathering, joining the wee folk to snatch a share of the offerings laid on the ground for them.

Chapter 31
Susan Fenner
Painting through the Veil

Portals of magick …doorways beyond
Found in a mirror …or a still, glassy pond
Open the doorways to otherworld's gleam; beware
…these light portals, are not always as they seem

Susan had been keeping to herself recently. She was loath to speak of what she'd witnessed in her dreams and visions, when she painted directly from her psyche. She would find herself in a trance state, deeper than ever before, remembering what Beth had told her about her state when she was weaving. How weird they should be so similar yet not blood related.

Alex often said to her that it was probably why Sarah had chosen her as her baby's surrogate mum. She'd smiled at the idea but wasn't comfortable with the thought that her dear friend had known the possibility of her own death.

She stepped back from the work in progress, critically studying the light effect she was trying to create. Once it had been so easy for her, now it took great focus.

She tried slitting her eyes, softening her gaze until her peripheral vision became cloudy. Breakthrough, she could see crystalline lights flitting in the corner of her eyes; if she tried to pinpoint them, they disappeared, aware of her seeking them out, the centre of her canvas opened up, segments peeling back like orange skin.

The effect made her feel a little queasy and she had to swallow hard to keep focus, not to lose the vision. She held her breath as a strange scene unfolded; it was horrific.

Huge forests lay wasted by blight, stagnant water seeped out of the ground, scum covered and sour and yet whole riverbeds were dry, empty dust channels. Small creatures and large, cowered under sparse cover or lay dying, caught in black, sticky webbing that smothered the light in everything that breathed.

Dark clad monsters roamed the land, lights flashed in the darkness as they hunted. With a cry, Susan realised that they were black clad humans, lamps on their helmets like miners; seeking food. They were stumbling around frenziedly, blindly, in a possible nuclear winter of acid rain and smog so thick they needed the lamps in what once would have been daylight, to find their way. She saw that they were emaciated, strained faces gaunt; their struggle to survive evident as two people fought over a scrawny dead rat.

Susan realised Dark Makers were swarming over everything, feeding the blight as the last remnants of the Makers fought furiously to protect a small being. About the size of a child, she slipped by in the darkness clutching something to her, light refracted from out of the core of it and she could see a long shard, perhaps a wand of what looked like glass; she was wearing a cap that sparkled too, bringing life to a sullen, dying world…

…and the Merrow, Mirdhaucha wept, her tears like small pearls, dripped on the barren land as she witnessed the Tree of Birthing topple to the ground. Cocoons holding Trueshapers in their state of renewal and their Littleshapes strewn on the acrid winds, one already blackened fell, the contents spilling. Sybille Madison's physical body crashed to earth; a cry of terror split the endless night.

She came too on the floor of her studio, her little terrier Jasper frantically licking her face; she realised the cry had come from deep within her. Tara came with great speed, manifesting nose to nose with her, demanding she breathe, soothing her in her strange tongue.

'Was that real?' said Susan, recovering herself a little. 'It was truly terrifying. Wait though,' she struggled to sit up. 'I saw the Merrow, she was holding something but it was as if she was trying to find somewhere to hide it and Sybille,' she sobbed. 'She fell …she…' Susan faltered unable to utter the horror she'd witnessed.

'What you saw are possibilities that can be created through mass fear,' said Tara. 'Not yet real but becoming closer to the truths people imagine as they fall deeper into despair for themselves and for the Mother, Mata, matter. As if having 'things' can save people from corruption and death, rather than clean food to eat and a healthy, sustainable planet,' she finished, sadly.

'Is this part of what Bethan saw in her aspect Leah?' Susan asked.

'Yes a version of potential in the thread of her reality, just as this is a potential of your thread; that is, if you believe it must be so, then so it must be,' replied Tara.

'What can we do to remain positive in the face of such frightful possibility Tara?'

'All that you are doing now, Susan, don't give up on the dream of beauty and peace. The Mother may not always be peaceful or gentle but She was always in balance and it's that balance that humankin must regain in Her and in themselves, in order to create what they dream of as their reality.'

Helping Susan to her feet, Tara poured her a glass of water and settled her on the couch, a cushion under her feet; she placed a throw rug over her legs, Alex crashed in through the back door.

'Susan, are you …I heard …I felt …Goddess are you all right?' He fell to his knees next to her.

'I'm fine Lex,' she said, stroking his mane of ashen hair. 'I'm fine. I had a vision is all; a powerful, dreadful vision but now I can begin to find those gateways again and we can help with the travel for those who can't shapechange.'

Tara grinned and 'high fived' Susan. 'That's the way Suzie, that's the way,' before she shifted shape and was gone.

'Gees, I wish she wouldn't do that,' said Alex, sounding just like his son; on another thread in the Skeins of Tyme Maeve stirred and woke, tears wet on her cheeks from a dream that was fast slipping away. 'Sybille,' she called out…

Chapter 32
Nina & Magdalena

She is so small ...her wings are frail
Once brightest of green ...they are now so pale
She is so tired and needs to sleep
...she will bury down into the deep
How will she live in the smoke and dust?
...the driving rains ...earth's rumbling crust.
Where will she go ...fragile as snow?
As you believe, so is she real
...you may not see her but you can feel
If you say no, she will simply go
...just disappear into the flow...

Nina watched as the now, somewhat fragile appearing Nangini, stood in the shadows of the old chestnut tree trying to gain Magdalena's attention. They sat shelling the last of the autumn harvest of peas, a task they both enjoyed. With their hands busy, they could put their mind to other tasks or chat about the lessons La Stregga had been teaching Magdalena of the Old Ways.

Nina was always more than interested, especially after her discovery that her Papa had made a deal with the elder Wytch for her return to health, despite the fact that her life had always been set to be a short one.

Her mind drifted as she shelled the peas, breathing in their sweet odour as she did. It was Lammas, a favourite time of year of hers. She loved the smell of wood smoke from evening fires and smoke houses as people prepared their store of winter meats, fish and of course, the rich aroma of roasting chestnuts that would be made into Maroni paste for deserts, full of nutty goodness to spread on Lammas bread.

Magdalena's thoughts wandered to her teacher; she had noticed that La Stregga's energy was failing and that she was on occasion, somewhat distracted, even fearful; jumping at sudden noises and staring off into dark corners as if seeing things Magdalena could not. She had been able to pinpoint the change in her mentor, since the ancient scrying bowl had shattered and a fragment disappeared. It was as if the essence of La Stregga had also lost a piece of itself, along with the lost fragment.

Nina wondered, not for the first time, why it was she could see Nangini, when Magdalena could not and said as much to her, pointing out exactly where the little Deva was standing but to no avail.

'I don't know why this is so,' she said to her young friend and mistress. 'I have tried but I feel uncomfortable with the thought of it. I feel if I see too much I will somehow lose touch with reality here and now. It's hard to explain but that's the closest I can be to defining what I feel.'

'No matter,' said Nina. 'I will be your eyes and ears where she is concerned, although it appears to frustrate her. When I ask her why that is she will not answer in any way I can comprehend.'

At that moment, Eduard strolled into the garden. Magdalena made haste to stand, bobbing a curtsey to him and making move to take the pea shells to the garden compost, to leave Nina and he to speak together uninterrupted. Eduard would have nothing of it, insisting she sit with them a while to enjoy the last of the autumn afternoon, sunshine.

As they chatted, his eyes kept straying to the little figure standing quietly in the shadow of the spreading tree; he became clearly, unsettled. Nina could see Nangini's lips moving but she was not privy to the conversation, as if the sprite had blocked her ears with cotton. She became concerned, when his face blanched at something she'd said.

Magdalena could sense that something was amiss but she still couldn't see what the distraction or cause for Eduard's change in pallor was.

'Signor,' she said with concern. 'Can I fetch you some water or a small brandy perhaps? Are you ill?'

Eduard turned to her distractedly. 'What? Oh pardon my rudeness but no Magdalena; I am not ill, just …I feel I may be seeing things.'

Nina laughed aloud. 'See Papa, I told you I could see the Nature Spirits and you laughed at me.'

'Oh, it's not that I disbelieved you Cara, I just didn't believe I would see myself. I am afraid that this spirit may not be all it appears. She has told me some frightful things and I am concerned for your and Magdalena's safety. Perhaps I should take you both away to a warmer climb for the winter?'

'No Papa, I love it here in autumn and winter and who knows how many I will see,' Nina said wistfully, with her usual candour.

Hush, Signorina Nina,' said Magdalena with alarm. 'Nothing will happen to you while I have breath in my body.'

Eduard's eyes grew wide with fear as he heard the words echoed that the sprite had said. Magdalena had no idea how prophetic her own words were. Nina looked deep within his soul and saw the possible outcome of her own and Magdalena's lives.

With the chill of the evening settling in, Magdalena took Nina inside to prepare for the evening meal.

Eduard sat awhile longer, listening to the rustling leaves of the chestnut as they blew in eddies across the garden, rubbing their skeletal remains against his legs. He could swear they took shape into small beings, little hands reaching out to him in supplication for help in their own demise or for something else; he could not be sure. He watched as they joined, forming the image of the Nature Spirit and blowing apart again, then all became still and he wept at what they had told him on the winds.

Chapter 33
La Stregga

Balance in the realms between dark and light
…singing in the time of equal day and equal night
Send your aid, however slight, to
…all creatures this day who are in true plight

La Stregga knew she was followed everywhere she went; she'd been a Wytch long enough to know that at times, it was not anything human, at others it was a man dressed in brown, monks robes. A follower of the White Christ, a large wooden crucifix hung over his paunchy belly; his beady eyes regarded her implacably from an unhealthy, sweaty face whenever he caught her eye.

Her patron deity had changed from a graceful, stern yet benign being; to one she hardly recognised who showed herself as haughty of demeanour and harsh, scolding her for the loss of the precious bowl yet showing her that she held the shards in her custody and what she planned to do with them. It was clear that somewhere in the threads, something was terribly amiss, if her Lady had become something so dark and hateful.

It was beyond La Stregga's comprehension to understand the strange scenes she witnessed of other threads in the great tapestry she knew life to be, other aspects of herself who were not very wise in their dealings or kindly, in their behaviour toward others.

She didn't know how she could change what she saw, until finally she made a journey unaided by her ruined scrying bowl to visit the woman who looked as she had when she'd been young. Her ancestry too was of the Italian lineage but there was no conscious knowledge of the information she had sworn to uphold. There appeared to be no memory of whom she was, only stirrings of fear and a vanity about how she appeared to others.

Surely, I have learned something in this life she would remember, La Stregga thought to herself, after speaking with the arrogant woman known as Anna Savage. She is so arrogant, Mother what shall I do? Why do some aspects believe that what they do or fail to do, will not affect the rest of the threads in their tapestry, in all directions? There was no reply, only the eyes of the monk boring into her soul. She shivered with fear and the bitter taste of foreboding.

I must warn Magdalena she thought. When she comes for her lesson tomorrow, I must tell her I have taught her all I can and that we may not meet again. The Lady knows she will be needed soon enough to tend her little Signorina, I have meddled enough and can do no more for fear that the rumours are true and that Wytches all over our world are being hunted and destroyed.

It was Lammas, the time when all made sacrifice to the land and in order to preserve the teachings, for now they must die; sacrificed for the good of many.

Changing direction rapidly she almost ran into the greasy faced monk, his filthy body odour washed over her like a bucket of slops and she thought she would vomit on his dirty, sandalled feet. She caught a spike of raw fear in his aura as he stepped back from her as if burnt. In his eyes, she saw the deaths of many of her kindred, brothers and sisters alike and so she drew herself up in pride of her ancestry and walked away.

Chapter 34
Sybille's Teachings: Air

Fire is harsh and anger sings
…don't go too close you'll burn your wings
Earth yourself go deep within,
…let water again become your kin
Let air breathe you, let laughter ring…

Air: our higher intellect and our intuition, all the winds and high places of our environment; it is classified as a male element, which is interesting, when trusting the intuition is something women are more likely to do.

Divination, higher learning and philosophy are all associated with the element of air. Again, if we only think laterally and are not open to a broader viewpoint, we may well be disappointed when our dreams don't manifest easily. Precognitive dreams, premonitions, hunches, gut feelings, are all for nothing, unless action is taken to either change what is not desired or to bring to fruition, what is.

Air blowing across the earth may fan the flames and yet is invisible, in and of itself. We may see the trees move but we cannot see the wind.

Sylphs, winged fae, spring, east.

Chapter 35
Changes

Can you fly?
Can you touch the sky?
No remorse and no goodbye
...can you simply close your eyes and fly?

Bethan sang as she worked. She'd decided to spring clean her cottage and with Lily and Morgan's help was well on the way to finishing. Morgan was cleaning the outside of the windows as she cleaned inside, they sang as they worked and the whole house seemed to light up in clean energy.

Post Ostara, the wheel of the year spun toward Beltane with still no concrete evidence of Sybille's whereabouts, only fleeting glimpses. Susan had told them of her visions of Sybille and so, somewhere in the Web of the Mother were the truths amongst the partial truths they were gathering. So much was dependent on their relationship to their other aspects and to each other, in such uncertainty.

Max and Lily were moving between Wells and the new shop in Glastonbury, travelling between the veils. Max, in finally overcoming his fears had learned to love Lily as she was and to trust her gifts more unconditionally. He had also grown very fond of Vanessa, treating her as a little sister, even at times behaving quite paternally toward her, something about her tugged at him.

They were all excited about the nearing completion of the shop they'd decided to name Greenman Ways, following the theme that Earthly Rites set with organic herbs, Lily's own jewellery, ritual tools, Beth's weavings; everything for a Pagan's needs.

Lily, Sam and Bethan had chosen art and books that would fit well in the UK market; Glastonbury was just the place.

It also meant they could remain working as a team, the distance being no obstacle when they could travel the corridors of the Skeins with ease.

Everything was set for the opening. Vanessa was particularly excited as she'd not travelled this way before but Flora was unusually reticent, saying she hadn't come to terms with her own abilities. She was soothed when Claire and Pwyll assured her, they would take her through, whether she could shift shape or not, taking her on little excursions to get her used to any, disorientating feelings.

For some, it felt as if 'time' shifted sideways and the distortion of vision, often made people feel a little sick. After a few attempts, she was as excited as the others were, and would make daily trips to meet with Lily, helping her set up the apothecary.

Sometimes she would dream of travelling and now that she'd experienced the shifting to other threads she would, on occasion, find herself as an observer of Nina's life.

Nina looked frail and Flora realised that Magdalena didn't appear to be anywhere around; she wondered what could have taken the young woman away from her charge. Edward walked the corridors at night, distraught and pale but Flora couldn't see the reason for this behaviour, which frustrated her no end.

One morning at breakfast with Cal, Sam and Vanessa, she was almost in tears as she clattered around in the kitchen trying to order her thoughts and shake off the disturbing dreams. Cal took the knife from her shaking fingers as she hacked with enthusiasm, born of frustration, at her freshly baked loaf, warm from the oven.

'Here Flo,' he said gently. 'Let me do that.' He glanced at Sam and she came immediately to take the obviously distressed Flora to a chair. Sitting her down she took her hands, Vanessa came to stand behind Flora, rubbing her shoulders in concern.

'Come on Flo, out with it,' Sam said. 'We can't help unless you tell us what's going on.'

'It's Eduard,' she muttered.

'What!' asked Sam questioningly?

'…Max is Eduard…' Flora began haltingly.

'Yes we know that,' interrupted Sam. 'Cal saw that at Yule and we've all experienced some travel before, except Vanessa.'

'Yes I know Sam,' said Flora, steadying herself with a sip of coffee before continuing. 'This is different. Eduard is different; more like Max, under the influence of the little Merrow.'

'You don't think he is, do you Flo?' Cal asked.

'I can't see what's making him so distressed,' she replied, 'but he's not himself and it's not just concern for Nina either, although she is obviously becoming ill again. Magdalena has disappeared from the scene and I can't seem to find her either.'

'Well,' said Sam, forcefully, 'I'm going to have to do a very specific journey and see what's going on with my aspect Magdalena then. It's funny you should mention that, 'cos I've been aware that something hasn't been the same for a while, La Stregga has changed too. She seems to have doubled in age and is frightened of something, I'm sure.'

'Well let's organise it with the others shall we?' said Cal.

Vanessa said nothing but they could see she was trying to remember something. They waited but she merely shrugged her shoulders, looking a little confused.

'I'm not sure yet,' she said in answer to their unspoken question. 'Perhaps I need to travel with you Sam? Is it possible for us to go together?'

'I can't see why not,' Sam replied, 'but I'm not sure what it is you want.'

'I don't know either, I just know I have something to do with these aspects of you and Max and I'm sure Flo's right, Nina's not her aspect.' More she wouldn't or couldn't say. Recovering herself, Flora rubbed her eyes and pulled herself together.

'Come on then let's have that breakfast and get to work then. Evening will come soon enough and we'll be off to finish the Apothecary. Can we get jetlagged travelling like this,' she laughed, breaking the tension.

Outside a small red fox sat waiting for her humankin to wake up and come home. Ruuark sat on the fence, muttering to herself in her raven tongue as the whole mob gathered. Tara grinned through the window at the friends inside before manifesting beside them. She sat at the table, startling Vanessa.

'Shoot, Tara I almost jumped out of my skin!' she exclaimed with a nervous giggle.

'Well Nessa,' Tara grinned at her, 'that's just what you might have to do,' before grabbing a piece of toast from Vanessa's plate and cheekily stuffing it in her mouth. 'Hmm, needs more butter,' she huffed and then paused, mouth full listening, and with a frown, disappeared.

'See you on the ethers,' they heard her say. Outside the raven crew took off in a raucous cloud the small fox, trotting rapidly after as they appeared to vanish into the 'Between'.

Chapter 36
Eduard Grimaldi

Last night, Lady Moon was an eye in the sky
...watching wild spirits as the wind blew them by
Sensing the veils thin, trees wept their leaves
...as Samhain approaches, the Lady bequeaths
...all life that is fading She will renew
...like silvery droplets of morning fresh dew

Eduard was restless. He had heard rumour of the Wytch hunters and knew he would have to get Nina away for a while. Torn between his feelings for Magdalena and the need to protect Nina, he was at a loss how to handle the potential of Magdalena being the next Stregga or how he could let her remain in the house as Nina's maid. He knew they were so much more than Signorina and maid; they had become best friends and sisters. He had hoped that Magdalena would become still more but he could no longer see the possibility in being associated with her in an intimate way. How could he marry her if she were to become La Stregga?

He paced up and down the terraced garden in the cold Moonlight, turning as he heard footsteps behind him on the gravel path. Magdalena stood a small bag in her hand, hesitating before stepping closer.

She stood tall looking him directly in the eye and said, 'Signor, I will be going now. I have made my goodbyes to Signorina Nina and she will need you now, more than ever. She is distraught, her Nonna cannot calm her and I must go. La Stregga is frail and I must go to her to say goodbye. Then I am leaving for the mountains to become a healer for a small community. Thank you for the opportunity of caring for your daughter; she is a sister to me.'

Hesitating at his silence, she stepped closer to see her words had stunned him. It was as if she had heard his thoughts but he had no chance to speak as she said. 'Signor you knew who and what I was when you employed me and it is my arts, together with the deal you made with my patron that have kept your daughter alive.' Still Eduard said nothing; she simply turned and walked proudly away.

He didn't see or hear her leave, keeping his face in the shadows so she would not see the tears coursing down his face and dripping from his beard as the vines above him wept their last leaves, with a sound like tiny, rattling bones.

Chapter 37
Greenman Ways

The beautiful village of Glastonbury, Somerset nestling in the valley between Tor Hill, Chalice Hill, Wearyall Hill and Windmill Hill, slept shrouded in morning mists. Mabon was past and the cold frosts of late autumn already made its presence felt across the county.

Mirdhaucha passed through the threads from her nest in the Lake of Seers, down through the Deep Channel in the River Brue, deeper still, following the springs to the Chalice Well. She sat, stroking the beautifully wrought well cover, before diving into the dark red spring waters. Her blue hair changed again to red as she emerged close to where the group stood lost in awe at, for some their first glimpse of the Serpent Way, as it wound its undulating path around Tor Hill.

'Home to so many myths and legends, it's a place of mystery. Pilgrims flock to visit no matter the time of year. Christians claimed it as their own, building the medieval abbey that's now in ruins, below the cathedral city of Wells and of course, the Tower, the remains of a church or possibly a fort, destroyed after an earthquake and the resulting landslide, in about 1275CE. This left only Glastonbury Tor or better said Tor Hill, remaining; Tor means 'a rocky outcrop', and really has nothing to do with the tower itself.

Long before the lands, drained for farming the hills appeared as islands. Where the Tower on Tor Hill now stands was once the Isle of Glass, Ynys Witrin, known too as the Apple-Place, Avalon, where the myths of the Celts are alive to this day and where legend says both Merlyn and Arthur might lie sleeping. Some Christian's say it's from here the second coming of their White Christ will happen. They call him the 'sleeping lord"

What have they not taken as their own, mused Morgan, listening to Max's narrative as he stood with the others looking out across the valley, drinking in the sight of the sun rising on The Tor.

'Erm …thanks for the history lesson Max. You sound as if you've swallowed the guide book,' said Lily as Max paused for breath. 'How strange though, I never thought to draw a parallel between Wells in Oz and Wells here, Bethy.'

'No,' replied Bethan, 'nor did I, but there's no such thing as coincidence, is there?'

'Well,' said Vanessa. 'Personally I can imagine Gwynn up Nudd riding out of the hill and across the land, this close to Samhain.' She shivered drawing the hood of her coat further over her brow. 'I swear I saw the Fae on Tor Hill when we arrived,' she finished.

'Mmmm, easy done,' said Samantha. 'What an incredible energy this place has and we're not even up on the Tor.' Her little sprites lifted briefly as one, at her words, settling again in a new shape around her. She could hear them singing a different song; home they sang, home.

'It truly is a magickal place,' said Morgan. 'It never fails to amaze me and I've been coming here all my life.'

'Yeah, I remember, Dad used to bring us here all the time, before he disappeared anyway,' said Lily.

'Well folks, I'm freezing,' said Flora. 'Travelling the 'Between' makes me hungry. What say we go find some breakfast?'

Vanessa giggled. 'What doesn't make you hungry Flo?'

Flo gave Cal a friendly punch on the arm as he laughed aloud at Vanessa's words. 'Oi,' she exclaimed. 'Don't encourage her!'

They wandered back towards the still sleepy looking town, although people were pouring warm water over frosted windscreens, a milkman delivered milk and bread to their doors and wisps of smoke were a appearing from chimneys, as the town stirred. They called into a little bakery to buy fresh croissants, buttery and hot from the ovens.

They had arrived the day before to finish the set up for Greenman Ways opening, taking a walk through the dawn light to explore and to blow the cobwebs away.

Strolling down the street to the shop, they stopped to admire their own handiwork. New signage, the window dressed for Samhain with candles, Book of Shadows, Quill Pens, Ink and handmade besom and a freshly painted, green front entrance. Painted vines, crawling up the architraves and under the eaves on the third floor, appearing alive in the early light, added yet more appeal to the pretty shopfront, as they surrounded it. Sam's sprites were attracted to them and arrayed them-selves on top of the painted vines, bringing them to life. They had to laugh at their antics.

Above the shop was a small flat with living and kitchen area and on the third, Lily had set up her little studio to take advantage of the light. There was a second room, a small bedroom. A classic Glastonbury shopfront, she had trouble believing at times she'd actually been able to acquire it. It fit well alongside the others in the street, all painted in pretty, pastel colours.

Further, down the road the Tor was visible, seem-ing closer in the sunshine. She opened the door and let everyone in ahead while she stood on the doorstep looking up toward Tor Hill; she did a little happy dance before going inside.

With everything but food and drinks organised for the opening, there was time to explore.

Morgana, Teddy and Honey, were well looked after with Susan's visits to the farm to feed them, the goats and hens too.

It was becoming easier however, as they gained confidence, to slip back and forwards through the veil and as the flat was too snug to sleep more than three, they would travel home the following day, returning for opening night. Tonight, Morgan was taking them to his cottage. They were playing at the pub; he had last played at the night he felt Sybille disappear. 'Unearthly Sounds' would make its debut in the UK.

Flo and Cal were returning to Springsmeet afterwards, while Sam, Nessa and Beth would stay at Morgan's cottage. Soon enough, it would be Beltane at home and Samhain in Somerset and so, just for one night, they put aside all else but some time to enjoy their music, their new surroundings and each other's company.

Arriving at Morgan's, they changed into fresh clothes for the gig and walked to the pub. Tara, Claire and Pwyll met them there as arranged but their delight when a tall, rather gaunt figure, stepped from behind Pwyll was beyond words. Bethan was the first to step forward to greet Maeve with a sweet smile and a hug, before all hell broke loose at the joy of seeing her again.

There was little time for more than a few words however, as they were called to the stage for their first set. Flo, Cal, Max, Susan and Alex took Maeve to a small room out the back, where they could still hear the music but muted by the thick, stalls, where they could hear themselves think.

'Are you home now for good Maeve?' asked Flora.

'No Flo,' she replied. 'I just have a night pass, courtesy of our Ravenkin. I won't be back for a while yet. Although I miss you all, I am as content as I can be and perhaps I will be of more use working from there than here. The Cybil has been teaching me, much as Sybille once did, but I am returning to Scathach's Hearth to train again. After that, who knows,' she shrugged her shoulders. 'I'm working with metal again and am really happy with the results. I wanted to bring one to show you but the elementals must still have other ideas at the moment.' Beth, Mor and Cal exchanged looks but said nothing.

'We miss you Red,' said Max. 'Whatever happens, perhaps you can come here to live for a while instead of going back home. I'm sure we can find something for you to do at Greenman Ways, although that's up to everyone, especially Lily, to decide.'

'I might just take you up on that Max, after all Ynys Witrin is where I am in its original state too,' she smiled, a smile that returned her face to the one they re-membered before the Merrow's attack.

While the group played their first set, they talked of all that had transpired and Maeve shared her experiences with Alma and how she'd come to realise that Alma and the Merrow had become one. When the first set finished, the others mobbed her, the telling began again and so the evening passed.

In the corner of the pub a tall lean man sat, his hair as burnished as Maeve's, note pad on his lap he appeared to be innocently jotting down his observations; his eyes never left Maeve's face. Casually standing, he downed his glass of cider before strolling over to the group, startling Bethan as she sat talking to Maeve.

'Hi Bethy and you must be Maeve,' he said, with a broad grin. 'How did you get here so fast I'm sure I saw you at Earthly Rites just yesterday? Do you have wings lovely Beth?'

With hardly a blink, Beth turned to him saying, 'Well hi yourself James and I could ask you the same thing. Tara said she'd seen you lurking outside the shop. What are you up to and why are you following us?'

'Oh curiosity mostly,' James replied. 'As I said to you the other evening I can smell magick a mile away and your shop reeks of it as in fact, my lovely Beth, do you.'

Beth subtly altered her position, the better to look James in the eyes. What he saw there caused him to gasp aloud as she changed, her skin taking on a greenish hue and her hair taking on a life of its own. Small shells and tiny crystals sparkled in the depths of her silvery curls and small nubby horns burst on her brow. Iridescent wings lifted to fold around her. James rubbed his eyes and blinked rapidly, so fast was the change manifested and gone. He stood quickly, almost knocking Maeve's drink from her hand, 'Arwen,' he said with a bow. 'Forgive me I didn't know. I was clumsy, how…' He trailed off at Bethan's peel of laughter at his discomfort.

Maeve smiled and said, 'Bethy aren't you going to introduce me to your friend, although he does seem a little familiar; and you,' she said, turning to James, 'should see her when she lets the antlers grow!'

Recovering, James held out his hand to Maeve, 'James Buchanan,' he said flashing his charming smile. 'I've been waiting to meet you Maeve Hedinger. I have a couple of questions I'd like to ask you.'

'Well I don't know why you think I would have the answers for you or why I should answer them just because you want me to, James Buchanan,' replied Maeve. 'Your charm won't work on me either. I've become immune to 'glamour,' she grinned back, openly teasing him.

Bethan laughed, not only at Maeve's confidence; she'd grown since she'd left but at their obvious attraction to each other.

James, taken aback at her disarming candour, joined in the laughter; he glanced at Bethan again to see her return to her normal 'human' state with ease and comfort. 'Lady,' he whispered respectfully. 'Can we speak privately at your convenience?' he finished formally.

'Tomorrow then, I'll meet you at Earthly Rites. Can I trust you James? There is much at stake here.'

'I can see that much has changed in you Bethy,' he said gently, returning to a more familiar tone with her.

'Oh you have no idea,' she laughed before moving away to speak with Tara, who glanced over at him a few times as they were talking, obviously about him.

'Do they know each other already?' asked Bethan of Tara. 'I've never seen Maeve so relaxed with a stranger.'

'Well yes and no,' said Tara enigmatically. 'They just have to remember when it was.'

'Tara!' exclaimed Beth in frustration. 'You know who I am; you can't play the same games with me any-more.'

'Ah yes Lady, I'm sorry,' said Tara in genuine sur-prise. 'You've been gentle Bethy for so long while you slept I forget myself but seriously, in answer to your ques-tion I can only repeat my answer. They have to remember their time together in the Skeins. There can be no prompting' …she paused, grinning at Beth. 'Not even from you Arwen but trust me, when they do remember they will both heal so much around events on this thread that all the others will form a beautiful tapestry. We can only hope they can grasp the potential.'

A large fox sat patiently waiting, in a night that had turned to drizzling rain.

Chapter 38
Sybille's Teachings: Earth

Earth you are, from earth you came,
…your intellect from air you gain,
Your fire should burn, with flaming ire,
…yet water has put out your fire

Earth: our physical body and our environment, it is classified as a feminine element, which contains all the others within its matter, 'Mata', the Mother.

When we ignore the needs of the physical and focus only on mental, emotional and even spiritual self, we forget that manifestation for us here on this plane of existence occurs within matter that is, if we wish to witness it, hold, smell, taste and hear it. We can attempt to manifest everything we need for our journey here using our mental imagery, our creative yearnings and our spiritual dreams of what we think life and being is. Nothing however will manifest in fullness, without the ability to bring it into the physical, for that is what this earthly life and body is about, bringing spirit into matter, highest truths into manifest reality.

Gnomes, leaf-sprites, deva, winter, south.

Chapter 39
Fragments & Scraps

Dare to wonder dare to dream
...when Moonlight pools and things unseen
...move and fly on gossamer wing
...as hidden Fae their anthems sing,
...to Lord and Lady fair and bright
...gathering souls to aid their flight
...to places green where magicks reign
...where all can heal their fear and pain

As agreed, Bethan and James met at Earthly Rites the following day; she suggested they take a drive to Wells and perhaps a walk through the forests of her home.

James agreed with alacrity but said, 'hold on just a little longer, there're a few things I'd like to pick up before we go.' He returned with a basket, which he packed into the back of Beth's car, before climbing in beside her.

In no time they were at Wells, outside Beth's little cottage.

'Oh Beth,' said James. 'This is so you, how delightful. Will you show me inside before we walk?'

'Sure, but does anything in that basket need to be refrigerated it's turning quite warm?' she asked.

'Well yes,' he grinned. 'There's a bottle of your favourite Elderflower bubbles, some of the first wild strawberries and some cheeses.'

Storing the things away, Beth showed James her little slice of paradise as she called it. He could see why she was totally in love with both her house and the lands around it. When she'd shown him inside, they strolled out to the table under the trees to chat. As they walked outside James sniffed the air, like the fox he resembled, Beth thought to herself.

'There's been something following us Beth,' he said, with concern. 'It was there in Glastonbury and it's still around now.'

'Yes, I sense it,' replied Beth. 'It's probably, from what I can pick up, the same Merrow that has caused so much trouble for Maeve and Max too. I have seen it many times through my wanderings through Ungwe.'

At her use of the name, James started a frown on his face. 'Then you really are who I think you are?'

'Oh well, I'm not sure you do know,' Beth said with a smile.

'I saw you Beth. You're Arianwen, whom I am under ancient oath to serve. I am not wholly human as you may have guessed but for now, you are the only one, other than the Shifters, who can know. We have not just been tracking Sybille but also the Merrow and the Dark Maker. I'm the fall back position Arwen,' he reverted to the formal title, 'you might say. I'm a tracker. I sniff out magicks that don't belong in a certain place and that's what I can smell right now, here. In fact she sits just a little way away and yet she's appears to be grieving, not quite what I expected, given her reputation.'

'Her name is Mirdhaucha, James and she is the Merrow who caused Maeve to be taken away to another thread to heal. I know she followed Maeve, even there but something happened she's changed.'

'There is more to her than meets the eye and I know Maeve has something to do with it, yet it's an old wound too, as if two threads have become so entangled they are no longer able to be separate. Does that make sense?' James asked Beth.

'It makes complete sense,' she replied. 'Nothing surprises me anymore and there are more than those two whose lives have become entangled. All of us in fact share aspect locations and they seem to move throughout the warp and weft, without much sense at this stage, although I'm sure they will soon. If we can just find Sybille, it'd be a start. I'm sure she has something more to do with the Dark Maker than we can imagine,' she trailed off as Tara and her mob arrived.

'Ah food,' Tara said. 'I can smell that you were thinking about it?'

James laughed, 'Yes of course. I'll fetch it.'

'What's going on Beth? Why is the tracker here with you?'

'We were talking about the Merrow and of Sybille's disappearance, Tara. Is he a fox?'

'Well not exactly my taste,' replied Tara, tongue in cheek, 'and I'd be surprised if you found him so when you have the Greenlord.' She giggled, poking Beth in the ribs as James returned laden with a tray.

'You know exactly what I meant, Tara,' Beth laughed.

'Of course I do but I live to tease,' she said with a smirk, 'and it worked.'

'What worked,' said James. 'Am I missing something here?'

'Oh no,' said Tara, grabbing a slice of apple. 'Beth was just saying what a fox you were.'

James scowled at her, 'You are meddlesome Tara,' he said but unable to keep a straight face, he joined in their laughter.

They sat in the sun, sharing ideas for the next stage of the journey until Morgan, Max and Lily arrived home. Exchanging glances with James, Max was curious to find him there.

'Well you do get around,' he said.

'Yes that's true. I like to keep up with what's happening,' replied James.

'Alright you two, hackles down,' said Tara. 'James, do you want to demonstrate why you're here?'

'Ah no, Tara,' he said. 'If it's all the same to you I'd rather keep it among the changers.'

'What' said Max, 'not another one? Soon Flo, Cal and I will be the only ordinary folk left. Oh and Nessa of course but we're still outnumbered.

'I didn't know there was a battle Max,' said Lily, grinning at James.

'I thought I could smell a little bird,' he said drolly, licking his lips and running his fingers over an imaginary moustache. Max was far from amused at the interchange.

'Well it just goes to show, the Merrow doesn't have to be around for long before you two are at it like fighting cocks,' said Tara.

'What, she's here?' Max looked around in concern. 'I thought you'd dealt with her when you took Maeve away, Tara?'

'The Merrow cannot be contained for long Max; she's a free spirit, a little magick or she was, before she became tainted and appears to be in some distress. Perhaps you could find a little compassion, which might ease the affect she has on you,' interjected James, harshly.

'Who made you the boss suddenly, James? You don't know us, or anything about us,' Max replied, drawing himself up to his full height.

'Whoa, both of you,' Beth intervened. 'Enough! Don't you think we have more than enough to handle, without fighting between ourselves? James, get it over with would you?' Beth commanded.

James shrugged. He wasn't happy at the results of his meeting with Beth. He'd wanted to keep his identity unknown for as long as possible no question of taint assumed about him. He couldn't question Arianwen as Beth shapechanged and with another shrug so did he.

Max nearly fell off the chair he'd just sat in and Lily laughed aloud, as James shifted into a large male fox. He'd only now come to terms with birdkin and now here was an animal shaper. He felt queasy and Tara quickly pushed his head down between his knees.

'Get over yourself won't you Max.' she said quite scornfully. 'There's no room for doubts or superstitions here and I'm over your weakness right now.' So saying she reached out and slapped him full across the face, before placing her fingers between his eyes and pushing, quite forcefully. 'Time to see true,' she said, 'and without questions.'

Poor Max, thought he would make even more a fool of himself; as his ears buzzed with noise, he was afraid he would vomit. Once his head cleared, he realised he felt different, more the Max he had been, when he'd first had the idea to ask Beth if he could renovate the old stables all those months ago; drawn to Wells and his sister, to spend time with her and to finish his book. The former, he'd had plenty of, the latter was sadly overdue but it no longer mattered and understanding finally hit him.

'I've been such a berk,' he said with a very sheep-ish grin.

'Yes you have,' they said in unison.

'Alright then,' said Tara, 'now, where were we? What are you doing here, foxy lad?' she said to James, with a less than pleasant smile. 'I get a little agitated around your kind I'm afraid.' It looked as if the Morrigan would make an appearance but instead, Ruark appeared and sat on the back of a chair, studying James carefully as he reverted to human form. Head on one side they regarded each other.

'Rowan?' said James. 'Where have you been?'

'Ruuuark,' was all she could reply.

James looked at Tara in consternation. 'So you still haven't found her Tara, or her bangle?'

It was Tara's turn to appear a little sheepish. 'Er no foxy lad, it disappeared after we found Rowan's body on the Wolds. You might want to speak with Cal too. He's the one, who found her, after that, the bangle disappeared. When I hid Rowan's body it was on her arm, I swear but when I brought her back, it was gone. Somewhere between the Wolds and the 'Between', it vanished. Although the bangle isn't much use to her without a body, now is it?'

'Yes but we wouldn't want anyone else to find it would we?' said Morgan, speaking up for the first time, 'but I think that might be exactly what's happened to it. It's time we took another good look in every place we can backtrack to,' he finished with some impatience. 'She's kin Tara and I know she has an important role in everything, including why she was killed and by who, in the first place.'

Tara smiled a knowing smile, losing all pretence of guile. 'Now we're getting somewhere,' she said. 'Now we can get on with things and we have foxy lad here to help with the search. He's a tracker after all.' Her smile cracked wider still and she fell about in stitches at her own cleverness.

'Is there ever going to be a time when you can just tell us straight what's going on and why?' piped up Lily.

'Errrrrrrrm, nope!' she chuckled with glee. 'Probably not, there'd be little fun in that!' As usual, she had the last word as she shifted and changed. Ruuark took flight after her.

'Alright,' said Beth, 'I'm hungry and that bottle of Elderflower should be just right to pop. If there's not enough to go round, there's another one at the back of the fridge.' Max and Lily volunteered to fetch them, leaving Beth and James with Morgan who had been very quiet, other than the question he'd directed at Tara about the bangle. He was fiddling with his own as he turned to James, observing the coppery bracelet on his wrist.

'So James,' he said directly. 'Tell me about yourself. I know Beth has known you for a long time and I suspect you know Maeve from another thread, but when have we met before?'

'I don't think we ever met formally Morgan although I do remember your Bran aspect and you may remember me as Jamie perhaps but I've always been a conscious changer, so the shape you see is the shape I've always had, along with my familiar fox-spirit shape, that is.' James replied quietly.

'So what role are you here to play in the ever more twisted scheme of things?' Morgan asked, his gaze not shifting from James.

'Well, Morgan, as I said before I'm a tracker. I find lost things; lost people. I'm here to help. It's not often the Mother intervenes but things are shifting, even in the 'Between' and more time can't be wasted in finding Sybille and healing the blight that's being spread, by more than just the Dark Maker now.'

'Thank you for your honesty, brother,' said Morgan holding out his hand to James.

'Thank you Morgan,' said James, shaking Morgan's hand firmly. 'That means a lot to me and might be the difference between win and lose, when it comes to the final threads in this weave.'

With a sigh of relief, Bethan sat back to relax. She accepted the glass of Elderflower champagne and sipped with apparent delight.

'Does nothing faze you anymore Beth?' whispered Morgan to her.

'No, what can possibly surprise any of us now. It's close to Beltane, I can feel the earth stirring as sure as my blood stirs yet we have to travel to Glastonbury for the opening, and for Samhain. A double delight for me,' she said. 'I get to see Hercurin twice and for opposite rites,' she laughed in delight. There could be no reply to such a comment as they relaxed and chatted, the day unfolded.

The small vixen sat as close as she could to the group without being seen by the Merrow, who also watched. James knew she was there and sent her a quiet glamour of concealment.

Tara sat in the tree above, unobserved. Ah the wily fox she sighed. As always, he's hiding something.

'Well it's time you had a little of your own medicine,' chuckled James in her head. With a raucous caw, she flew away.

Chapter 40
Maeve

Foxes aren't sly they're clever and bold
…listen to their tales, cunning wisdoms of old
…lost in the folds of the times in between
…as they slink through the veil stealthily, rarely seen

Tara had surprised Maeve as she brought her from the Seer's Isle to Scathach's Hearth with, 'just a detour, is all,' she said with her best poker face. Maeve was not convinced.

'Yeah, sure what are you up to Tara?'

'Ta dah, surprise!' Tara yelled with glee as she broke through the veil outside the Journeyman Pub, Maeve in tow.

'What?' giggled Maeve. 'You gonna shout me a drink then?'

'Ha ha! No silly, look.' Tara pointed through the window of the pub.

'Oh is it really them?' Maeve almost screamed with delight as Pwyll, Claire and Tara dragged her inside. She felt almost shy seeing them again, fearful they'd judge her for what had happened but no, they were the same, generous, loving bunch of people they'd always been.

Embraced, welcomed and grilled for answers about where she'd been and what she'd been doing, Maeve simply relaxed into the gathering, savouring the twenty-first century food, smells and amenities.

'Oh,' she squealed like a little girl, 'taps, toilets, running water!'

She had to remind herself that it wasn't the 'done thing' to eat everything with fingers and a dagger, grinning at Sam as she speared a piece of meat on her fork. Sam raised an eyebrow in question, indicating the meat with surprise.

'Ah,' mouthed Maeve across the table to her. 'When in Rome, Sam, when in Rome and at least this meat's cooked through!'

While the music played and the conversation washed over her, everything from politics to magicks, she was content to simply listen and watch.

She observed James surreptitiously from beneath her fall of wild hair. She realised he could almost be her brother-friend Jamie from Scathach's Hearth, the male to her female; same stance, slightly arrogant presence and yet she knew there was a gentle interior. He teased her unmercifully and she knew there were moments that there had been other meetings throughout the threads. How and when or where, she couldn't remember, only that they had shared more than family, were more than siblings were to each other.

So who was he here on this thread, she wondered, it was only a matter of hours since she'd left the isle and yet here he was in another skin same and yet more mature, more sophisticated, worldly but still her friend for all that. When she returned to Scathach's Hearth, she would ask for help from Bran or from the elder seer, to find their shared thread. She felt it would unravel more of the answers she needed, to make sense of her life there and here. After all The Cybil had opened her sight to so much more than it had been on this thread, even more than Sybille had but then that had been her own doing, as she well realised now, remembering Sybille's nickname for her had been 'wild child'.

Vanessa approached her, introducing herself.

'You'd already been moved by Tara when I joined the grove, so we haven't met but I feel as if we have.'

She told Maeve a little of her story, needing no prompting, listening with interest and sympathy as Maeve told the tale of the Merrow, even sharing with her the loss of her little friend Alma, who became the Merrow; they were comfortable in each other's company. As Morgan and the others watched, they could see how much Maeve had changed or perhaps she'd just found a better space to be in, despite the pain of her journey. They couldn't help but notice James watching her with intense focus.

Seeing Morgan watching Maeve, Sam reached out to brush his arm. 'Are you okay?' she asked.

'Sure Sam thanks. It's just good to see her so at peace. When I tune in via Bran, she really had a desperate time when the child died and changed, and I really don't think that part of the story is over yet either. Somehow she's come through it though, and I'm happy to think that I've had a hand in helping her heal and can continue to perhaps, if she needs me. More than that no, there's nothing there for this thread where she's concerned, and looking at James over there I sense there's another story about to unfold.'

'Yes, agreed,' said Sam. 'I just wish we could find what links everything and all of us together, other than the obvious of course and to the thread that joins us to Sybille.'

'We will Sam,' said Morgan. 'It's so much more complex than I could ever have imagined but I'm sure one day, we'll look back on all of this with a sigh of relief, 'cos we finally understand what it's all about.'

'Yeah, let's hope,' replied Sam, 'and make it soon please.'

They smiled at each other in a moment of under-standing, one that deepened their friendship further, Sam's leaf sprites hummed with pleasure, so loudly Mor-gan could hear them.

Chapter 41
James Buchanan: Enigma

We are they …the magick the Fae
…we are the masters in the Skeins of Tyme
We created the realms of this world
…but we are the ones who have lost the rhyme
When we awaken …when we remember
…all is not lost, if we were to awake
When we remember…when we awaken
…we will recall, it was all for Her sake

James had only met Sybille once on this thread and he'd been a boy really in human terms, but even back then she'd seen the potential in him as a changer and seer, known his blood was not all human, but then whose was? Their journeys on other threads had been similar, he had in some way, looked after her, even rescued her but he knew this time he couldn't rescue her alone and that he would never meddle again, even though his human aspects were as always, tempted. It was this part of being human, that was a constant source of irritation to the 'Shining Ones', the 'Tuatha de'.

No, he had meddled in his wily, woodsman way, seeking to avert the death of a friend, one of his shapechanger-kin, but the arrow had knocked her down and he'd been unable to find her. Now he could smell her essence again, closer than before but strangely, he couldn't identify the source and so he needed the help of the others who had gathered, as much as they needed his.

He wasn't arrogant; he'd just been to places in the threads where they hadn't yet been, other than Bethan or Pwyll of course. He'd conversed with the Fae, both fair and dark and was on the trail of one whom he thought, might well be a key to find Sybille. More than that, this particular key could be the one knot in the thread that might untangle the rest. Bethan's mother, La Stregga, Magdalena, Nina, Eduard, even Brandubh; he knew the group had uncovered their links but still they needed help in the hidden ones, those that the Dark Fae had carefully hidden and whose minions, albeit unconsciously, were no less dangerous for that.

His reaction to seeing Maeve again, had surprised him. Perhaps she'd forgotten him for now but the memory was there. She was searching for it; he saw that now as she looked across the room at him from under her lashes, questions in her eyes; lowering them again when he caught her watching him.

It was like a dance he thought, a game of déjà vu. Who knew more, who would admit to knowing, who would remember first? At times exhausted by the endless dance, he thought of her, she was something more special than he'd realised even then on the other thread, their time together thrust upon them like pawns in a game. Ah, yes he thought, humankin love to meddle but with all their promises of not interfering, the shapers and the Fae, he reminded himself, were the worst.

He turned again to look at Samantha; yes, he knew her story too, but was not at liberty to solve her mysteries for her. He sighed; she'd been a delight to interview on the night of Sybille's book launch and he'd been frustrated, in being unable to help her find her aunt, whom he could see she missed. He didn't know where Sybille's physical form was, but he knew it was in neither warp nor weft of these threads; her pain at even speaking of her, told him that.

Then there was Bethan, his friend from years ago in this thread on the Lady's Wheel and so many others. Here she was Arwen Arianwen Isil'Lindir, his Lady and patron's daughter. Oh the twists and turns of warp and weft he sighed, closing his eyes for a moment as the inner fox of his nature stirred, straining to emerge at his distress. Its physical counterpart sat in the laneway behind the Journeyman Pub waiting, as he smothered the need to move on. All his senses told him of the twisted path; the Crooked Path, the Fae were leading the group on. He pleaded in the name of all names that they all remain as whole, as they were now, before their tasks were complete.

Chapter 42
La Stregga

What vows have we made that will bring us to grief
…when broken and saddened we find no relief
…when fate is our undoing
…and the north wind blows strong
…even deep in the dreaming
…we knew it was wrong

La Stregga had no warning, no premonition, until the thunderous knocking came on the door. She was still recovering from the huge shock, after the bowl of her ancestors had shattered and a couple of shards had disappeared. It was as if, with their disappearance, she had lost all her powers of seership and spell-craft, even her health was diminishing. Nothing seemed to work for her on any level and she knew that her patron Lady was angered at her incompetence.

She stumbled to the door; spying through the peephole. Trembling with terror, she opened it to three burly guards and the monk who had been hounding her footsteps constantly. The younger of the guards stepped forward, opening a parchment scroll with a flourish, obviously relishing her discomfiture.

Shrinking down within, she feared the worst and after reading the scroll, said in a small frail voice, 'No, this is not me. I am no Stregga; I am just a humble old midwife who tries to help the needy with her knowledge.'

'Ha,' the elder soldier said gruffly, looking at her more closely, 'you delivered my entire brood ancient mother but I also remember people saying you had provided them with a talisman or a spell for love, on occasion.'

'Nonsense,' she retorted with a harsh, false laugh, 'that's not my way at all. I am a simple woman, a healer; I know nothing of such evil magicks. It's not me you seek!'

She shrank back as the other soldiers went to grab her before gaining an outward semblance of composure; she drew herself up to her full, if diminutive height.

Unable to think straight she panicked and in one moment, denied her birthright, denied she was La Stregga and with the last, unforgiveable betrayal, her successor...

'You must be looking for Magdalena,' she cried breathlessly, before clamping her hands over her mouth in dismay; her cowardice was unforgivable...

The men looked at her in horror and the monk smirked blatantly, in triumph; La Stregga realised with horror, Magdalena was who he'd been after from the start. The guards, having no choice must follow up on her accusations, dragging her with them to find the unsuspecting Magdalena.

Chapter 43
Potions or Poisons

...worlds within worlds ...lives within lives,
...fly swift as a bird ...be a fish as it dives,
...smell the soil ...burrow deep
...hear the earth ...does she sleep?
...nestle in ...worming down
...be the bug in the ground,
...be a cell in her skin ...go within ...go within

A few days before Beltane eve, and before Greenman Ways would open, Samantha sat in the garden at Covenstead Farm leaning against a vast apple tree, doodling little pictures of her leaf sprites as they cavorted around her in the wintry sunlight, with boundless enthusiasm.

Occasionally one would pause, strike a pose for her and zip away again; their bell like voices filled the air and Sam, with peace. She was supposed to be working on the Grimoire and incense blends, for both Beltane and for Samhain in the UK for the opening of Greenman Ways, but she'd become distracted, caught up in the playfulness of the sprites as they changed their colours from the grey-greens of winter to the emerald and white of spring.

Her tattoos came alive and she could feel a couple working at the nape of her neck, burrowing under her now, shoulder-length hair, giggling while they painted new designs on her skin, skilfully tying her hair in little elflocks that were almost impossible to comb out; she didn't care. She'd all but given up anyway, thinking she'd more the look of Beth's wildness every day; gone the neat as a pin girl who'd arrived at Covenstead, grieving for her missing Aunt.

Now, with more than eighteen months passed, Sam often wondered why someone like Annie Savage hadn't put in a missing person's report to the police. Tara had said the Gods had their methods, just as Lily and Morgan were able to come and go between countries unnoticed and Maeve, not reported as lost either, merely 'away.' Glamour, Tara said, had its place in keeping secrets but also in protecting their own kin.

With a sigh of regret, she put aside the drawings and pulled the Grimoire towards her. As she flipped through the pages, it was as if they came alive for her but she still couldn't work out why she was suddenly the magickal potion maker, when it was Flora who knew so much. She could only imagine it was because of the reticence of her aspect Magdalena that it was her task to learn, or remember it now. After all, she'd been an herbalist then and performed the same things Flora did now. Still, she thought, what should I mix for Samhain this year?

She heard her name called and saw Vanessa coming toward her, carrying a steaming mug of something fragrant. She thought, another budding herbalist, before waving to Vanessa.

They chatted a while about Samhain. 'It's always been my favourite rite,' said Vanessa, 'along with Lammas, Imbolc and Beltane, the Greater Sabbats, but Samhain has always been special. Perhaps a bit morbid of me really, but it has the essence of all that the Way is about, cycles, life, death and rebirth, with no judgement of a natural process. Well that's how I see it anyway,' she broke off in embarrassment. 'Sorry Sam, ignore my blabbering, you know all this stuff better than I do.'

'Oh, that's not necessarily true Nessa. I avoided it all until it was unavoidable, after my Aunt disappeared. I'm glad I have a good memory and remember what she taught me. I understand it now so much more but it's a horrible way to learn.' Sam smiled at Nessa a little ruefully. 'I regret not having had the need then and that it had to be a tragedy that brought me here, yet I'm grateful for all that I am and all I'm remembering now.'

Nessa reached out to Sam for the sadness she heard in her voice, touching her hand gently she said, 'I do understand, although I would've found my way here anyway, at least mum let me come to the Lesser Sabbats as a kid. Lately she's been strange and withdrawn and I think something serious is going on with her; I'm not the one to ask at the moment, although it might have been different once,' she sighed. 'She's knows more about what's going on than she's saying. Something has frightened her, but her guard goes up as soon as anyone says anything like that to her. She gets all prickly; that's a dead giveaway.'

'Isn't it curious that we mostly have parental issues,' mused Sam. 'Bethan lost hers basically, but at least had Susan, Alex and Max. Maeve, well that's another story altogether, poor love. Flora and you have Harry to contend with but Flo, luckily for her, has supermum, Claire…'

'Ah yes, she is, isn't she,' said Nessa interrupting briefly. 'Supermum and lucky'.

'…Lily and Mor, well that's an amazing story and I wonder who their mother really is and then there's mine. I never really got to know them but I did have Sybille, even if I didn't appreciate her then. All I know is, when they were at home they were talking 'at' me about a career in law and that writing and art were the devil's work. Thinking back, they must have had their heads on backwards, 'cos the law is the last thing that's holy,'

Nessa giggled as Sam trailed off thoughtfully. 'There's something else too that's surfacing. I remember them taking me somewhere every week, a doctor, psychologist or something, who said I was 'troubled'. Can't remember anything else though but I'm sure it's on the way to the surface now. I do know they were church members too but I'm wondering if it was more some sort of cult, rather than a church really. Fanatical and fearful and utterly controlling and whatever their beliefs were, they still liked the fame and glory of their 'pilgrimages', over raising a 'troubled child'. Sam made parenthesis signs in the air on the words troubled child, with a watery smile at Nessa.

'Perhaps Tara can help you bring the memories out Sam, she's magickal with that. She helped me as a kid when I had oral exams due; I would clam up with nerves. She never put the memories there or enhanced what I knew, she just helped me remember and stay focused on the knowledge rather than the fear.'

'I hadn't thought of that,' replied Sam, 'but yes, when I feel ready I'll ask her to help, perhaps when we have Samhain and Beltane behind us. Now, on that note, we'd better look at those brews. Let's start with Samhain seeing as it's your favourite. That is, if you'd like to help Nessa?'

'Oh yes please,' she exclaimed. 'Is the Pope a Catholic?'

'Fair question Ness, fair question,' Sam chortled.

It was with heads together over the Grimoire that Nessa, without agenda, put her hands on Airmhid's ancient leather bag, running her hands lovingly over the soft, supple leather. In an instant, with a flurry of leaves and blossoms Nangini stood eye to eye with her. She looked deep into her before drawing the bag gently but firmly from her hands to place it in Sam's, drawing closer still to whisper. Vanessa had to strain to hear what she said.

'Not for you little one, not this time, the price is too high,' she said to Vanessa, before turning to Sam.

'There is something I must ask you to make. It needs to be a very potent soporific, pain removing but it must also reveal truths to the one who must take it.'

'But surely you are better qualified to do this Nangini,' said Sam.

'I may not meddle, not even when someone is in danger or dying. We may not alter things. Only you can alter your threads by changing your mind and focusing your will, attuning it consciously with a greater will, such as your patron or of the Primordial One. Will you help in this without question?'

'I've trusted that the Spirit of Nature, always has the answers but isn't it wrong to make something as dark as what you're suggesting?' asked Sam. 'What are the consequences of this for me? Won't I be putting my integrity at risk?'

'Only if you know who it is for and have negative intent,' replied Nangini.

Vanessa couldn't help herself, she cut in with a nervous laugh, 'why that sounds like something Tara would say!' Nangini only looked at her sternly.

'There is no time for hesitation, you must choose now,' she said to Sam.

'Well we were just speaking of Samhain, so I guess a blend of what would be used for a revealing spell, and a potion to dull the senses for a priestess experiencing her initiation at Beltane, would be a combination to fit what you've asked for.'

'It would,' replied Nangini, 'it would.' She nodded in satisfaction and disappeared.

'Hmm,' said Sam. 'I'm not sure of the ethics of this Nessa?'

'Can we argue this? Perhaps we should speak to Beth; even Pwyll or Tara?' said Vanessa.

'No,' said Sam, 'something tells me I must trust this process and see how it all unfolds.'

'Okay, I'm happy to help if I can,' said Vanessa.

'Thanks Nessa but I have a feeling that this is for me alone. You can help with the two blends for Samhain and Beltane though, and then I'll take it from there with a mix of both for Nangini. Quantity balance will be the key to this so I'll have to be careful to get this one right. Somewhere in the threads, someone will need this for a very specific purpose and I'm sure it will be revealed who and why in the next few days.'

Walking back to Covenstead, carrying the bag between them, Samantha noticed that it seemed much heavier than when she'd brought it out earlier, despite the fact that Vanessa carried half the weight.

Curious she thought to herself as the little fox trailed them home.

Chapter 44

Herbs & Brews

Herbs that harm and herbs that heal
…some to numb and some to feel
Nature has all the answers hid
…but will not reveal her secrets 'til respectfully bid

Samantha and Vanessa settled in to mix the herbs, resins and essences for the rites for the rest of the afternoon. They found the work relaxing and rewarding; Flora found them in the herb room laughing over a curiously shaped root they had found in the bag.

'I'd never thought of Mandrake as a Beltane herb but looking at the shape of this one I could change my mind,' said Sam to Flora as she held it up for inspection.

'Hmm,' said Flora. 'It is a bit phallic isn't it,' as she joined in the shared laughter. 'I don't think it would quite have the properties though! If I were to prescribe it for my clients with fertility issues, I'd be struck off!'

'It says here, it's a plant once used by women who couldn't conceive, so I guess that's very much a Beltane herb?' said Vanessa. 'There again, it's also said to be an herb of visions and can be used as a plant familiar. So that would mean it could become a communicator for between realms, wouldn't it?' she questioned Sam. 'So, Samhain for instance?'

'Oh wow, I wonder how that would work. We've been so focused on animal and bird spirit familiars, we've forgotten the plant and mineral realms,' said Sam. 'This could put a whole new light on our approach to the ritual. If it's another herb of vision questing though, how do we work with it, 'cos it's not one to ingest.'

'I don't know Sam,' replied Flora. 'We really need some help and none of the people we know who have magickal gifts seem to want to help. They simply keep saying it's our task to solve, but what if we're not up to it. The thought freaks me out more than a little.'

'Nangini won't let anyone else near the bag either, why is that do you think?' said Vanessa. "Didn't Airmhid give the bag to you Flora?'

'Yes she did originally but it would appear that there are other hidden reasons for giving it to me. Sam, as Magdalena wouldn't acknowledge Nangini, for whatever reason. Nina did, but if she's not my aspect I don't understand, other than perhaps the herbal medicine tie we share, rather than a soul aspect tie. Maybe I was the go-between for Sam to remember and Nina for Magdalena to remember, although we still don't know if she did or will. Wow that sounds convoluted,' Flora laughed.

'It does, but we get it,' Sam grinned.

Sam drew the bag towards her, stroking the soft leather almost lovingly, it seemed to vibrate beneath her hands, giving off a subtle aroma of woody loam and forest glades. The light dimmed and the sound of Flora and

Vanessa's, voices chatting happily diminished. She received a brief glimpse of Nina, pale and apparently grief stricken, in a cottage Sam didn't recognise. Nangini tended her and a large male fox was sitting on the threshold as if guarding the entrance. He turned and looked at a leather bag, placed on a chair in the cottage and she could feel his energy as it surged through the Aether; she knew he could see her and she him. He grinned; a foxy grin in acknowledgment and nodded.

'Why that's James,' Sam said aloud in astonishment, ripping herself back to the moment.

'What?' said Flora.

'I just saw James in his fox form, with Nina. She appeared frail, Nangini was tending her and James's standing guard but I don't understand what any of it means or where they were. It wasn't at her father's house that's for sure. What's happened to Magdalena?' Sam finished, in concern, pulling the bag closer to her chest in comfort. 'This,' she indicated the bag, 'or one like it anyway, was there in the room so at least it's safe.'

Rubbing the bag again as if it held the answers, Sam hefted it in her hands gauging its weight; it was definitely heavier. With a small frown of puzzlement, she opened the bag, rummaging through the content. Nothing appeared different about the pouches of herbs, other than that they were giving off a more pungent aroma. She tipped them onto the table unceremoniously and turned the bag inside out, running her hands over the lining.

Deep in the base of the bag, she felt a hard lump and not wanting to rip the bag she carefully felt around it. Sure enough, a seam, more loosely sewn than the other well-made stiches, gave a little under her probing fingers. Reaching for her small Boline, she slit open the stitching carefully, almost reverently, as the bag released its fragrances and an object fell out of its hiding place. Her sprites collected busily, humming softly as the package tumbled out.

Flora and Vanessa looked on silently; they knew Sam wouldn't be doing this without good reason.

Wrapped in a soft, indigo blue velvet pouch, embroidered with the interlinked initials MG, was an exquisite, hand tooled leather book. It shone with life and energy as if brand new and Sam knew instinctively whose energy it was, Magdalena's; she remembered; Magdalena Grigori.

With trembling fingers, she held it out for the others to see the cover; they gathered close around her, awestruck by the beauty of the little book, it appeared to pulse in Sam's hands.

Wiping hands become damp with nervous excitement, Sam opened it, carefully turning each page, astounded by the artisanship of the little illuminations in pen and coloured inks, so like her own work of late and lacy border workings, identical to the tattoos on her arms.

Her leaf sprites stirred, attuning to her thoughts, the energy emanating from the ancient book exciting them into action. They gently gathered, lifting and turning the pages until they found what they sought; a piece of parchment, worn and faded fluttered out of the book settling on the table in front of Sam. Putting the book down carefully, she picked up the parchment, tenderly opening it to read aloud, 'Oak for endurance, Ash for power, Hawthorn for enchantment at the Beltane hour, Holly brings challenge let justice prevail, Mistletoe brings trance to see 'tween Samhain's veil.'

Written, in the same careful script as the book and in Italian, yet Sam understood readily, the language a cell memory of her other self, Magdalena.

Sam didn't know whether to laugh or cry so did a little of both as the others gathered round to hug her.

'That's it,' she crowed. 'That's the recipe we need to make for both rituals and then if we add a little more Mistletoe and add some Mandrake root we have the mix Nangini wanted!'

The door opened and Claire, Lily, Bethan and Susan came in quietly, drawn inside by the previously silent house. They'd knocked, called and helloed but no one had answered until the sound of Sam's cry of triumph had led them to the herb room to share in the excitement of solving the blend's contents and the discovery of Magdalena's book. Sam carefully wrapped it again in the pouch, replacing it in the lining for safekeeping; she was elated and her sprites were already busy working on her body again, she could feel their little spiky thorns creating intricate patterns on her skin. She wondered briefly, what the finished tattoos would be like this time, before drawn along with the excited group of women, to the kitchen.

Today they'd agreed to meet to finalise their plans, the men, due to arrive from their various tasks and chores, had agreed to be the cooks for the evening and pizza was on the menu, the scent of wood smoke and bay leaves filtered in from the little clay pizza oven, outside.

Sam was strangely quiet as Cal approached her with a healthy slice of succulent roast vegetable and herb pizza. She barely heard him, lost in thought about what she'd seen that day and what role James had still to play in the scheme of things. He nudged her gently, flitting the steaming slice under her nose to ground her back to the moment. She laughed as she centred again, telling him what she'd seen. He listened, as always with an open mind but said nothing, as he'd promised Hercurin, about the vision. Instead, he rubbed her arm in a friendly man-ner and moved on to serve the others. Sam's eyes followed him. She'd sensed his reticence but thought how normal that was for Cal. 'When you're ready Cal,' she muttered to herself.

Chapter 45
Beltane: Maeve & Jamie

Heart of the wildlands ...spirits of old
...what do you teach us, so gentle yet bold
Whom do you call on as this new spring breaks?
Who will hear you ...who will awake?
Will we stay sleeping or will we wake up
...to dance in your meadows ...to drink from your cup
Will we remember ...as time's speeding by?
...remember the greening ...and fly

Deep in the Mysts of Tyme, the land knew the calling and the people responded. Beltane was the source for which the fertility of the lands rested and, for the folk bound to the land by love and fellowship, it was the source of their personal fertility too.

On a thread in the weave, Maeve wandered the hedgerows with the other women of her tribe, gathering hawthorn to make wreaths for their hair for the following morning's romp at Beltane. She was young and free and knew nothing of other lives that ran and interwove with this thread, concurrently. This would be her coming of age and she already knew the man she was destined to meet would be there on the following day.

She trusted that now her first bloods had come and gone the pairing would be natural, spontaneous and right, the other girls had laughed at her naivety. The Cybil had chided them a little, reminding them that Maeve was a seer and would know the 'one' when he came, saying quietly to her priestesses that perhaps he would be Fae, which would strengthen the blood of the tribes again with such a pairing and, the resulting offspring.

They would come to the dance arrayed in their finest and prettiest cloths, such as they may be, bedecked with hawthorn garlands, the tree covered in ribbons. A maypole was not then a known thing as who would do such a thing to a tree, when a living one would honour the land with her flowers and berries and be a source of nutrition, even healing when the healers took their share for tonics and May wine.

Careful not to prick herself or rip her clothes, Maeve pushed deeper into the hawthorn thicket where she could see a beautiful sprig of blossom she thought The Cybil might like for the Beltane Altar. As she did, she noticed a large male fox curled asleep in the leaf litter at the base of the tree. He was the largest she'd ever seen and knew he could be fierce when cornered so she started to back out as quietly as she could; too late, he opened one amber eye and regarded her with an almost human knowing. She could have sworn he smirked at her as he lifted his head, raking her from head to toe with his gaze.

'Well!' she exclaimed. 'If you were a man I'd slap your face.' His grin widened, showing sharp white teeth and she retreated rapidly vowing to ask The Cybil about fox-spirits. She'd heard that in some tribes he was a revered being, a Cunningman in disguise.

Hearing the other girls calling, she picked up her basket and ran, feeling his gaze on her back like a warm hand.

With the gathering done, they cleaned the Hearth and shared common space thoroughly, spreading sweet grasses and thyme over the floors. Excitedly, they went to their beds knowing that the morning would bring a new cycle into being. Giggling together, they shared their dreams, late into the night.

Maeve woke early, hearing the sounds from the communal hearth and cooking smells wafted on the faint breeze of bread and simple stews for the feast later that day. She wandered down to the lake unseen to bathe, noticing elderflower wines and meads hung tethered, cooling in the lake.

Stripping off her clothes without a second thought, she didn't see the fox who sat under an apple tree, his gaze not leaving her face. Stealthily, moving back from the tree, he disappeared into the thicket to re-emerge dressed in his best humankin clothes and a broad grin. He carried several rabbits and a bow with a quiver of arrows, slung across his broad chest. He was nut brown from sun exposure, freckles scattered across his nose, tall and strongly made, he was the centre of attention as he sauntered through the Hearth to present his catch to the cooks.

Just past dawn, the tribes gathered from all around the isles. Hawthorn tree bedecked with ribbons, held the focus of attention as the maidens and young, fertile women, formed a circle around it, facing inward and the lads and men in a circle behind them.

On a cue from the piper, they all turned to face east as the rising sun spilled golden light across the dew-bedecked grasses. Each man held a ribbon of green; fertile mothers, who wished for another child held a red, and the maidens, a white.

They began their intricate circle dance, weaving and threading over and under, the three colours of the Summer Lady and Her Greenman Lord.

Danced over centuries on this spot, facing Tor Hill with steps unvarying, the energy rose from the heart of the land, through their dancing feet and up their spines. Warmth blossomed in loin and womb as they circled and spiralled, around the ancient thorn until the ribbons ran out, leaving the tree wrapped in coloured garlands in a knot work design; the phallus enfolded in the womb of the Mother.

Silence fell as the circle formed anew, the young men on the outer, the maidens on the inner who, taking off their hawthorn wreaths threw them over their shoulders toward the waiting men. Some knew exactly where their intended partner would be standing, while others such as Maeve didn't know if anyone would catch their wreath that day.

Shrieking with laughter, the women, pretending fear at the chase, fled the circle their bare feet made no sound as they disappeared toward the orchard, the lake and the surrounding hedgerows with their partners to be, in hot pursuit.

Maeve bolted, real fear at not knowing who was pursuing her gave her feet wings and on reaching the thorn, where she had harvested the bough of blossoms the evening before she tripped, only to be caught in strong, calloused but warm, brown hands. She was pivoted around to meet the eyes of her nut-brown man; she'd dreamed of him, tall and Fae. Her foxy-lad, the words echoed through the threads, vibrating them, causing other aspects to toss in their sleep in longing as she sank to the ground to offer her maidens' blood to the earth and her body to her lover.

Small Makers flitted around them waiting for the moment to become human if the omens were right. Tara's laughter echoed throughout the entire weave.

Chapter 46
Samantha's Doubts

Darkmoon days ...go within
...forget the hype, forget the spin
Contemplate your inner self
...search inside for inner wealth

Acting on Vanessa's suggestion, Sam sought out Tara. She wanted to get it over with, end the self-doubt that had plagued her about her latent abilities and what her parents may or may not have instigated in their bigoted fear of her, 'troubles'. She wanted to remember everything that had happened in those early years of childhood before Sybille had taken her to stay at Covenstead and her parents had gone off on their jaunts without a care, presumably.

What memories was she dredging up from the fringes of her psyche?

Tara was not happy about helping, fearing she would be interfering but Sam simply said if she wouldn't 'regress' her, she'd just go to a hypnotherapist who would.

'No, no,' Tara had replied hurriedly. 'You don't know what they'll find or if they'd understand Sam!'

'Well that leaves you then doesn't it?' Sam grinned smugly.

A couple of days before Samhain in Somerset, Tara took Sam to the Chalice Well. It was sunset and the hills were silent as a heavy mist floated in, bringing the frosts with it. It was freezing, and Sam wondered why Tara had decided to work with her outside in the cold rather than at home at the farm in Australia or even at Greenman Ways.

'You need no witnesses for this Sam; you may not want to speak of it at all, who knows.'

'I don't think I have anything dark buried Tara but I do have a right to know what memories, if any have been tampered with. I merely want the truth about me.'

Tara looked at her and Sam could see the Morrigan was not far away, as she reached out to tap Sam sharply between the eyes. Sam felt the earth spin away and she was flying in an unknown form. She couldn't make out what it was only that she'd flown out of her bedroom window. She'd been fast asleep, a little girl of no more than five. The vision faded but she felt that perhaps Tara **had** meddled, resolving to ask about it when she returned to her senses. It didn't feel as if it were part of what she was searching for, now anyway.

Her vision cleared and she was a child again, a little older this time. She was practicing her flute and as she played, she could see the leaf sprites were with her even then. They were distracting her by drawing images on her hands in time to the music she played. She realised it must have looked strange to the music teacher as she giggled, wriggling her fingers when the sprites tickled or pricked them.

At one time she'd fumbled her fingering because of it and had giggled again, the teacher thinking she was doing it deliberately, actually rapped her on the knuckles with her conductors' baton and all hell had broken loose, the sprites attacked the woman's hand, biting her fingers and pulling her hair. Sam giggled in her trance at the memory and Tara smiled watching her recapture what had been the real delight of her childhood.

Her parents, hearing of this began to observe her closely. On occasion Sam knew her parents could see the tattoo-like drawings that would appear and disappear, depending on Sam's moods and that they were disturbed terribly by the fact that they could see something that, to them was un-godly, whereas Sybille would encourage Sam's drawings and writings about the little sprites, creating a little book of her tales. Her parents would often raid her room when she was at school and destroy all her work; cruelty takes many forms.

She became careful, carrying her drawings with her, leaving some at Sybille's and putting on an earnest face when she was practicing her music, so as not to create any further suspicion. She had a new music teacher and made sure, no matter what the sprites were doing, not to respond.

Together with some hypnotherapy sessions and her continuing to ignore them, the sprites finally appeared to have left her. She was bereft but after a while, she forgot them, the hypnotherapist convinced her they were only a figment of her child's imagination. Sometimes she would look at her drawings and wonder how in the world she'd ever come up with such fantasy work but it remained with her and it became her goal, to be an illustrator and writer.

Her parent's death left her strangely numb and was once again, subjected to psychologists and therapists by her school teachers, who concluded that she was simply masking her grief. Sam finished her studies of the law abruptly, starting the course in journalism, where she finally found her niche with the edgy journal she still occasionally, wrote for.

No, there was nothing dim and dark there, just a sadness that she'd pushed her friends away and lost her child-like joy, becoming the serious young woman whom Beth, Flora and Maeve had originally met. One thing for sure was that she'd blocked out the sprites on this thread just as she'd blocked Nangini on Magdalena's thread of life.

As she came back to the moment on the cold hill by the well, she sighed in relief, forgetting the moments of flying as it slipped to the back of her mind again.

'Time enough for that,' Tara muttered.

Deep in the well, the small Merrow listened quietly. She liked the nest she'd created for herself, lining it with little trinkets and pieces of fur or feathers. Among her prized possessions were, a coil of silvery hair, pulled from Arianwen's pretty snood where it had caught. She remembered the unusual anger Arianwen had displayed as she'd pulled the cap from her hair, practically throwing it in a box. She had wondered about it and finally snatched it from where Arianwen kept it hidden; she'd never worn it again.

Mirdhaucha loved it and would wear it often, even though it made her head feel odd and never where M'lady might see it. She knew the pieces were from the shards she'd filched from the old woman's shattered bowl and given M'lady and she remembered seeing the tall red-haired woman Maeve, working with the pieces, some-where in the twisted threads. Ah Maeve, there was a memory, a stirring where her human aspect had been; again, she wept, she did not know why.

Chapter 47
Beltane at Covenstead

He walks the land again tall and strong
...so many myths say he's evil and wrong
One look at His face, the warmth in His eyes
...will show you the truth of His ways
As He walks with the Lady, trust in that smile
...as He shows you the new greening days

Beltane, usually such a huge and somewhat raucous gathering was thoughtful and somehow more conscious; focused.

Flora and Cal, immersed in each other were probably the most light hearted of the group. Max and Lily were obviously making progress in their own relationship challenges but it was evident that Lily was not yet ready to recommit; not quite yet.

Beth was ambivalent about her plans for the morning and none questioned her when she wore a subtle smile like a badge of knowing. They knew her Greenlord would be waiting for his Lady.

Sam, Vanessa and Morgan were happy to boost the gathering with energy but had no other thoughts about partnerships, only friendships. Sam would sometimes observe Max and Lily, knowing she'd been right in withdrawing her energies when her sprites had shown such animosity towards him. How could she not trust the loyal little creatures that had stayed with her, even when she'd forgotten them? They in turn were becoming more noisy and boisterous, playing games that appeared almost amorous to Sam; they had her in stitches as they parodied humans, smacking their lips and blowing kisses around. She couldn't stay despondent long with such enthusiasm. It was as if they were trying to distract her from her thoughts.

With Flora and Vanessa's willing help, Sam had created the herbs as instructed, for Beltane. Ever since then, a chant had been circling repeatedly in Sam's mind. She even thought she might ask Bethy or Mor to create music for it, it had such a pretty ring to it. '*Oak for endurance, Ash for power, Hawthorn for enchantment at the Beltane hour,*' she crooned as the sprites danced around her and now they would put the first half of the blend to use at their Rite.

They gathered at dawn in the Grove on the hill at Covenstead. Susan, Alex, Claire, Pwyll, Lily, Max, Flora and Cal chatted, laughing happily, as they made their way up the hill. Bethan, Sam and Mor said they'd dance for the fun of it, Vanessa had opted not to join in the May Dancing but would preside as the Virgin May Queen and would she said, gleeful indulge in ordering all the men around for the day, with a naughty giggle.

Just as in days in other threads and other aspects, where Maeve and Jamie joined the dance, the men and women of Covenstead faced the Hawthorn they had arrayed with ribbons, blossoms opened to the morning sunlight as the men stood on the outer and females within, their circle. The Fae were gathering; Aithlin, Circaea and others of their kin stepped forward as the veil thinned. They circled and the ribbons intertwined, white under green, green over white and red, the thread of blood from maidenhood to motherhood, binding everything in the cycles of the greening time.

In one coordinated movement, they turned to face each other, the bond between the group felt as a tangible energy surged between them. The traditional May wreaths, exchanged between those already coupled; Lily and Sam threw theirs wildly over their shoulders as they turned to face the men.

Unplanned and un-choreographed Max caught Lily's with a flourish and a bow, Alex stepped to catch Sam's but Morgan stepped between and advanced toward Sam with a determined and solemn air.

He bowed and placed her wreath in her hair, grown long and tangled as the wild sprites played; he dared their wrath as he did.

'Lady?' He said, a question in his voice.

Sam felt suddenly weak at the knees as she recalled memories of different threads and a man, a Cunningman named Bran. She faltered, as he looked her in the eye as if daring her to remember what he couldn't, then a sound broke the silence as Hercurin entered the grove, wild and brown he approached Bethan and all else was lost in the celebration as he joined their rites. He stayed a while to celebrate the spirit of the land with elderflower wine and honey cakes before unceremoniously, grasping Bethan by the hand, running off with her amidst catcalls and gales of laughter.

They stood in their circle holding hands, giving thanks for the day; they all knew that night would be a different ritual, a serious stepping between the veil. Claire and Pwyll carried around the wine and cakes again as they shared their dreams for a fertile year to come and sang together before opening the circle and leaving their offerings for the wee folk of nature…

'Cherish each other …love one another …the law is 'harm ye none!' Gift to each other the truth of yourselves and earth's greening will be done. Find you the innocence of gentler days …come to the forests where Faefolk play. Live in the moment as if t'were your last day and earth's greening will be done.'

Chapter 48

Bethan & her Greenman

Hear the winds calling a sultry refrain
He's out and about ...the prelude to Beltane
You can hear Him now in the rustling of leaves
As He sends small reminders that tug at your sleeves
He whispers, 'I am the essence that lives ...all unseen
...I am the memory of all that is green
Take up the mantle of earth's greening time
...smell the wild's fragrance like sweet summer wine
Come to your circle in Hawthorn arrayed
I will meet you in the Greenwoods
...where my music is made

Hercurin grabbed Bethan's hand, his lady, Arwen Arianwen Isil'Lindir, Spellsinger, an aspect of Arianrhod the Lady of the Silver Wheel. She always came to him in this form, and in those times he could hold her in her physical body after the blending of spirit in matter had occurred; all aspects combined to make her vessel.

Now she was more, there need never be separation again as she flowed between her physical and Aetheric forms seamlessly.

She was laughing as she changed, shifting to her Greenwoman essence to match his fluidly, no pretence and all shyness gone, although she trembled when his eyes grew serious, drawing her to him.

Union, complete and utter as Hercurin, holding Arianwen's hand, stepped back into a huge oak in a forest so ancient it was there before any other life form had created itself.

Union; bark, leaf, branch, stem, flower; sap flowing, rising to the surface and bursting into life force; oneness.

Merging, face to face, mouth to mouth, breast to chest, cup to blade; no cell separated, no illusion left in their 'becoming'.

Chapter 49
Samhain Opening at Greenman Ways

Step through the mists to the lands of the Fae
Step from starlight into bright day
A mystical dance will unfold as you stray
...through the Tor on the hill where the Wildlings play

 Despite the seriousness of Samhain's fast approach, Lily was beside herself with excitement for the day ahead. She'd tweaked, fussed and moved stuff around and finally, Sam had taken the small figurine of a seated faery, gazing raptly up, lap harp across her knees, out of Lily's nervous hands, placing it next to where Bethan would sit to play that night.

They'd decided not to have the full troop playing, just Bethy and Mor as backup. They wanted a wistful note, as it should be for All Hallows. Lily had even wondered at the omen of starting something new at the waning year. They had all agreed it was unusual, Ostara or Beltane being the traditional times but as Mor reminded them, it was Celtic New Year and things begun now took a year to come to fruition. In a new business that was expected as a minimum time to kick-start something; Lily was reassured.

Sam, observing Mor, had thought how typical of the man, always finding just the right things to say but never giving false hope.

They moved through the day, patiently encouraging Lily to delegate things to them, rather than trying to do everything herself. In the end, the men polished Athame, metal chalices and any glass surface or window tirelessly, until she was happy.

Sam's eye for detail had her helping with displaying the beautiful goods to perfection, until the place was shining and pulsing with energy. Candles were set to light when the day faded, early here in the approaching dark times. Bowls of crystals invited touch, small statues of the Faery sat on shelves, between jewel coloured book covers and cabinets, gleaming with their silver and crystal content. The look was similar to Earthly Rites, on the other side of the planet and yet uniquely different, bathed in the bright colours of Lily's choosing.

A flicker on the Aether made them aware of the arrival of Susan and Alex, as they appeared to step through a painting at the back of the shop. It depicted the Grove at Covenstead with a swirling portal leading into a corridor of blooming apple trees and into Greenman Ways.

'A brilliant touch,' crowed Tara as they arrived.

All things came together for the opening and the Rite, as they prepared to welcome in a New Year, a new business and hopefully, more new information about Sybille, who Nina's aspect could be and how they could bring the seemingly endless saga, to a successful completion.

When the store was jam-packed with visitors, some just curious and others excited about the goods offered, young and old alike, fluttered like birds among the books and magickal tools on display. Sybille's book, 'Earth Rites' was on show in a prominent position; an older, rather distinguished gentleman with a neat braid of snow white hair, stood looking at her photo on the back cover. Seeing his expression of bewilderment Lily approached him.

'Have you read any of Sybille's works?' She asked him conversationally.

He seemed a little startled at her direct question but turned to her with a steady and direct look. 'Well that's just it and I suppose you're going to think me loony tunes but, I dream of her.'

'I'm sorry?' exclaimed Lily, taking a step back in surprise.

'You see, you do think I'm crazy,' he grinned, a winning grin.

'No quite the opposite, but there is someone I would like you to meet to tell about your dreams. She will understand completely I assure you, if you're willing to share.'

'Well I do like riddles solved and she's an intriguing lady. I met her when she came to the UK and we, shall we say, collaborated, on both her and my own books.'

'Then come with me, I'll freshen your glass and find Tara. I'm sure she'll help solve it.'

Meandering her way through the crowd, she smiled as she came across various members of the group and found Tara in a corner with Pwyll and another of the shifters that seemed to be everywhere that night. Taking Tara aside, she pointed to the man in question and Tara reflectively studied him.

Ah, I see,' she said a little distractedly as she walked toward him. Lily could see his eyes open wide as she approached him with the glass of red wine she'd taken from Lily's hand; she passed it to him and his hand was shaking a little as he took it. He placed it carefully on a counter where he couldn't knock it over, before offering Tara his hand. 'Robert Cromlech,' he said politely, 'author and lecturer on paranormal studies.'

'Tara,' she said smiling. 'Tara Saark.' His eyes grew wider still at her name. 'Yes I know,' she said.

Tara took a deep breath before asking him to come with her, somewhere where they could speak. Beth began to sing softly, her only accompaniment her lap pipes. She followed with her eyes as Tara took the man to a small reading room at the back. He paused by the painting of the grove at Covenstead, shaking his head in bewilderment.

'More riddles,' he said.

'Yes I know,' replied Tara again gently. 'Come on in and take a seat. We won't be disturbed here unless someone decides they need a snooze,' she laughed and he visibly relaxed. 'Now tell me about your dream.'

'Well,' he paused, thinking how careful did he need to be but throwing caution to the wind dove in with his telling. 'It's a series of dreams and you are sometimes there, plus many of the people in this room. We're standing at a gateway; I don't mean a physical one and it's very like the picture in the back of the shop here. We seem to be waiting for something or someone but I can't tell at what time of year it is exactly. There's a strange odour on the air, acrid and it's dark. All I know is it's bitterly cold, cold that could sheer the flesh from bones.' He shuddered visibly at the thought before continuing. 'A person, a shape at least, appears in the gateway, says she's the way shower and that we can step through now; it's safe. Other beings are moving around in the doorway, one is a small fragile girl of no more than 18, 19 years; she's searching for a book. She looks as if she's been very ill and seems to be grieving; she carries a secret and a burden. Then there's a couple, both alive and vibrant, red-haired and so alike they could be brother and sister but I know they're not by the way they are together; so in love and she's pregnant, it's just visible. She's not here tonight but he is; reminds me of a fox.'

'Ah, the foxy lad eh,' Tara grinned. 'Go on, Robert. I can call you that?'

'Rob, will do,' he said before continuing. 'There is a small child size being following everyone in turn, sticking her nose into things and making a proper nuisance of herself.' Rob paused for breath. 'She is sad too though; she's forgotten something she needs to retrieve, something she shouldn't have had or given away in the first place. There's a small human element that obviously still governs her conscience.'

As he continued speaking at length, Tara saw his eyes glazing over, the deep green becoming almost violet and then a veil of filmy white covered them, making him appear blind. She didn't dare touch him to see if he was okay as his trance deepened. A true dreamer she said to herself, how wonderful. I wonder how open he'd be to joining the Grove. What an asset with him and Bethy working together. She delved deeper into him as he was speaking, searching for aspects or shapechangers in his ancestry. He was quite an enigma. She focused back on his words.

'There's another there in the shadows, a dark Fae and what appears to be her son. She's cunning and not all she seems. Even what you may think you know about her is nothing, compared to what she hides within and she's dangerous. She has the child creature under her power but she's trying to break free, as the human side emerges again and there's a dark haired woman who is entirely under her glamour. One of her daughters is here, a lovely girl meant to be a secret; she must be protected.'

His eyes focused on Tara briefly again and then he was gone again.

'So many wonderful souls gathered together and so twisted have their paths become for them, so twisted they can't recognise each other readily but they must. It's imperative they do and then there's you Tara Saark, never interfering per se and yet at times you can come close to crossing the line toward manipulation but then you're not human and your mistress and you are one.'

Rob fell silent and she thought he'd fallen asleep but he roused after a few deep breaths and directed his clear green eyes at her face.

'I'm speechless Rob or should I say Robyn? You're a rare one and no mistake. How did you find me here tonight and why did you pick Lily to ask your question of?'

He grinned broadly and his face became youthful and clear before falling back into its age lines again. 'She is shaper and yet so innocent in many ways; I didn't want to be recognised,' he replied.

'Well Robyn, you've been sprung but your secret's safe with me, especially tonight of all nights.'

Rob just smiled and taking her, hand kissed it in a courteous fashion. 'We are found in all places and all threads; taking different forms and yet still one but you still haven't answered about my dreams.'

'Do you really mean you don't know about Sybille and what's happened,' Tara said aghast. 'I thought you could help us with your seership.'

'There are things hidden that probably only Primordial One knows, the threads are so twisted.'

'True but you, surely you know more than you're sharing?'

'Yes my dear of course,' said Rob, 'but there again so do you, and that's the fine line I mentioned before.'

Tara laughed at that, a deep chortle of appreciation. 'Come on Rob; let's take you to meet the crew. Will you come to their rite tonight?'

Rob laughed, his face handsome, craggy and wild like the land he came from. 'Oh I can guarantee you I'll be there.'

When Tara and Rob emerged from the room, the shop was already emptying. James was the first to approach, shaking hands gravely after being introduced. He felt he should know the charismatic elder. Max came next but recognised him as **the** author Robert Cromlech, whom he greatly admired for his works on the energy of standings stones, Dolmen and their Numen or Genius Loci. In fact, he was currently reading Spirit of Place, Robert's most recent book.

'Why, didn't you work with Sybille on occasion?' said Morgan stepping forward to meet Rob.

'Yes that's right but where is the lady, she's disappeared off the radar for a quite a while. Is she well? You seem to know her?'

'I've never met her in the flesh,' said Morgan, 'but she was …that is, she's my mentor.' Rob raised an eyebrow at his slip but made no comment.

'Isn't it strange that in the Gaelic your name means 'flat stone' or Dolmen,' said Morgan, quick to recover.

'Clever lad, but of course I can hear the Welsh in your voice; and is that your Da?' He indicated to Pwyll standing watching with Claire, Flora and Cal. Bethan was nowhere to be seen nor were Susan, Alex, Lily, Sam or Vanessa who were clearing the decks in the kitchen to make way for the Samhain Rite and the 'dumb feast', to follow.

'Yes, that's my father and I believe you met my sister Lily earlier on.'

'Indeed I did, lovely girl.'

At that moment, the rest of the group emerged from the kitchen and James came in from outside, brushing light snow from his hair and shoulders.

'Can you believe it,' he said, 'it's snowing! It's going to be a cold Rite folks and I…' He trailed off as he saw the man standing next to Mor and Pwyll, looking at him with apparent interest.

'Oh sorry, James Buchanan,' holding out his hand. 'And you are?'

'This is Robert Cromlech, James,' Max introduced the older man. He wrote…'

'Yes I know, Spirit of Place, wasn't it?'

'Does everyone know my work, I'm flattered,' said Rob.

'I was saying before how odd that a man with the name of Cromlech should be writing about stones,' said Morgan, passing the ball to James neatly.

James grinned broadly. 'Yes but doesn't 'Crom,' also mean 'crooked', he quipped. Rob didn't smile at this merely looked at James carefully.

'Well it suits one on the 'Crooked Path', very well. He smiled innocently at them all.

Laughter is contagious and Tara stepped forward to ask if they minded if Rob came to the Rite. They were wary but after Rob shared a little with them of his Truedreaming and Tara vouched for him quietly, they demurred, welcoming yet another thread in the tapestry to the group.

Chapter 50
All Hallows in Glastonbury

The wild folk ride through forests green
...once a year they're easily seen;
...they come from beyond the in-between
...breaking through the veil
Their horns sound bright ...their voices light;
...riding through the dark of night ...faces ghostly pale
The Wild Hunt rides ...hounds at their sides
...to chase the dark away,
...as the Green Lord comes a-gathering in
...all who were led astray
She waits for them in a lightened glen
...where the Fae folk play
He leads them through the forests fair
...to the Summerlands faraway

A group of thirteen walked by lantern light to join the throng of people walking the Serpent Way to Tor Hill. They could join with other groups and factions or they could find their own place to be still and listen, on the Celtic Festival of the Dead.

Each of them thought about the previous year and how raw they were in comparison to now. They would never stop learning and mustn't be over confident, but a little goes a long way and was necessary on this night of all nights.

Morgan remembered the raw circle casting of those who were unused to working a Grove, and yet such courage was shown that night as the Hunt pressed in on them from all sides. He remembered Bethan as the crown of her head burst open with her own light. Her horns rose from her brow for the first time; he would never forget the sight, seen with his mind's eye. Colours had danced around her as she stood in the cold, pure air. He wondered if it had hurt that first time.

In her inner sight, Bethan was back at the last Samhain night, when she'd felt the pressure as the horns had sprouted from her head …spreading wide; silvery antlers that held weight; a weight that had her standing taller as her energy shimmered. Then she was literally there again in bilocation, running through the forest toward the sound of the Wild Hunt's horns. She carried the wand that Maeve had made for her and wore the cap of Lemurian crystals; a part of her wondered where it was as she'd not seen it among her things recently, vowing to look for it on her return.

She flew across the ground to stand again in the circle where the Wytches waited, and a white owl glided down to land on her shoulder; she smiled at Claire who acknowledged with a nod of her head and a rustle of feathers. All the while, she was Beth standing on a hill above the town of Glastonbury.

High Priestess and Priest were waiting and the words repeated again. 'There She is; She's come to us.

Welcome Arwen, you honour us with your presence.'
…and she was stepping with grace toward their circle, dressed in a deep blue robe, a sickle Moon shone silver on her brow between the raised antlers …and in the forest she heard the sound of the Horn, calling the Wild Hunt to the chase.

Once again she was spinning in a circle, blue flames flying from the end of the wand to fill a safe circle for her friends to stand as the hunt rode by…
…she spun and the dark was attracted as much as light to her casting…

…the Priestess and Priest uncovered their heads and it was Sybille but the Priest wasn't Pwyll this time …it was Robert Cromlech…

All around on hilltops, standing stones, in back gardens and centres dedicated to the Old Gods, beacons and bonfires flared, signalling the time of vigil and introspection as the veil thinned and the trooping Fae and the Lord and Lady of the hunt emerged, to gather in the dead or those gone astray.

I give myself to the Lord and Lady; I reach within to find the
flame. Deep within the eternal silence
…only in the Lord and Lady's name
None shall step across the border, between the lands of man
and Fae. None shall come to create disorder
…for lives shall fall in disarray

On Tor Hill, Samantha collapsed with a cry of pain and outrage. Morgan and Tara caught her as she fell.

Chapter 51
Treachery

In the depths of your sleep,
...in the dark of the night, remember ...awaken
...the room filled with light
You are only lost if you believe it is so
...untangle your thoughts and let go ...just let flow
...the snarls and the tangles will all melt away
When you know that your power is all that holds sway
...all the things that you dream
...all the things that you know
...they are real ...so is She ...so let go ...just let go.

Magdalena couldn't stay away, she had to pay Nina a final visit to say goodbye. La Stregga had said she could teach her nothing more and that she was ready to become La Stregga to a small village in the mountains that had need of one. She had said it was for the best, using her feelings for Eduard as an excuse to convince Magdalena that she must move on or she may well endanger Nina.

Nonna let Magdalena in by the back stairs to avoid seeing Eduard and she was consoling the distraught Nina as they said their goodbyes when thunderous knocking on the door and cries of 'open up, open up,' had Nina dragging Magdalena, toward the closet.

Nonna was in the hallway and made to open the door in alarm but Eduard gently put her aside, a finger to his lips to quieten her. He opened the door and half expected the soldiers to push their way in but they bowed with respect to the stately man.

'What in the name of all names is wrong with you? My daughter is ill and must not be disturbed.'

To Eduard's horror, they pulled the silent and shrunken La Stregga forward. Tears were streaming down her face but Eduard said nothing, only looking at her in consternation.

'What are you doing with this old woman; she is the midwife who delivered my own sweet Nina ...what harm can she possibly have done?'

'It is not you we have come to see Signor, with respect, you have a servant by the name of Magdalena whom this old woman has accused of witchcraft.'

'WHAT! What have you done?' he said turning in horror to La Stregga.

'Have you been aware of this Signor,' said the elder of the soldiers pulling himself up stiffly, 'and you haven't reported her?'

'No, No said Eduard hastily, I know nothing of this, she doesn't work for me,' and once more, one she loved the most, denied Magdalena.

'She was witnessed evoking small demons in the trees in the town square in full daylight,' said the soldier.

'If that is so, why then they must also be able to see these er ...demons, would you not say? Who are these witnesses,' queried Eduard.

'Hmm, I cannot say Signor but you are correct and this too shall be dealt with no doubt but first, where is the maid? Then we shall leave you in peace to care for your daughter Signorina Nina,' said the soldier again, respectfully.

Eduard, his heart breaking at his own treachery, looked into the eyes of the soldier and stepped aside, his shoulders slumping in defeat. He felt constrained, forced to choose his daughter's wellbeing over his personal feelings of love for Magdalena.

She stood at the window above, looking down on the scene below. Her own teacher, her one source of strength in a world blown apart after the death of her parents, years ago, who had raised her and taught her everything about the natural world and yes, about magicks.

Nonna, flew up the stairs with unaccustomed agility for one her size to warn them, bursting into the room where Magdalena and Nina stood looking down on the scene below, rushing to pull Nina away from Magdalena as the soldiers pushed past Eduard and trooped up the stairs. The door burst open and the three soldiers filed in.

A rush of air and a humming, like bees filled Magdalena's ears; she thought she was would faint. It was only the invisible hand, suddenly holding her own that steadied her, as the energy of the little diva Nangini flooded her with strength, while slipping a small packet into her hand. Finally, she could see her, feel her presence; all too late, she thought as she watched the soldier's faces for just a spark of emotion.

Magdalena raised her chin proudly and said not a word as the soldier read her the accusations levied against her …she was numb.

As they led her away to the screams of grief from Nina and Nonna, she fleetingly met the eyes of both La Stregga and Eduard; she simply shook her head in confusion. She only had a moment to secrete the small packet Nangini had given her into the folds of her many pocketed skirts; its contents were the least of her concerns as the soldiers led her away.

Weeks passed and with Samhain's approach, Nina's strength failed rapidly. Magdalena went to trial, convicted of witchcraft, and condemned to burn.

There was no defence brought in her favour and no time was wasted either, no one came forward to visit her or to speak for her; her role as assistant in birthing local babies and the hours she had spent with the sick and dying, all for nothing.

Accused of Wytchcraft but her own teacher was free. There was nowhere to go with her pain and grief at the betrayal …and then there was Eduard; what she felt for him turned to dust; despair overcame her.

What is the point of living when there is no one who cares enough to step up to help? When did the

Wytch become the scapegoat for all the fear that men had of women who knew the keys to healing, the plants to cure, and the words to mend? What indeed, happened to the Cunningmen and the Druid healers of old, the Ovate, male and female alike, who were the teachers of their time in herbal lore and psychic phenomena, the walkers between the worlds?

When were the Pantheons of Spirit, who helped us to create ourselves forgotten, and with the forgetting, when did the memory die that we carry the same spark within as created them? Our only fall was into matter, "Mata," the Mother, and it is in Her embrace we have always lived, together with the animator's flame of the wild forest, the Spirit of Place; indeed wasn't that our choice too?

If they exist then in truth we can awaken, we can remember all that we are, not in an egocentric or hierarchical manner, but in sheer awe and delight at our own magnificence as creatures born of darkness and light, matter and spirit and of joy not fear.

Brave thoughts at least, she said to herself as she pulled the small packet of herbs from the depths of her skirts, sniffing carefully to identify their content. Ah, she thought, so even the sprite knows I am to die then! Magdalena smelt belladonna, monk's hood, mistletoe and something else that had the stench of death to it, fly agaric perhaps; it couldn't be worse than the flames. She curled up in her cloak on the damp, rank pallet of mouldy straw and reached out to her aspect on another thread in the tapestry, whispering to her, 'Help me, help me please. Let it be quick and let me be brave. He cannot see my fear.'

'Sleep child,' Nangini whispered, spreading her hands over Magdalena's head and calling the sprites to help soothe her. 'It will be so, fear not.'

She slipped through the warp and weft, in search of Samantha to see if she'd progressed with the blend, she'd asked her to make. She had not said it was for Magdalena, there would be the right occasion for that if the clever Sam didn't work it out for herself.

Arriving at the thread where Sam dwelt, she could sense the air of excitement that emanated from the house. Cautiously slipping in through the old stillroom, Nangini made her way to the herb room. Sitting on the table was a bottle of liquid that almost glowed in the dark and tied to it in a cursive script was a parchment tag that held the words…

Oak for endurance Ash for power
Hawthorn for enchantment at the Beltane hour
Holly brings challenge let justice prevail
Mistletoe brings trance to see 'tween Samhain's veil
Added at the bottom was…
'Mandrake brings the visions to guide her on the way,
I will wait to meet her on the thread we live today.'
Nangini smiled and took the bottle to Magdalena as promised, singing the chant of birth to her.

Sam stood in the shadows and wept for she was
to kill herself. She realised why Flora, Vanessa and Nina
were instructed not to work with Airmhid's bag of herbs;
they wouldn't have been able to forgive themselves even
though it would bring Magdalena relief. She hoped it
would be as merciful for her when she experienced the
dream for the last time.

Chapter 52
Sybille's Teachings: Fire

Spirit sings within your frame
…on your loom and through your pain,
Water washes all things clean
…air brings truth to you again.
Fire is needed, earth to ground,
…when the web you weave, all things abound

Fire: our brain synapsis, our circulatory and neural pathways, classified as a male element it is our 'fire in the belly.'

We can dream of creating amazing things and be strongly inspired but we also need the physical get-up-and go that makes us take action on something. Earth and fire combine like left and right brain hemispheres to galvanise us into taking action and to bring it into manifestation on any level; a dream remains a dream unless do.

If we want a new job and know, exactly what we wish for it cannot manifest unless we physically start looking in the jobs vacant pages.

Fire brings the passion for life and never allows for boredom because it makes us too busy ever to be bored.

Undines, salamanders, summer, north.

Chapter 53
Nina's Strength

As we believe, so it is true
...even shape is illusion ...knowledge hidden in you
When you remember ...when you awake
...who will you be ...what is your true shape?

La Stregga took to bed in her grief and shame at her betrayal of one of the sisterhood and her own acolyte too. She was visited by a dark Fae who laughed at her pain, 'You have crossed the line that must never be crossed and henceforth you are mine,' she said harshly before disappearing from sight, 'I will see you in the nether country cowardly one.'

Eduard was beside himself at the vehemence his daughter showed him for not finding someone who would stand up and defend Magdalena. Even her Nonna would have none of it, saying that she always thought there was something odd about 'the girl.'

To which Nina retorted angrily, 'well 'the girl' saved my life when the Dottore would have bled me dry with their leeches! If it were not for her and...' she trailed off, unable to speak of the small nature sprite that came with other herbs for her.

Nangini had not been around since Nina had seen her slip a small packet into Magdalena's hand on the horrific night she would never forget. Now her helplessness was more than she could stand. She had made a promise to carry the Littleshape of Sybille within her but she thought that it must end, that she could not fulfil that agreement, so weary and spent was she.

One night, the one before the day she feared the greatest, when her dear friend would be given to the flames, the one known as Silver visited her, shining with light but wounded to her core. Black ichor poured from a gaping wound in her belly, confounding Nina that she could still be alive. The beautiful being came to her, soothing her in a language unknown…

'Hini lle na erin thaliolle; I' ai lle mani kirma en lle erin coi sina dagor, vee' na lle. Lle lasteva na beleg, lle lasteva dina khil I' men Kurini, Magdalena. mani lasteva aut n'ala lle.

He coia lasteva il ten' kai; re coi 'e I' n'at coiamen 'ar yamen lle ele 'e kaimel, manke lle yuuyo oment 'ar mello-nim. Thaliolle mani, thaliolle, Nangini lasteva kol lle yulna en kaima tanya lle en 'ten lle sanga n'at sangan tul're n' I' nyeer en llie sel'er.' …and yet she understood…

'Child you must stay strong; the one who is a part of you now must survive this ordeal, as must you. You will be tempered and honed; you will quietly follow the ways of La Stregga, Magdalena, who will go before you.

Her life is not for nothing; she exists in that other time and space you have visited of late in your dreams, where you both met and shared friendship. Courage little one, courage, Nangini will bring you a draft for sleep so that you may not hear the crowds as they gather tomorrow or feel the pain of your sister.'

Despite Silver's gentle reassurances, Nina was not convinced or calmed at the thought of what her friend was about to face and that she would never see her again in this life. Nina turned her face to the wall, denying her father access to her room and refusing to eat until the stern face of Nangini manifested before her; admonishing her for her selfishness when she had promised to be the host for the Littleshape known as Sybille. Her life extension was because of her agreement and it was a rare and honourable thing she did, eventually enabling her to make huge strides ahead in her own spiritual advancement.

'But I didn't choose this,' she screamed at Nangini, '**LET ME DIE.** I didn't choose to have my father and La Stregga, betray my friend for their own selfish reasons. I will not stay in this house a moment longer than I have to. If I may not die, I will live elsewhere, perhaps I shall go to where Magdalena was to live as La Stregga.

Who is this person whose spirit I carry within me? She must be important indeed that others must die and another carries her spirit, after her body is lost to this world.'

'Nina, your words come from grief, but whom do you refer to and to whom do you speak?' Eduard questioned as he came to check on her.

There came a rustling sound and he could see the small spirit Nangini watching him; Nina simply turned her face to the wall. Little did Eduard know but it would be the last time he would see his daughter in this life again.

The following day, before Magdalena was to breathe her last, Eduard went again to Nina's bedroom door. Her Nonna alerted him, that the door, locked from the inside, was something Nina never did and she feared for Nina's wellbeing. She couldn't hear Nina within, the little Signorina was not replying to her knocking.

In fear for what they might find, Eduard and the Nonna broke open the lock but only to find an empty room. A valise was missing, some clothing; only that which was old and warm, the newest clothes left hanging tidily in the armoire. A few precious items such as her pens and parchment and a few books were also gone. All else had been left and there was no sign as to how she had managed to leave without being seen or heard; the windows too were locked from the inside, so had not been her escape route either, although that would have been difficult for her in the frail condition she'd been in, the day before.

Eduard was distraught, his little girl and his love would both be gone from his life unless he acted now. Pushing past Nonna who was wringing her hands and sobbing he ran to the guardhouse where Magdalena was imprisoned. He begged the guard that he may speak with Magdalena but they refused, saying that she was attempting to find her peace and to let her be, that there was nothing he could do for her.

He spoke to them of his daughter's disappearance and they responded immediately, knowing how frail the little Signorina was and having daughters of their own, were compassionate men.

A search ensued and continued for days until the first snows covered any possible signs of passage; the girl had vanished without a trace.

A large red fox and a smaller young vixen trotted briskly down the road toward the mountain passes, hurrying before the snows would begin to fall but knowing that in doing so it would stop the search as the trail became impassable. Overhead raven flew, carrying small bags between them through the veil, which they deposited in a little stone cottage in the mountains in readiness for its new occupant.

Chapter 54
Samhain: Final Thread

At the end of our dreaming, where do we wake?
Is the truth of our waking more than we can take?
Was the life that we dreamed real or a fake
Did we change in the dreaming?
…to correct past mistakes

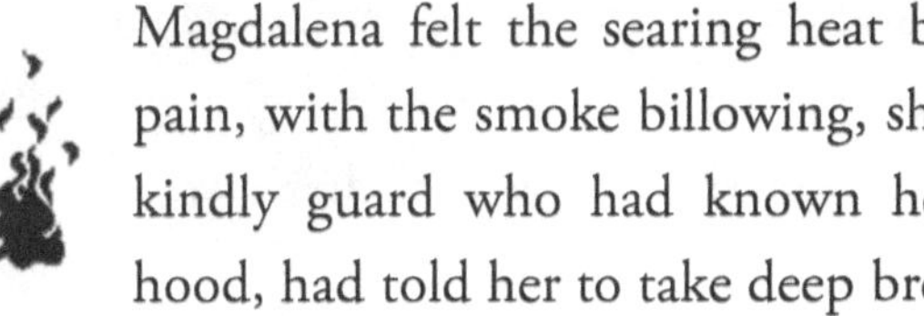

Magdalena felt the searing heat but at first, no pain, with the smoke billowing, she choked. The kindly guard who had known her since childhood, had told her to take deep breaths, to inhale the smoke that would make her unconscious as the flames rose from the faggots to her feet and upwards.

More he had not said, but she had heard that the smell of burning human flesh was similar to that of roasting pork and the thought made her retch. How could she be so clear in her head at the stupid thought that the smell of pork was worse than the smell of her own flesh burning as the flames edged toward her feet, blistering the tender flesh, licking at her hungrily?

She could see dimly, as her sight became blurry through the smoke pall, a million small beings working to fuel the flames to make it quick now that there was no other recourse. They began to become frantic, as they licked at her hungrily, not with malice but to ease her way.

Why hadn't the herbs worked; she had managed to take them in a goblet of wine the guard had brought her. 'For courage,' he had said with a knowing smile more like grimace as he dropped his tear filled eyes from hers. Had there been something else in the wine she thought in her last moment of lucidity? Would it counteract the others?

Now it was happening, it was real. Her bowels cramping with fear, turned to water and she could smell her own urine and worse, above the smoke stench as her body let go …for the last time she thought quite consciously, before the herbs finally took her away from all pain and suffering…

…her last cry was **'Lady why, what did I do?'**

From somewhere deep within from another thread, she heard a chant and grabbed hold of it, letting it take her away.

Blessed oblivion finally came and a cloud of raven lifted off from the rooves of the buildings in the town square. They weren't after carrion but it appeared briefly to those watching that they took the shape of a dark, feather cloaked female, who breathed in the fragments of soot and ash that blew up from the pyre.

With Magdalena's final scream of pain and fear, La Stregga's life snuffed out, no more than a candle extinguished in a draft, her heart simply stopped.

Annie Savage woke screaming, gasping for air as her aspect slammed into her on the Aether, binding with her as one as La Stregga's own thread in the tapestry, frayed and finally snapped.

Aelish watched, observing their mutual discomfort at being two in one body, with cold-eyed dispassion. She chanted quietly as she stood in the shadows...
...two in one and one in two ...the gift of life they gave to you ...as above so below ...your heart is light when their truth you know ...as without so within ...cast your circle ...let them in...

...all things come around, there's never a need for us to meddle, when we know nothing of the other's journey, just as the wheel turns on from life to death and to rebirth but Aelish had forgotten this; or chose to.

Chapter 55
La Stregga Nina

Stir up the storm sprites
...dance on the wind
...follow the music to where magick begins
Always remember, 'with harm to none'
...then follow your dreams 'til they simply 'become'

 Nina woke on a soft bed, snugly covered with a goose-down quilt. A single candle burned and the wind howled down the chimney; a fire glowed in the hearth.

For a moment, she felt happy, warm and comfortable before the rush of memory overcame her. Nangini moved rapidly from out of the shadows to administer some drops that would restore her to sleep.

'How long have I been here she asked?'

'Many days child,' was the reply. She closed her eyes as a tear escaped to roll down her face. Her friend Magdalena would be dead, gone from this life, how would she cope with the acknowledgement of her sister's excruciating pain?

'I will help you understand and learn through strength to bear it,' said Nangini.

'Have I not been strong?' Nina replied.

'Yes you have child and now one more sleep of healing and you will feel even stronger I guarantee you.'

With a stroke of Nina's brow with her rough little hands, Nina slept a different sleep, lucid and life affirming.

She dreamed she was walking through thick snow, not in her human form, rather that of a fox and she'd not been alone. A tall man with burnished hair had taken her through a misty veil and along narrow mountain paths, emerging through the forest at the stone cottage where she slept, a large fox to her vixen. He'd not spoken to her other than to say he would escort her to safety and a place of peace, where she could heal before meeting with the people who would be her new tribe.

She recalled asking where she was, what people, and how would she live but he said only, 'All in good time little Nina.' He'd settled her in the cottage where a fire was already burning and the space warm, the bed too, heated by a stone water bottle. She fell immediately into a deep sleep.

Deep within her knowledge stirred, arcane knowledge, astrology, herbal lore and the laws of the Wildwytch were fuelled by memory from the depository placed there by the silver haired woman whose spirit she held entwined within her own for safe-keeping, until such time as her body was found and restored. What would happen if that did not she could not countenance.

She was innocent Nina Giraldi yet a new confidence was growing, alongside the grief she felt for her friend Magdalena but that was something she knew would never go away completely and which she must live with, if she were to be more than a person whom grief had broken.

On other threads, in other aspects she knew where La Stregga was, the one who had betrayed her friend but she also knew that life and the Dark Goddess would catch up with her, that she need do nothing except heal to become La Stregga for her own community. Become what her friend could no longer be and yet she knew her friend was carrying on the journey in another thread, working toward the same ends to help and to heal.

She'd never really done much for herself. Her father; she thought of him with only a pang of remorse, Nonna and Magdalena had taken care of all the day-to-day things she'd needed. She'd learned by observation the simple tasks of running a home, had enjoyed bread and pasta making, simple cookery and had been active in the herb and vegetable garden when her health was strong. Now she needed to stay strong to learn all over again what it was to look after a productive garden and to tend simple folk with herbs when called upon. She wondered what it would be like in such an obviously extreme, cold climate but even here, spring would come.

Daylight filtered through the louvered shutters as she woke, the fire was out and the room was quiet. Kindling and firewood were stacked in abundance along one wall by the hearth and a fire laid, ready to light. She thanked the thoughtful one who had done this for her. On the table were fresh bread, goat cheese and milk, a small, wizened apple she recognised as Nangini's offering, sat together with a large pitcher of icy spring water.

She noticed an ancient leather bag, placed with her own meagre valise on a chair. She was curious but first she needed to light the fire, heat some water and find the commode. She paused a moment thinking of her friend, it was a little like sticking her tongue in a sore tooth to see if it still ached; it did but somehow it had been eased by the rest and the drops Nangini administered. She realised she would survive; she would cope, for nothing could be worse than what Magdalena had experienced.

Wrapping herself in the quilt and slipping bare feet into her boots, she looked around the small cabin, liking its simplicity in size and contents. Warm coloured, woven rugs scattered the floor and bright copper pots hung above the hearth. A scrubbed table with simple chairs held centre stage and a shelf with clay cups and brightly coloured platters, artfully displayed, drew her eye. By the hearth, two comfortable chairs stood covered with fine, warm throws; they would make a cosy place to sit and read, she thought.

Bright light poured in as she opened the window and pushed open the shutters, hastily closing the window again as icy air rushed in. All around was white, blinding white. Pines and mountain ash formed a circle around the cabin as if by design, and she could see a small circle of stones with what appeared to be a stone Altar at the eastern edge of the clearing. 'Later,' she said aloud, 'I'll explore later.' She felt a frisson of excitement at the thought.

Nina stirred the embers in the grate a little and found enough spark to bring the fire to life with the addition of a few more sticks of precious, dry kindling. A small being startled her as it flew up out of the fire, looking at her with intelligent bright eyes; a salamander she thought a winged salamander, as they regarded each other with equal interest.

Filling the kettle that hung at the hearth, she swung it over the fire to heat, looking around the cabin for some tea. Not only was there tea in a well-stocked dry pantry but fresh coffee too. She would hoard this carefully she thought but today a cup of hot coffee would be just the pick-me-up she needed.

Finding all she needed for her simple breakfast she washed in tepid water, enjoying the freshness on her skin and feeling invigorated, she settled to eat more than she'd eaten at one sitting for a long time. Something within her, despite the nagging ache of grief was changing and she was excited by her apparent restoral to health.

Life could begin again and she was determined to grasp that new start, the only thing still confusing her was who it might be who shared space within her and whether she would be able to actually speak with this being.

So Nina's new journey began and she sang quietly to herself as she pottered, exploring her new space... a

chant kept buzzing around inside her head so she pulled
paper, pen and ink out of her bag to write it down...

Oak for endurance Ash for power
Hawthorn for enchantment at the Beltane hour
Holly brings challenge let justice prevail
Mistletoe brings trance to see 'tween Samhain's veil
Mandrake brings the visions to guide her on the way
I will wait to meet her on the thread we live today.

Epilogue
Beltane: Samantha's Thread

Dance the last dance of
...on delicate wings in an azure blue sky
Soon the first mists and frosts of the time
...will cover the land in icy rime
She will sleep the long sleep in enchanted pools
...her wings folded tight as the planet cools
...and then in the spring her offspring emerge
...to fly trembling again, on the brink, on the verge
For nothing ever truly dies
...as we dance the last dance of Dragonfly

This time it was real. Samantha knew it was no dream as she gasped for air, drenched in sweat and her own urine again.

Once more, she was on the great pyre, alight. Strangely, she felt no pain, rather drugged and numb. Yes, she could feel but not to the degree, she should. With the sounds of the screaming crowd diminishing, she heard only the crackle and pop of her own flesh burning, the smell cloying like pork fat, even over the stench of soot and smoke.

When the smoke parted like a veil for a brief moment, her last fleeting recall was of a pair of soft grey eyes looking at her, watching her burn with utter sorrow and horror. 'Forgive me Magdalena,' he mouthed to her before the smoke finally overcame her and she was floating free of her burning, blackened body.

'**Eduard,**' she screamed inside her head, the words so loud they brought her back from the dream instantly. Brushing her sweat soaked hair from her face, she cried aloud. '**Max, it was you!**'

She'd never managed to fathom what this dream actually meant until now. She began a chant that resonated in every cell of her being... *'Oak for endurance, Ash for power, Hawthorn for enchantment at the Beltane hour. Holly brings challenge let justice prevail, Mistletoe brings trance to see 'tween Samhain's veil. Mandrake brings the visions to guide her on the way and I will wait to meet her, on the thread we live today.'*

When she'd thought about the concurrent lifetimes experienced, anything could happen. Her deepest fear had always been that she'd actually relive this again physically. She'd wondered if she were to merge with her other self, how in the world would she ever cope if that were so.

Now she had, she could feel the fear and pain of her aspect Magdalena, struggling to make sense of where she was as she too picked up the chant, holding on to it like a lifeline.

With a rush of wings, Tara and Morgan were there beside her; her sprites gathering around to soothe her reddened, blistering skin. Flora was there, birthing them through all the pain, wrought by the acts of mad-ness and bigotry. She held Sam while she cried and Magdalena mercifully slept, finally at peace within her twinned soul.

To help counteract Sam's own blend that Magdalena had taken, Flora gave Sam an antidote and as it took hold, Samantha flew.

She saw a vast tree and a sleeping woman, a small child-like being wept pearly tears of loss, two foxes ran free through the wilds of a different forest in the Skeins of Thyme, her friend Maeve found love and a raven sat waiting, its silver streak flashed brightly before it followed Samantha's flight 'Between'…

…continued in
Silver's Threads, Book 4 …Silken Web

About the Author

Penny Reilly Author 2014

Renowned as a clairvoyant and a teacher of the Western Mysteries at Daylesford School of Arcane Knowledge, Penny Reilly is an initiated Bard in the Tradition of the Druid. Moving on this year to the Order of Ovate, Penny has a passion for the Old Ways of the British Isles; she will be returning there this year to carry out research for her nonfiction books and her second 'Cloak of Magick' series to come. She feels that the gentle path of the Druid, Pagan-Wytchway is the path to take for a sustainable future, connecting us to the land, no matter where we live on the planet. She describes herself as a 'nature writer'.

Her own visionary experiences are very much a part of her storyline, poetry and lyrics …this is her fourth published book. She has previously written articles for alternative magazines, blogs regularly about her ideas and way of life, writes for 'starts at sixty' lifestyle blog and has over 6,000 followers on her poetry page 'earthly rites', her school and her author pages on Facebook.

Penny moved to Sydney, Australia in 1980 and to the central highlands of Victoria with her husband David, 18 years ago. They share space with an 'all sorts' terrier, an old tabby cat, a small flock of hens and a fat wombat fondly known as 'Chocolat', who has adopted them. Keen gardeners, they are becoming self-sufficient on their beautiful rolling acres on the Great Divide; their blended mob of children are long 'grown and flown' the coop.

You can find out more about the author, her books, poetry, tours and workshops, through her website, amazon.com and social media pages

http://www.silversthreads.wordpress.com/
http://amazon.com/pennyreilly
http://facebook.com/pennyreillyauthorpage
http://facebook.com/earthlyrites
http://facebook.com/daylesfordschoolofarcaneknowledge
http://www.goodreads.com/pennyreilly
@PennyReilly.twitter